Rough Water Baptism

Albert Norton, Jr.

eLectio Publishing
Little Elm, TX
www.eLectioPublishing.com

Rough Water Baptism
By Albert Norton, Jr.

Copyright 2017 by Albert Norton, Jr. All rights reserved.
Cover Design by eLectio Publishing.

ISBN-13: 978-1-63213-268-0
Published by eLectio Publishing, LLC
Little Elm, Texas
http://www.eLectioPublishing.com

Printed in the United States of America

5 4 3 2 1 eLP 21 20 19 18 17

The eLectio Publishing creative team is comprised of: Kaitlyn Campbell, Emily Certain, Lori Draft, Court Dudek, Jim Eccles, Sheldon James, and Christine LePorte.

Without limiting the rights under copyright reserved above, no part of this publication may be reproduced, stored in or introduced into a retrieval system, or transmitted, in any form, or by any means (electronic, mechanical, photocopying, recording, or otherwise), without the prior written permission of both the copyright owner and the above publisher of this book.

If you purchased this book without a cover, you should be aware that this book is stolen property. It was reported as "unsold and destroyed" to the publisher and neither the author nor the publisher has received any payment for the "stripped book."

The scanning, uploading, and distribution of this book via the Internet or via any other means without the permission of the publisher is illegal and punishable by law. Please purchase only authorized electronic editions, and do not participate in or encourage electronic piracy of copyrighted materials. Your support of the author's rights is appreciated.

Publisher's Note
The publisher does not have any control over and does not assume any responsibility for author or third-party websites or their content.

ROUGH WATER BAPTISM

Chapter One

The airplane seemed as if it were about to land right on the water. Even craning his head against the window, Tino couldn't see far enough ahead to dispel the sensation. And yet, he was relaxed. It was perfect. Just the way to enter into his new life. The proximity of the glistening waters below heightened the sensation of floating free but alighting here, in San Francisco, only because he willed it so. The grass apron to the tarmac blinked into view. An instant later, the wheels made contact.

Tino wanted to jump up and collect his bag, but first there would be the interminable wait for the passengers ahead of him to file out. Beside him sat an older woman, looking ahead as if seeking instruction on what to do next in life. She made no move to stand. Tino had worked his charm on her for the first fifteen minutes after take-off from Austin. But then he'd let the conversation lapse. She reminded him of his mother.

The woman now turned to Tino and said, "My daughter is picking me up."

"Great. I hope you have a good visit."

"I've only been here once. It was terribly confusing in the airport."

Tino couldn't picture trundling through the airport with the lady, showing her the obvious places where arrivals were greeted, or the private car lanes outside. "I'm sure it's like any airport. Just follow the signs to ground transportation."

The woman looked at Tino expectantly, clearly wanting him to offer help. He pointed toward the crowded aisle. "It'll be less stressful if you're ready to go when the people in the aisle start moving."

"Oh, yes." She looked about her on the floor, though she already gripped her purse and a shopping bag firmly in her lap.

It was a nice little ego bump, seeing his name on the placard in the arrivals area. On the way into town, he bantered with the limo driver. The driver's Jamaican accent was interesting for a while, but not so much what he had to say. And anyway, Tino was soon engrossed in the scenes outside his window. Everything he saw confirmed this was the place to begin. He felt it in the very atmosphere. Austin had its charms, but Tino always intended it only as a way-station. A place to pause, shake off the dust, and move on, leaving the past behind. What a contrast San Francisco was, not only to Austin, but to the place he'd grown up—New Albany, Indiana, pressed hard against the Ohio River. In Tino's imagination, it pressed hard too long against his desire to be free. Too much history there to feed an ambition unconstrained by convention. Here, the very air was lighter. He felt free.

Tino was animated by a special sense of adventure, buoyed by the grand sweep of possibility in front of him, with no limits, no burdens, and no baggage. It was already late in the afternoon when he arrived—a sparkling sunny afternoon of course—but there was time to explore a little. The limo driver deposited Tino's bags inside the door of Tino's temporary abode, a third-floor flat rented by the week, in a historic Victorian overlooking Golden Gate Park. Tino tipped him, then skipped out into the buttery sunshine. Across the street, tall eucalyptus trees at the edge of the park caught the late-afternoon light in their upper reaches.

Tino was well disposed to San Francisco even before seeing it for the first time. He had months before formed the idea of starting afresh. Far from New Albany. Far from Texas. It was more than starting fresh, really. It was escape. And it wasn't just escape in the overwrought way we sometimes use the word. Tino was breaking bonds that seemed oppressive. He did not travel on the wings of raw ambition alone. He was not so much arriving in San Francisco as severing old ties that might cling and cloy. Tino meant to wall off his past. Even before arriving, he sensed an openness waiting for him here; an unquestioning latitude for his affairs. Tino felt his presence in the Bay Area was pre-ordained, as though his flight from the past could terminate only at the endless sea.

He followed sidewalks that would take him through a corner of the park to its easternmost edge, along Stanyan Street. The conifers and cultivated underbrush were taking on a shadowy blue in the gathering gloom, despite the shards of orange light penetrating randomly. Tino rounded a corner in the park and encountered an artist who was beginning to put away his materials.

"Do you mind if I look?"

"Not at all."

"Kind of late, isn't it?"

"I was on a roll."

"A dancer. But there's no dancer around."

The painter was wrapping wet brushes in a paper towel. He looked over at Tino with a half-grin. "I painted the form of the girl inside. I talked a friend of mine into coming out here for a little bit before sunset one day so I could get the coloring right. Today I was just finishing out the background."

"It looks like— Sorry, I was going to start talking about something I know nothing about."

"Tell me. I want to know."

"It's a dancer in the woods, but not one of those wood sprites in an old-timey print where she's brightly colored and the woods are dull. She blends into the wild surroundings. Like she's supposed to be there."

"Something like what I was going for," the man said. "I would hope to capture the best of all that we are—like the dancer—and no interruption with the nature around her."

"Well, I see it. I like the face. She's not an angelic presence of some sort. She's a hungry, alert woman."

"Good," the painter said. "I wanted her at home in the woods, but she aspires to something beyond."

"I think you succeeded."

"My name's Hanny," the painter said. "Mark Hanigan."

"Tino Croscetti."

"You've given me a big boost today, Tino. You have no idea."

"Likewise."

"Live around here?"

"Actually, I'm new to town. Just arrived."

"When you say 'just arrived,' you mean—"

"Literally," Tino took out his phone and looked at the face plate. "Less than an hour ago."

"No kidding. Get some coffee with me. I'll be the Welcome Wagon."

"Sure."

After dinner at a place not far from Haight, Hanigan oriented Tino to how he would make the turn on Lincoln to get back to his rental unit. "Art show," Hanigan said. "Bridgewater Hotel. Four o'clock."

"Got it," Tino said. "I will see you there." Tino had a deep conviction confirmed by experience that whatever came his way, he, Tino, would ride the crest of the wave. Opportunity might come from any direction. Tino had an innate sense that all would redound to his benefit, as if events within his orbit occurred just for him.

The next day, he awoke early to the sound of a Pacific breeze at the window, catching the sheer curtain lining, swooshing it against the edge of his soft bed. It was otherwise quiet. There was a blue coolness, better appreciated under the heft of the thick comforter. The room Tino awakened to was spare, but artfully so. Subtle differences in off-white color were softened yet further by the indirect lighting. A tableau of cool, meaningful shadow presented itself to him. The walls, the bedclothes, the ceiling, the trim—all were in pale shades, except for the dark-stained wood floor and the frame of the bed. And the picture across the room, beyond the foot of the bed, above the mantle and the fireplace. A woman in a garden, but she had a cloak, worn almost like a cape. Red. No, burgundy. No, a satiny blood-orange, it might be, in stronger light. It stood out, a slash on the wall, intense against the surrounding muted colors.

Tino lingered over the visual sensation, under the warm comforter, in the whelming quiet. He embraced the contrasts between the cool of the room and the warmth he felt in bed; the merely suggestive sounds outside now, and the mid-day noise that would follow; the substantive but pale color, and the provoking red of the painting. His was a full-scoped sensuality. Even his anticipated rising in the cool room appealed to him, when the cold floor and the hot shower would play their parts, in turn.

Tino breakfasted as the sun was coming fully into its own, at a trendy diner with pretty waitresses hurrying about. Afterward, he had time on his hands. Not time "to kill," though, because life was not that way for Tino. Not because of raw ambition or an innate industriousness that made him restless. Rather, because at any moment circumstances might adjust in his favor. Anxiety was not a part of his makeup. Opportunity and optimism were. This resonated with people. Tino expected to be accepted by everyone he encountered. And so, usually, he was.

As he walked, he fiddled with the card in his pocket. A card for the breakfast restaurant, with his waitress' phone number handwritten on the back. The morning was well along now. The hills of San Francisco were steep, surprisingly so, though he'd seen pictures online before arriving. He went up and down, but the net trend was downhill. At openings in the streetscape, he could see the San Francisco Bay off in the distance, but its nearer boundary was obscured by a distant tangle of bridges, wharves, and buildings.

Tino walked, headed generally in the direction of the bay, ending up at the Embarcadero. He happened upon an expansive and busy farmer's market. The bright light there contrasted sharply with pools of shadow cast from awnings placed by the various vendors. There was a general move of people in and around the vendor booths. Tino felt a part of the ebb and flow of humanity.

In the walk between rows of vendors, Tino observed a fall of mahogany brown hair, swinging forward from the shadow into the light, and the shapely skirt-and-blouse-clad figure of the young woman behind it. She turned slightly, in Tino's direction, but she was looking down to attend to a display of vegetables. As she did so, Tino caught the soft features of her face. A kind face. And beautiful, in an innocent, fawn-like way. The girl rearranged carrots and potatoes that nearly filled wooden boxes tilted toward the trade. Then she looked up. She saw Tino. Tino smiled with an open countenance, expecting that when her eyes met his, they would be friends.

The girl smiled back, and then caught herself, suddenly self-conscious, straightening up and reaching a little too quickly for more potatoes higher up on the tilted display case. She dislodged them, creating a little potato avalanche. Tino had seen this unfolding, and his hands were there, at the spot she couldn't quite reach, and the potatoes were saved.

Tino looked up. The girl's lovely face was inches from his. She had stopped in her reach forward, just as Tino had. She continued to look down, though, at their hands and at the produce, for what seemed to Tino a telling moment too long. She then glanced up at him. Her wondering eyes were the color of her deep brown hair. Dark, full eyebrows and long lashes added to her aura of simplicity and honesty. Then she straightened again, and her face was again in shadow. Tino felt sure he detected color in her cheeks not explained by just the sunshine beyond her booth.

"You saved the day," she said.

"For these guys, anyway," he replied as he rearranged potatoes in the box. "I deserve a reward for my gallant efforts. I demand to know your name."

"Cassandra. Cassie." She recovered herself as she said this and came around the outer edge of her booth so she could help Tino.

"I could almost have guessed. You look like your name." He smiled again in a way that put Cassie at ease. Not a leer nor suggestive nor aggressive. "My name is Tino."

"Thank you, Tino."

"Is this your little kingdom? Potatoes and carrots?"

"And bread," she said, gesturing to the next table.

"Oh, now that is impressive."

"You should have seen it this morning. I came with twelve different kinds today. What you see is all that's left."

"Your specialty?"

"You could say that. We bring from the garden whatever is in season, but we always bring the bread."

"Who's 'we'?"

"Well, Mom, Dad, sometimes my brother, Billy. Just me today."

"From?"

"West Marin. Near Olema."

"Am I in the way of customers? Let me step back here." Tino stepped to the side of the vegetable display.

UGH WATER BAPTISM

behind it. "It's okay. It's been slowing down

those loaves," he said.

at her table of bread and back to Tino. "No, With that, she took a loaf and unwrapped it behind her booth. "You'll like it. And here. r where I live. That part of Marin is famous ed to talk, Tino began bagging potatoes and though the booth was as much his. The time as time to pack up. Tino helped, following pickup truck with a topper covering the bed, npty boxes and the remaining vegetables and

"Will I see you when I come back here?" Tino waved toward the public part of the market.

"Most days it's open."

"And I can call you."

"Yes." She looked down again, but for just a moment, and looked up. Bolder now.

Tino took her hand, pulled it up and engulfed it in both of his, held next to his chest, for just a moment. He smiled into those dark eyes and then looked down. Tino had intuited the impact of this blend of affection and restraint. Cassie's eyes spoke delight.

Chapter Two

Elise wheeled her father in the direction of his good friend Gerald, who was making his way over from the bar. They converged near a planting of intricately-cultivated ficus trees.

"Professor Brinkley. Emeritus. So glad," Gerald said. As he reached to shake her father's hand, Elise watched a little wave of cabernet sweep up and over the edge of Gerald's glass. It plopped onto the terrazzo floor, leaving little blood-like drops. Neither of the men noticed it.

"Such formality. It ill becomes you, Mr. Teague," her father said.

"It's owing to the surroundings, Potter. All this sophisticated art. I'm pleased to see you, Elise. How are your studies coming along?"

"Very well, thank you." Elise smiled serenely and made a deferential gesture that might almost have been called a curtsy, in an earlier day.

"Potter, you don't deserve a daughter such as this. Never marry, Elise, I want to always imagine you strolling around your father's loggia in a long, white, pleated gown, with a laurel wreath crowning your fair hair."

Elise smiled an indulgent smile, and as the two men turned to conversation with each other, swept her eyes around the room. Huge canvases adorned the main walls, but on smaller, movable display walls irregularly placed around the room were pictures in various media, all of them abstract. A common theme included dashes of brilliant color juxtaposed against a duller background. The artist, Mark Hanigan, held forth near the center of the room, hands tensely clasped behind his back, his dark beard thrust forward. He was a former student of her father's, well-liked despite his inexplicable turn from her father's discipline, neuroscience, to art.

Just as Elise began to turn away, she observed a young man approach Hanny from the other side of the room. She was struck first by the young man's classic good looks. Wavy, gold-brown hair, long but not bedraggled, swept back carelessly but artfully. A broad smile with gleaming white teeth as he smiled and shook Hanny's hand, covering their clasp briefly with his left hand also. Masculine, but kind. His bearing was confident, assured, yet not preening nor overbearing. A fine picture of a young man. An artist himself, perhaps?

Elise turned quickly away, but out of the corner of her eye saw the young man turn to glance at her. Had she turned away in time? Or had he caught her looking? She set sail toward a knot of guests clustered at a far corner of the room. She slowed, open to an encounter with a friend or an acquaintance, calculating that she could divert her attention to one of the displays there if no social liaison appeared. On the neutral background of the display board next to her was a series of three smallish unframed canvases. It was a triptych of oils, each of which vaguely suggested a horizon, of just such a non-color hue that one was drawn to try to separate out what might comprise its constituent colors. In each was a foreground sprig of color, what might have been a sagebrush, or just an uprush of color, but of natural-looking eucalyptus color at the edges and an increasingly intense exotic color mix toward the middle. Elise had never developed a great appreciation for abstract art, but this drew her eye.

"It's really not bad. Better than I thought it would be," a voice next to her said.

Elise turned and gave a one-armed hug to her friend Mary, who was holding a glass of Chablis in her other hand. "Hanny did well," Elise said. "I'd love to see his art take off. Is that okay to say about art? Are we supposed to say something like 'break a leg,' like we do for actors?"

"I'm not the right one to ask. I'm such a philistine. I just love the atmosphere," Mary said. "And speaking of art appreciation, did you see his friend?"

"Not sure I know who you're referring to."

"Liar. You know exactly. The Greek god over there. He's fabulous."

"Maybe a little too fabulous?"

"I don't think so. He has a kind of carelessness about his looks. He doesn't seem to cultivate the look, he just has it." Mary was looking past Elise and swayed a few inches further to one side to see the young man without pointedly staring.

"I'm over here, Mary."

"I'm using you to line up my quarry. That's what friends are for."

"Let's talk again before you leave."

"Okay. See you in a few, Elise."

Mary wandered off, and Elise turned her attention back to the paintings. She stepped back to try to take in all three at once, to note the differences in presentation among them. The horizons varied slightly, but all had that color that seemed not to be a color. The sprigs or bushes or upsweeps of paint each differed in their vivid colors at the midpoint, though each fanned out to the neutral color at the edges. Each was spaced at a different point on its seeming horizon, each picture almost but not quite in symmetry with the others.

Elise sensed a presence at her elbow and turned to the face of her friend Joy. It was like turning into the bright sunshine.

"Elise," her friend squeaked. Her lips were pursed, and her eyebrows raised. There was excitement in her every gesture.

"Joy in the evening," Elise said, giving her a quick hug.

"I am so happy to be here. This is wonderful."

"Have you met the artist before? Mark Hanigan? He used to be one of my father's students."

"I was with you, silly, when we visited his studio."

"Oh, how could I forget you were with me? He'll be glad you came to his debut."

At that moment, the man himself walked up. "Elise. It means a lot to me that you're here." Hanigan turned to Joy. "And thank you for coming. You came to my studio with Elise, a few months ago—"

"Joy!"

"Oh, of course. Everyone's name should match them so well. And you had someone with you that day. Your special friend, I think."

"Fiancé. David."

"You couldn't drag David here today? I don't really blame him."

"He's working. Or else he'd certainly be here."

"Hey, Tino, let me introduce you around," Hanigan said. He was speaking to someone behind both Elise and Joy, so they stepped slightly to the side to open up the little circle. "Meet my friends Joy and Elise."

The man behind them stepped forward and greeted Joy and then turned to Elise. Elise found herself face to face with Mary's Greek god. Up close, he looked even more perfect than when she had spotted him across the room. It had to have been her imagination, she thought, but in the microsecond of their face-to-face encounter, their eyes met in a way that seemed to exclude their surroundings. She felt momentarily off-balance.

Small talk ensued, and then Hanny excused himself to circulate among the guests, as the occasion required. Elise was diverted by one of her professors. She exchanged pleasantries with him and then turned to include Joy and Tino, but by then they had drifted away. There were more guests now, probably because it was near the end of the work day. The exhibition was theoretically scheduled to close soon. Elise realized the timing was probably deliberate so the exhibition would carry on into chic "overtime." Good for Hanny.

Elise had been back to check on her father only once, and it was time to circulate back that way again. She traversed the now-more-crowded exhibition floor. Through the traffic, she spotted Tino again, seated and speaking animatedly near the spot she'd left her father. As she approached, she could see it was, in fact, her father who engaged him. They seemed to be having one of those exchanges that was a notch more intimate than usual cocktail-party chatter. That, combined with the fact that Tino was seated to be on the same level as her father, made them an island of conversation. Elise paused next to her father, thinking she would interject to see if he wanted anything, but there was no pause in his exchange with Tino. Rather than stand awkwardly above them, Elise sat opposite her father in the only place available, next to Tino on a low divan. Tino shifted over for her as he listened to her father. There was only a small space remaining on the divan, however, and she could feel Tino's body next to hers.

"You see, all of those thinkers were brilliant, no doubt, but they sometimes spoke of things they knew nothing about. Do you know Aristotle thought women were somehow less than fully-formed humans? That the moon and planets had godlike consciousness? And yet we revere Aristotle, and rightly so. He didn't know what he didn't know. Aristotle is cited for thinking there is a *telos*, a grand purpose, in everything, even the rocks and trees. And yet now we know that's all wrong. It's the same with how we think of what motivates us, how we decide there's a purpose or will inside of us somehow. Just not true."

Tino said, "Your critics would say that's dehumanizing, I imagine. That it means we're a collection of nerve endings and stimuli, and nothing more."

"Ah, good. Well done," the professor responded. "Determinism. A curse word. To that, I would just say there's plenty of mystery remaining without shrouding it in falsehood to make it even more impenetrable. We should follow the evidence wherever it leads. There's mystery enough to explore without looking for it in a god or concluding we're all little gods ourselves."

Elise's father paused and looked at Elise as if seeing her for the first time. Elise was preoccupied with her proximity to Tino and didn't immediately speak up.

Tino said to her, "The first thing Professor Brinkley told me was that you were his daughter."

"Yes," she said brightly. She didn't continue, as much due to the company as to the weightiness of the conversation she was breaking in on.

"Elise is the sunshine of my life."

She said, "I came to see if you wanted anything. Do you want to circulate around a bit? A drink?"

Tino added, "I could help you around."

"No, son, then you'd be behind me and we couldn't talk. Thanks, no, Elise. Anyway, it'll be time to go, soon. I'm fine. You two run off and let me talk to crusty old men. And young sycophants."

Tino laughed. "Let me turn you a little bit this way, so the sycophants can find you."

"Thank you. Go in peace." The professor made a vague cross in the air, two fingers up, as if he were the Pope.

"Can I get you something?" Tino asked Elise, motioning toward the bar as they walked past.

"No, thank you."

"What brought you here? Do you know Hanny?"

"I met him when he was a grad student. My father was his advisor."

"So he's a neuroscientist as well as an artist?"

"No, he took a break and hasn't gone back to it. Went to go find himself."

"And has, apparently. I like his work."

"Me too. I hope he succeeds. I wouldn't have the courage to try something like that. The world of art seems so fickle. I mean the business of art. Are you an artist?"

"No, but you're the third person to ask me that this afternoon, so maybe I should take it up."

"You already look the part. So how do you know Hanny?"

"I'm new to town. He sort of took me under his wing."

"Sounds like Hanny."

Elise paused before another panel of pictures and found some good things to say about them. Tino likewise commented on them, first disclaiming any special knowledge of art, in an endearing expression of humility. Elise noticed that the spike in attendance was short-lived, and now the crowd was beginning to dissipate somewhat. While they were talking, Mary hove into their orbit, glass in hand. She was a bit overeager to meet Tino.

Later that evening, Elise, seeing that her father was installed in his capacious and ornate study, went up to the loggia on the building's flat roof. Part of this area was covered, the loggia roof being supported by columns suggesting a Greek temple. Much of the half-wall surrounding the loggia was covered in slow-growing vine that would cling to the brick, bearing tiny leaves all year. Elise spent a lot of time here, overlooking the city and East Bay in the distance. She remembered Gerald Teague's comment, about wearing a pleated dress with a laurel wreath about her head. But here she was, in jeans and sandals, wearing a thick flannel-lined shirt she'd bought at a discount store.

Elise thought about Tino. A gentle but strong man. Good looks like his were a plus, but not of the essence. What was of the essence was a certain kind of assertiveness, like she sensed in Tino. Elise was not unhappy with her life, but she didn't think of it as being adventurous—still less romantic. She entertained now the scandalous idea that a man might invade her life and turn it upside down. She was open to the idea that the course of her life might be suddenly redirected by anything—why not a young man? This openness to unexpected change felt vaguely scandalous because she had absorbed from the very air around her the conviction that she was supposed to be the master of her own fate.

Daylight had faded. Lights now ringed the bay. The blueness of the water had darkened to black, and now the bay was pronounced by its absence of light, except where ships anchored a little to the south. The air was soft. She had always looked upon the lights of the bay wistfully, especially the lights on the ships. Perhaps they were only floating warehouses, but they represented more. They went here and there all about the globe. They, or rather their lights, represented to Elise a connection to the great beyond. The beyond for which the San Francisco Bay, and the Golden Gate, and the Pacific itself were the passageway. An invitation to mystery. Adventure.

There was a great big world out there. She would have her part in it, but it was foreign to her nature to think of the world as something to be conquered. She wanted only to find her place in it. While she did not want that place dictated to her—and especially not by a man who would be only her equal—she understood that much of life was an accident. A million variables conspired to create the place in life she occupied at this moment. There was more to it even than the family and place and time into which she was born. Her friendships had formed her. Her study. Her entertainments. The culture at large. Perhaps this was the point of her father's determinism—the incalculable number of such influences generated the sense of mystery to which we are all heir.

The mystery might be only an impression, however. A mood, an awareness that not all the events leading up to this moment—Elise in the loggia overlooking the bay—were known. It was interesting to think, in the abstract, that she was what she was because of the one particular combination of events in the universe preceding this precise moment. But that would mean space and time were mysterious only because they were not fully known, not because they held some answer to the "why" in every person's mind. Elise could well enough say she stood in this posture at this moment, thinking these thoughts, because of an infinitely complex combination of particles of matter moving in space, but if that was the only explanation for "why," then there could be no purpose to human life at all. Mere presence does not explain purpose.

So was there something to the criticisms of her father's brand of materialism she'd studied? Perhaps a religious sense of mystery exists only to preserve us from a slide into nihilism. It might function as a buffer against the effects of realizing the pointlessness of existence. But why? And how? Why would the absence of meaning or purpose move us to despair? How would believing a lie pull us out of it? Why do we carry a sense of the ineffable, which we approximate with words like beauty and mystery and purpose? It would seem to be unnecessary and even debilitating baggage. Is religious feeling hardwired into us by evolution? Or does the feeling exist because God does?

Elise heard a muffled popping sound, like distant gunfire. She turned, alarmed. She was looking toward the south end of the bay and was immediately treated to a vibrant display of fireworks in the sky above the city's baseball stadium. She remembered talk of the Giants having a shot at the World Series. They must have come through. This unexpected display lifted Elise from her brooding thoughts to a quiet, inner celebration. The bursting colors made her think of the little bursts of color in Hanigan's paintings surrounded by the muted non-colors behind. She was quite a bit uphill from the source of the fireworks, but they weren't lost against the lights of the city, nor of Oakland on the other side. The backdrop to the firebursts was the inky blackness of the bay. Serendipitously, from this perspective, the city lights only framed the fireworks display.

Serendipity only? Elise hadn't known there would be fireworks, yet here she was at what must have been the best place in the city to view them. The firing seemed random, but it wasn't. Someone fired the rockets in a prearranged direction, on a planned schedule. Each rocket was prepared so as to present a planned pattern upon explosion. The resulting display was orderly, and the beauty was derived from that purposeful order. The thrilling sight caused Elise to look around, instinctively, for others who might share it with her. She could see no one else on the balconies or rooftops near her house. She was alone in the loggia, as if the fireworks were only for her.

Chapter Three

Joy's tiny apartment was on the second floor of a building on a steeply angled street. On the uphill side, David could see, at an angle, into the bay window. He looked up now, on the off chance she might see him approaching. He continued down the sidewalk and stopped at the alley gate. She might have seen him after all, he thought, because he was instantly buzzed in. He closed the gate behind him and scooted up the exterior steps, entering at the kitchen.

He saw a light under the bathroom door. "You're early!" came Joy's voice from behind the door.

"Only a bit." He wandered over to the pair of secondhand couches in front of the bay window. On a side table were some magazines. He picked them up, pulled Joy's Bible out from underneath, and put them all back, this time with the Bible on top. Yesterday's newspaper was on the coffee table. David opened it to the editorials.

"David, put that down," Joy said when she emerged. "It'll put you in a bad mood."

"Not while I'm with you." He smiled and stood to embrace her.

Joy allowed herself to be swept up in his arms and kissed. A passionate, movie star kiss. But then she said, "Put me down, I'm not ready yet."

"You look ready to me," David said, but she was already returning to the bathroom. He stepped over to the window so he could look up and down the street. It was a fine afternoon. A golden light caught on all the west-facing angles. In moments, all would be in blue-gray shadow. The apartment was so small that they could easily continue to speak, he at the front, she in the bathroom at the back.

"Tell me about this Tino character," David said.

"Elise thinks he's mysterious. I only met him once, at that art show you didn't want to go to."

"Is this the artist friend?"

"No, someone she met there. She didn't want to jump into a serious one-on-one date."

"So she likes him. And I guess that makes us just props. Do I have a script?"

"Stop it. It'll be fun. You like Elise, right?"

"I do. Enough that I wish she had a spark of spiritual interest."

"Now don't get all broody."

"What do we know of Tino's spiritual leanings?"

"I don't know. How do I look?"

David turned to behold Joy again. "Well," he said, hesitating just a half-second too long. He hastened to add, "Wonderful. But you looked wonderful a minute ago."

"All men are useless."

On the sidewalk, David tested the iron gate behind him and turned. Joy's back was to him, chin up and taking in the sweep of the world outside her apartment. She turned back to him. "It's beautiful," she said. "Can we walk?"

"Sure. Kind of a hike, though. Aren't we going to North Beach?"

Joy just looked at him and gave one of her little nonverbal gestures, something between a wiggle and a shiver, that said life is too amazing to get bogged down in words describing it. She stepped out in the direction of North Beach, a smile on her face. David loved this about her. As much as he was prone to taciturn introspection, she was the opposite—warm, compassionate, and more alive with more company.

"Yo, slow down," he said.

"Yo, speed up."

"Where do we meet them?"

"At the restaurant. Pajoli's."

"Expensive?"

"No," Joy said. "I looked it up. Mary thinks he's a Greek god."

"Mary thinks—who's a Greek god? Tino?"

"Yes. Keep up, David. Tino."

"So is he? A Greek god?"

"I don't know. I'm engaged, number one, and number two, uhm…"

"My blinding good looks chase all such thoughts out of your mind."

"Uncanny. That is precisely what I was going to say."

"I don't suppose he would influence her away from the party line."

"What's the party line?"

"You know. Brinkley. There is no God. We're all about the learning, the erudition, the mystery of science, and the humanist tradition."

"You're against learning and erudition?"

"According to the Brinkleys of the world, it's not fashionable to actually believe in God. We're all supposed to be machines, there's nothing else."

"I'm teasing you," Joy said.

"I know you think I should just lighten up, but I think it's disheartening. I can't imagine going through life thinking everything is just a function of our biology. Nothing is important. Things only seem important because of our wiring. Isn't that what Elise's Dad teaches?"

"They're still alive."

"Okay, so—"

"So there's hope for them while they're alive."

"Well, Brinkley has built a whole career on this nonsense. He's bricked himself up pretty tight."

"Not Elise, though."

"No. But this way of thinking is ingrained. It's kind of an inverted faith. There's no God, and there's no heaven, and there's nothing but people interacting with people. We're all atoms bouncing off each other in a big, meaningless box."

"Sounds broody."

"Let me just brood till we get to the restaurant."

"You can brood till we get to Chinatown."

"Deal."

Pajoli's was a modest café in the heart of the tourist district of Little Italy, north of Chinatown. They exchanged introductions and pleasantries with Elise and Tino before settling in to study their menus. David was well acquainted with Elise already. He had often referred to Elise, Mary, and Joy as being the "Axis powers," eliciting the expected eye-roll from Joy. Tino seemed a nice enough guy. David was prepared to find him off-putting, at first, because he had the look of the artsy, avant-garde hipster. Or maybe it was just the hair. Tino seemed a normal enough guy, and not a mindless Narcissus.

"You're a brave man, Tino, going with the cioppino."

"Why? Too hot?"

"No, but it comes in a big bowl, lots of marinara, all kinds of seafood."

"That's what I was going for."

"Oysters and clams still on the shell. It's tough to negotiate. Messy."

"Oh, I see," Tino said. "Not something to order on a date. But see, you're helping me out even if I do order it. Now Elise's expectations are lowered. If I get the sauce all over myself, she won't hold it against me."

"Mmm," Elise hummed, expressing equivocation.

"Thanks," Tino said to David, "but I see I'm on my own."

"Are you an art connoisseur? Joy said you met Elise at Hanigan's art show."

"No, not at all. I'm basically the man in the gray flannel suit."

Elise said, "You're not a stodgy conformist."

"He's being ironic," Joy offered.

"No," David said. "Double-ironic. Right? We conform to the fashion of not being in conformity? 'We're all rebels together.'"

"Clever," Tino said. "Makes me want to go out and get a gray flannel suit for real."

Joy asked, "You're new to the Bay Area?"

"Just arrived a couple of weeks ago."

"Did you come for a job?" Joy asked this innocently, but David noted just the slightest hint of discomfiture in Tino's face, probably because he otherwise seemed so at ease in his surroundings. And then, Tino didn't exactly answer the question.

"Actually, I'm going to be doing some independent work, a liaison of sorts, so I guess technically I'm a consultant."

"So no boss," David said, still curious but not wanting to appear to be prying.

"We all have bosses," Tino said with some emphasis. "But I don't have to punch a clock and do face-time."

David asked, "Permanent job, or just something for now?"

"We'll see," Tino said. "One day at a time. I'm grateful for good friends. Dr. Brinkley, for example."

Elise turned to Tino, looking at him quizzically. "My father?"

Tino smiled his ingratiating smile. "He's the only Dr. Brinkley I know."

"He helped you find a job? He didn't mention it to me."

"I was fortunate he thought of me and gave the word in season, and it went from there. He's a good man."

"Well, we'll get the whole story when you're more into it," David said, by way of letting Tino off the hook from further grilling.

At this, Tino turned the table, asking all manner of questions about Joy and David. About Joy's work as a nurse at St. Francis. About David's fledgling career as a software developer. About the Bay Area and things to do. About the attractions of the surrounding area—Napa Valley, Marin County, and beyond. Even Joy's and David's church, which was located, oddly enough, in Berkeley, on the other side of the bay. Tino deflected the invitation to go, not trying too hard to make up excuses. Elise smiled, as she had herself politely declined such invitations from Joy more than once.

The next day was Sunday. David looked forward to Sundays all week. Much of his waking energy was spent on the success of the Galilean Community Church, which he had joined back when they still met in the pastor's living room. David had even had a hand in choosing the name for the church. They chose "Galilean" not only because Christ grew up in the region, but because that's often what the early Christians were called. David liked a name evoking that early period when Christians were still getting their feet under them, fleshing out a full theology, but in love with the presence of God among them. To David, their little church in Berkeley felt like the catacombs of old. Not because they met in secret, but because they seemed invisible, so it amounted to the same thing. Church with all its trappings existed in San Francisco and in Berkeley, of course, but to David's mind, too many churches favored a watered-down version of Christianity more palatable to modern sensibilities. He wanted communion with God, not a self-referential, vague spirituality. They met in rented space which was, ironically, a historic church long-vacant before their arrival.

Every Sunday, David took a personal inventory of how he'd done in his progress toward knowing God. This usually occasioned a pang of self-criticism. He was slow to release the idea that he was in some way responsible for the salvation of those with whom he came into contact. David's desire to show others the truth had given way over time to a sense of resignation. He might be trying to water dead seeds. The story he articulated was familiar—too familiar—and it carried baggage, whether warranted or not. David's Christianity seemed to meet a strong headwind.

"David," Joy said when there was a break in the service for everyone to greet those around them, "That's Mark Hanigan!"

People were already beginning to take their seats, in a halting, looking-around sort of way. "Let's catch up to him after," David said.

After the service, David and Joy had to break somewhat abruptly from conversation with a friend on their same row in order to catch up to Hanigan. Hanigan had attended alone, and it appeared no one had detained him in conversation. Fortunately, Joy had none of the inhibition that had slowed David down, and she soon had Hanigan by the elbow, near the door.

"Hey, Mark. I'm so glad to see you. Joy."

Hanigan looked at her with a half-smile, and then at the people standing around, as though surprised to find himself there. "Joy. I'm glad to see you, again," he said. "Very different context." At that, he extended his hand to David, who was walking up, a few steps behind Joy.

"My fiancé, David," Joy said.

"You came by with Joy and Elise a few months ago, right?"

"Yes, good to see you again. Sorry I couldn't make it to your last show," David said.

"Only show, so far. But maybe you can make it to the next one."

"Glad you came," David said, nodding back toward the interior of the church.

Hannigan looked around, quickly, as though wondering who else might have seen him here. "Thanks," he said. "Kind of new to me, truthfully."

"How'd you end up all the way in Berkeley for church?" David was trying not to sound inquisitorial, but he was thinking it unusual that Hanigan was so far from home when he apparently hadn't been invited to come with someone. Joy had half-turned to speak with another of her acquaintances.

Hanigan looked David in the eye purposefully. The artist's intensity was in his eyes. "I came here for church because of what I read on the website. I have actually gone to some other churches, closer to home, but—" here Hanigan hesitated, not wanting to offend. "It was like the lights were on, but no one was home."

"I know just what you mean. It's real, or we're wasting our time."

"Yeah. Good," Hanigan continued, now emboldened. "If all this is true," he gestured to their surroundings, and then lowered his voice, almost conspiratorially, "then it's a lot more radical than just going through certain motions every week."

"Or dressing up nice for our neighbors."

Hanigan nodded but seemed again to want to be elsewhere. "Well, look, good running into you." He made as if to step through the door.

"Wait, Hanny, we're opening another campus, in Twin Peaks. Maybe you'd want to come to church there?"

"That would be very close to me. Maybe so. Will that be on the website, too?"

"Yeah. In fact, I'll be posting it myself in the next few days. You'll check it out?"

"Sure. I will." Joy had returned her attention again to David and Hanigan. Hanigan nodded to her. "'Bye, Joy. David."

A moment later, David turned to Joy. "He was eager to get going."

"But he was here. I wonder why he came all the way over from the city?"

"I asked him that while you were circulating. I think for the same reasons we do. Looking for the real thing."

"Ready?" Joy asked, and she bounced out the door. David followed, thinking as he did how the whole world felt a little different with these first few steps out of church on Sunday. He wondered if the bounce he felt at the moment was what Joy felt all the time.

Chapter Four

Tino opened a small office and continued a deep study of San Francisco political affairs as he awaited more detailed instructions. On a Sunday morning, he answered an unknown number.

"Tino, Gerald Teague. It was a pleasure meeting you at the art show. Do you remember me? Dr. Brinkley's friend?"

"Of course. Very well. Dr. Brinkley said you might call."

"He speaks well of you. Any friend of Potter's is a friend of mine. I wonder if you might meet me for lunch?"

They ate at a restaurant overlooking one of San Francisco's many small parks. The lunchtime conversation was about Teague getting to know Tino, though early on, Teague got Tino's commitment to an after-lunch stroll in the park. Tino understood that would be where their business conversation would occur.

"Tino, your advent in San Francisco is auspicious. Brinkley thinks, and I agree, that you could be just the man for an assignment you might find interesting."

"I'm all ears."

"Tino," Teague began, but then interrupted himself to point to a bench in an out-of-the-way spot along the trail through the park. "Sit for a minute?"

"Discretion is called for," Teague resumed. "We—that is, Dr. Brinkley and I and others—feel a public calling to advance the city's interests in ways that may not be obvious to the man in the street. Someone needs to look beyond the routine minute-by-minute affairs of the city, to see the big picture, and that it's moving in the right direction. With me so far?"

Tino nodded. He was thinking this would be a function for city hall, but obviously, Teague meant something more. "I suppose there's always back-channel work to be done, in the best interests of the city."

"Exactly. Good. We're a democracy, but there is also a place for, and a need for, civic-minded leadership to cut through partisan wrangling."

"I can absolutely assure you of my discretion."

"Well, let's start with an issue requiring intelligent and deft diplomacy. Are you familiar with the debate going on about vacation rentals in the city?"

"I've read about it."

"I'll give our view of it in a nutshell. San Francisco is obviously a major tourist town. It's important we draw business visitors, conventions, events. But it's also important the city remain one of those places people visit from time to time and cherish in their hearts—I'm being serious here—cherish for being something special, something that doesn't exist anywhere else. Not for nothing is there the old song, 'I Left My Heart in San Francisco.' Familiar with it?"

"Oh, yes. People have a special feeling about San Francisco. It's why I came here."

"It's a cultural thing, a unique positioning of the city we like to cultivate. Good for visitors, good for our self-image. Anyway, as you might imagine, the hotel industry is a big thing here."

"I'm sure it is."

"But imagine a map. San Francisco sits atop a peninsula. It's almost surrounded by water—the San Francisco Bay on one side and the Pacific on the other. A finite amount of real estate. On top of that, the city is concerned with the availability of ordinary residential housing space consistent with the current character of the city. So the city has historically exercised control over hotel starts, to prevent a creeping hotelization. There has to be a place for residents."

"So there's plenty of business for the hotels already here, I would guess."

"Yes, there is. It's not cheap to visit and stay in San Francisco. But neither is it cheap to live here. There's been a reasonable balance, though, so far."

"But what about short-term rentals?"

"Ah, well…the high prices for hotel rooms entice people to want to rent out their own places—not to residents, but to visitors. But that would defeat the control the city tries to impose, to prevent residential real estate from becoming, in essence, hotels. So historically, city ordinances prohibited that kind of short-term rental."

"Doesn't that solve the problem?"

"Well, it should, but now there's a new game in town. Disruption, I think, is the new word for this kind of thing. Now we have all these websites making it much more feasible for property owners to rent out their places to visitors instead of to long-term residents. What used to be an occasional thing that didn't need policing now becomes a problem. There was some political pressure, and the city messed up. Perhaps we should have been more vigilant. The city changed the rule so people could do short-term rentals, if they were renting out their own place."

"How was that messed up?"

"Well, once you give an inch, they say, why not a mile? It just begged the question, why should they not be free to rent out all they want?"

"So the city is trying to put a genie back in the bottle?"

"Yes, and that's where we come in. The city can only do so much with rules and regulations. We need some private-side cooperation. The hotels compete with each other, but they have to come together to fend off the websites. There's some delicate maneuvering, but we've mostly managed it." Teague stopped and looked around. "This isn't something for the front page of the newspaper, you understand. People jump into subjects like this uninformed. The law is sometimes on the side of whatever populist notion is at the forefront. But we needed to act to do what's best for the city. The tricky part has been getting the websites on board."

"Why would they get on board? Wouldn't they want the business?"

"Competition is a funny thing. Right-wingers always say it's great, but businesses aren't motivated by competition for its own sake. They're motivated by what's best for their bottom line. The websites are interested in having more individual property owners list their property. But they also compete with each other, and if the law keeps all websites out of an area, that's better than competing and losing, especially if they can be compensated for it some other way. Website businesses are especially vulnerable to this. One business can take over a particular space—look at Google. So the websites are willing to give up on trying to get into the city, if they can get some protection from hotels in areas around the city, plus some payments for giving up the opportunity. Of course, all this depends on the city holding to the prohibition."

"And the hotels pay?"

"Oh, they pay. They go on competing with each other, but they pay the Dane-geld to keep the disruption out of the city."

"I can help with this."

"Tino, this is where utmost discretion is called for."

The work Tino undertook was somewhat clandestine, and he liked it that way. Evidently, Dr. Brinkley was politically connected in the city. So was Teague, of course, but as Tino was quickly learning, the real power was that which moved silently in the background. Teague's task was to relay instructions and make introductions. Tino intuited he might compromise Brinkley's and Teague's confidence in him were he to inquire more deeply into their connections to this job and their own interests in it. Tino knew this opportunity did not arise only from his sunny affability and lack of prior allegiances but was based on an expectation that he would be reliably discreet. He was to be a foot-soldier, of sorts, and those for whom he carried out his duties were to remain a few steps removed. A matter of plausible deniability. In his office, Tino included the trappings of routine work for the city, including maps and organizational charts and ordinance books and files and more maps.

All of this Tino did on his own fund, again intuiting this was expected. Fortunately, it was made possible by the preparations he made even before arriving in San Francisco. The fund from his father's estate was now being employed in exactly the way he had hoped. It was seed capital, of a sort, and thinking of it that way helped Tino justify its questionable provenance. It had not exactly been bequeathed to him. Tino wasn't using it for boring investments or to supplement a small salary. He expected a many-fold financial return, and eventually that most significant of returns: power. He well understood the opposing spectrums of risk and reward. He also understood the law stamped a point on that spectrum, beyond which one was not supposed to pass. But to Tino, the law just demarked a transition to yet higher risks, and yet higher rewards. Everything, he knew, was for sale.

During this time of setting up shop, Tino was intensely aware he was being tested. He would provide to his mysterious directors no reason for questioning his loyalty or discretion. He met openly, and often, with Teague, but they discussed Tino's role only in general terms. They would discuss the needs of the city and desirable policy directions for it, for example, and occasionally they touched on the positions of various district supervisors, and the mayor, on this question or that, but it was left to Tino to snoop on his own to fully grasp the inner workings of the city's politics. This Tino did with some zeal, letting slip from time to time in his meetings with Teague some of what he'd learned, thus inspiring ever greater confidence that Tino had the wit and intelligence to handle nuanced matters, in addition to the requisite discretion.

Tino realized it wouldn't hurt these efforts to act upon his attraction to Elise. He thought of Elise as a classical beauty. Quiet but observant eyes. A graceful walk. She was polite but not officious, serene but not aloof, elegant but approachable. She was not the type to make her interest in Tino obvious. At the same time, he sensed an expression of interest by him would not go unrequited. This need have nothing to do with Cassie. Cassie was not the love of his life, either, but rather a very pleasant diversion. Only days after Hanigan's show, and as soon as he had set himself up with some standing in San Francisco, Tino asked Elise to dinner. On that occasion, and more to follow, he arrived at the Brinkley house and greeted and chatted with Elise's father. They never discussed San Francisco politics, or Tino's possible role in them. And yet Tino knew Dr. Brinkley had quietly sponsored him.

Not long after his first meeting with Teague, Tino called Hanigan.

"Ah, Tino, you haven't forgotten me," Hanigan said.

"Never, my friend. You represent San Francisco to me. Our experience together is indelibly imprinted. Let me buy you dinner this time."

"I've actually gotten something started here. You should join me."

"Well, I wasn't calling to invite myself to dinner."

"I know."

"But I can be there in twenty."

"Perfect."

Tino stepped out of the cab on the far side of Haight-Ashbury, right on time. Hanigan's apartment was on the third floor of his building. The building had a small interior courtyard open to the sky. The arrangement provided for sunlight on two sides of the apartments surrounding the courtyard. The uppermost level was in the poorest condition, and Hanigan was the only tenant there, occupying half the top floor. There was a wide walkway around the open space to the courtyard below. It was devised so that most of the walkway would be covered by the roof extension, but a few feet closest to the interior rectangle would be exposed to the sky.

"Come in, come in," Hanigan said when he espied Tino ascending the steps. "I realized when we hung up that your standards for pasta might be higher than mine."

"I'm sure it will be fine. I was going to get a bottle of wine—"

Hanigan was shaking his head but smiling.

"But I remembered you've given it up, and I didn't want to get flowers—that would be weird—so I brought this." Tino handed over a loaf of bread, which had been given to him freshly-baked by Cassie the day before.

"You're a class act, Tino."

"So this is where the magic happens."

"You haven't been inside before. Yes. Well, not magic, but this is where I spill paint."

"Ideal, I would think."

"It really is. I couldn't ask for a better setup. My speculation is that whoever built this place was an artist. The apartments on this floor are smaller, so there's more room out here, with natural light."

"But still some cover in case of rain."

"Well, it is San Francisco. I can't just stop every time it rains, or I'd never finish anything. And I'd rather be out in the air than under glass."

"Maybe you can show me some of your work."

"I keep work in progress in there," Hanigan said, pointing to one apartment door, "when I'm not actively working on it. And finished work in there," pointing to another door further down the walkway. "How about we eat first?"

They proceeded to a door between the two Hanigan had pointed out, entering a surprisingly spare room with a table and chairs, kitchen hood, counter, and shelves for kitchen items, and then a seating area under the wide windows on the far wall. On the wall opposite the kitchen were cheap bookshelves, groaning under the weight of books of every kind and description and condition, covering the wall from right next to the entrance, all the way back to the window, except in the middle, where there was a narrow opening leading to a bedroom and bathroom.

"Simple but serviceable," Hanigan said. "I had to trade off some elegance for sheer square footage."

"Plus light."

"Yes. Light. Make yourself at home. I've got to attend to this pasta."

"No problem. Can I look over your shelves?"

"Sure, help yourself. I keep saying I'm going to purge books, but I can't quite bring myself to do it."

"You know you can get all this on one of those reading devices."

"Not the same, brother."

Tino turned to the shelves, hearing Hanigan clank around in the kitchen behind him. After a few minutes, he turned back to Hanigan, with a volume on comparative religion in his hands. "Is there anything you don't read about?"

"I'm just a curious fellow. And I haven't read them all. Sometimes I get books by the basket-load at used-book sales."

"Well, it's a relief to know you haven't read all of them. I'm a little intimidated."

"My mother used to say, when she was alive, that some people are naturally smart, and some people need all those books."

Tino smiled appreciatively. "I'm sure she was very wise. Here's one on trees and shrubs of coastal California. And Daniel Defoe. Shakespeare, of course. Who's Patricia Churchland?"

"Oh, that goes back to my neuroscience days. She puts forward a pretty stark case for materialism. Just like Dr. Brinkley."

"That's his favorite topic. He's got no tolerance for beliefs about heaven, or God, or leprechauns."

"He loves to say 'leprechauns' in the same sentence as 'God.'"

"So it's a whole developed philosophy, I take it. What we see and hear and taste and touch is all there is."

"Right, and the thing I had the hardest time with, that the mind and the brain are the same thing. In neuroscience, the prevalent point of view is that all of consciousness is something that resides in the brain. Material. Neural impulses and chemicals."

"Not how you see it, then?" Tino asked.

"I think there's something too limited about that kind of materialism. If you could untangle every electric firing in the brain, and the content of every cell, I still don't see how that can account for human consciousness entirely. Intellectual processing, maybe, but not our full awareness of ourselves and the world around us. And the main reason is I don't think it can account for the interaction of consciousness, one person to another, communicating like we are now. There are too many features of a person's consciousness that require something beyond what is material, in the brain."

"So you're a heretic. Is that why you left neuroscience under Brinkley?"

"Not just that. I think all along I was really trying to figure out what a person is, and at some point, I decided it wasn't just wiring. It seems to me that if you mapped out every circuit and chemical in the brain, you still wouldn't find the person."

"And at that point, neuroscience lost its appeal."

"Very astute, Tino. Plus, I think in Brinkley's world, there's a zeal to get to the conclusion that the mind and the brain are one and the same, and that zeal gets in the way of evaluating the evidence for it."

"So it requires faith."

Hanigan beamed at Tino. "A lot of irony there."

"So you want to know what the essence of a person is. Not finding it with neuroscience. With art, you do?"

"Maybe. Maybe. But that's an insightful question, Tino. I'm still working out what it is I'm trying to express with art. And if I don't have anything to say, why am I trying to be heard?"

"But in doing art, are you necessarily answering that question? I mean, maybe the point is there's not a philosophy to express, but rather just an impression to impart."

"But if I'm just imparting an impression, then there's no content to what I'm saying aside from the impression. I'm not even saying something about why the impression matters. Maybe it's like engaging in idle chit-chat. Pointless but for the fact of communicating. But I love it that you can track me on this. I sometimes feel like I have no one to talk to about it. Certainly not other artists. It's a dog-eat-dog world among artists. We don't sit around sipping espresso together."

"Maybe the point of art, or at least your art, is to express something that can't be expressed some other way."

"Ah, I like that. If I could put it in words, then my art would be writing, not painting."

"'Course, that leaves the possibility that the meaning is in my interpretation rather than what you intend to express."

"Lots of debate about that, in art and philosophy. But if it were entirely true, I think it would just make me an interior decorator."

"Are you trying to express that there is no meaning?"

"No, but that would seem circular to me anyway. The meaning would be that there is no meaning."

"Not if I'm free to say it means whatever I want it to mean."

"I hear that point of view. But I think it's pointless to do all this if I'm not trying to communicate something. I mean something other than that there's nothing."

"But there's something to idle chit-chat, too, isn't there? People talk about the weather to make a connection with one another. Talking is the point, not what's said."

"I don't know if that level of communication would be enough to count as art, but I take your point. Just wanting to convey anything at all suggests something about human consciousness. The social part of it, to be understood even about abstract things. And that's my dilemma about the viewpoint of the Churchlands of the world. I believe we have consciousness, and it exists apart from brain functioning. I came to the conclusion that whatever I was looking to neuroscience to find, I wouldn't find there unless I accepted a completely reductionist point of view in advance. Radical materialism."

"So you left off grad school in neuroscience and landed at art. Are you fulfilled now?"

"I don't know what that would feel like. Or maybe I am and don't realize it. Or maybe my way of being fulfilled is to try to scratch that itch any way I can get to it, and art is the closest I can get for now."

"You're a tortured intellectual."

"Yeah. First world problem."

"Well, Brinkley was at your shindig, so I guess he took your departure in stride."

"He's been great, actually. Despite my apostasy. He tells me he considers me an ally, whatever that means. He helped me get my show going, and showed up himself. Added a little intellectual heft."

"And he brought Elise."

"Yes, lovely Elise. How's it going with her? Have you seen her again?

"Yeah, couple times. A few times."

"'Couple.' 'A few.' Trying kind of hard to be casual, Tino."

Tino smiled, allowing it to be an affecting, bashful smile.

"Can't blame you, though. Come on over, it's ready."

After dinner, they strolled through Hanigan's "finished work" area, an apartment like the one Hanigan lived in, but a little smaller. Many of the works were packaged up, so it was too much trouble to get to them. Then they went over to the works in progress. Tino found this room more appealing. There was more disarray, but it had more of the bohemian artist feel. Hanigan chatted as they looked through paintings, talking about how his thinking had progressed.

He deliberately painted abstractly, but tried to get as close to representational work as he could get, without crossing a line. He didn't want to represent a ship's bow, or a sagebrush, or a sunset, so much as to hint at it. His best work at this stage, Hanigan explained, would cause you to work a little at what ultimate reality might be suggested. Not a boat hull, for example, but a curve which might make you consider the form of the boat hull.

"A Platonic ideal for the curve of a boat hull," Tino offered.

"Good, I like that. I may incorporate it into my next pretentious brochure."

"Use it with my blessing. What's this? Someone else's work?"

"Ah, that," Hanigan said, as if he'd been caught cheating. "Something traditional."

"Yours, then?"

"Oh, yes. Recent, in fact. Not sure why I went with this. I went completely off track to do it. I was working hard on other things. Maybe I was just trying to clear my head, but not quit working altogether."

The subject of the painting was an older man, looking back over his shoulder, with suffused yellow light from above catching on the side of his nearly bald head and the tops of his ears, and strands of curled hair in bushy eyebrows, each strand distinct. A tremulous chin, but above that, an expression of faded desire and resignation, and yet at the same time an unvanquished ethereal spirit.

"It's good, Hanny. Really good."

"Don't tell anyone. I haven't figured out where this came from."

"Your secret's safe."

They stepped back out onto the wide walkway. It was darker now, but lights of the city reflected off the low clouds and back into the open-air studio, creating an effect of gauzy, muted iridescence, almost tangible in the air.

"I'll head back. It's been good seeing you, Hanny."

"Thanks for coming. Every time I see you, I'm glad you happened upon me in the park that day."

"You're much too generous. See you, buddy."

The next Saturday morning, Tino crossed the Golden Gate Bridge and took Highway 1 north to Olema. He was on the very edge of the continent, above a vertiginous drop down to the water on his left side, with a vast sweep of infinite Pacific in view. The new car handled the tight turns beautifully. The sun shone. He was alone, but he was on the way to visit a young beauty, who would be all smiles at his arrival. All was right with the world.

As he approached Stinson Beach, the road descended from its cut high on the mountainside down to almost sea level. At this level, Tino could no longer see the wide expanse of the sea but could catch glimpses of the shimmering water through narrow slices in the sagebrush, laurel, live oak, and Monterey Pine. Skirting Bolinas, Shoreline Drive ceased to follow the shoreline and instead followed the St. Andreas fault through a V-shaped cleft in the countryside— rolling chaparral rising to the right and majestic dark conifers steeply uphill to the left. The turn to Cassie's house was along this road, but Tino missed it and rolled into Olema proper, a couple miles further on.

No loss. It was good to get his bearings from this direction, anyway, since he'd approached Olema through San Rafael on previous trips. He turned back and found the drive, a modest packed-gravel side road, leading to a modest house. Not visible through the oaks, until he was at the house, was an irregular-shaped garden space comprising a couple of acres, all together. Behind that, mountains separating them from Drake's Bay rose steeply. Tino's car would be visible to the house as soon as he turned from the highway. By the time he pulled into the circular drive, Cassie was standing out front with the family's dog, Dewey. By now, Dewey was well familiar with Tino, though not with the car, so he barked until Tino climbed out, and then he trotted up, wagging his tail. Cassie wound her arms around Tino's neck, inviting a kiss with available lips and half-lidded eyes. Tino obliged.

Looking about, Tino could see no other cars. He inferred neither parents nor brother were at home. He felt a sense of inevitability that all things worked in his favor. He had not planned this detail, but he wanted on this occasion, as on all occasions, to avoid awkwardness.

This visit with Cassie would be more than a walk through the woods or coffee in Olema.

"Ready?" he said.

"Hmm, just let me get my bag," Cassie said, sliding reluctantly off him and then trotting up again to the front porch. "C'mon, Dewey!"

Tino had admired her sunny freshness as they embraced, and now, as she returned to the house, he admired her from behind. This night they would spend in a hideaway he'd picked out on Tomales Bay, a little further north. It was a vacation rental with, according to the online pictures, big windows in the bedroom and downstairs living area, all overlooking the bay, Hog Island, and the Point Reyes peninsula beyond that.

Chapter Five

Elise twirled before the mirror in her long gown. It was something in the family of colors of champagne, honey, and wheat, with a soft belt a few shades darker.

"Well of course it looks good on you," Mary said.

Joy's reaction was, "Oh my, this won't do. You can't outshine me—I'm the bride."

"Don't be silly," Mary said to Joy. "All eyes will be on you."

"And you only need one set of eyes on you anyway."

"I knew you were a closet romantic, Elise."

Mary looked at Elise with mock surprise. "No, Elise must have read that somewhere. She's an ice princess, aloof in her tower."

"Not so lonely anymore, I don't think."

Mary shifted to mock indignation. "Oh yes, about that, Elise. You know you stole away my heart's desire."

"Girls. Truce," said Joy. "This is all about me. Me, me, me."

"Joy, you're going to be a bride. You have to practice blushing."

"Mary, I don't think blushing is something you can practice."

"And this isn't the 1950s," Elise added.

Mary was not to be put off her theme. "Elise and I can make you blush, I bet."

"I'm sure you could."

Elise felt some pressure over her final-semester school work, but she was determined not to let this time with her best girlfriends slip by. She sometimes did feel like that princess of Mary's astute imagination. She lived a privileged existence. She took care of her father, getting him to and from his post at the same university she attended. She knew he approved with some pride her choice of classics as a field of study, his own self-perception being that he was a Renaissance man, even at this stage of his life.

It is ever true of us that our self-perception in youth does not depart us in old age, even when we are too old, infirm, or feeble to live it out. Age overtakes our bodies, but not our pride. Elise had observed a slow physical decline in her father over the years, but she perceived there yet remained for the great Professor Brinkley a self-identity wholly wrought up in his intellect. She pictured him, on those days when he did face a classroom of neuroscience graduate students, rolling forward and back before them with all the stature he might have possessed if walking. His standing among them did not require standing.

Elise shared in her father's prestige, not merely because she was his daughter, but because she was his daughter in this particular relationship. Her physical caretaking of him made them closer than they might have been otherwise. She understood he had long ceded to her this superiority of bodily strength, but she thought perhaps it caused him to place his self-identity even more in his towering intellect and the reputation that followed him as a result. Elise saw herself as her father's complement—young, fair, even-tempered but not docile. And so she appeared to others, she knew, especially as she was so often with him, navigating for him the steep San Francisco streets, strategizing how to get from the university to various functions to the house with the singular loggia and the stately office.

Elise had a peculiar benefit from being so often at her father's side. It cast her in the respectable light of doting and helpful daughter, but it also placed her in the company of her father's colleagues and friends, who admired her youth and beauty, certainly, but also her poise and her measured reticence when among those much older, who considered themselves intellectuals. She was a delight to them and was made welcome. As she had blossomed intellectually herself, during her undergraduate years, she won some measure of respect among them in her own right. The world was at her feet, and she was mere weeks from graduating and stepping out into it.

The loggia symbolized all this for Elise. Every time she entered it, she was reminded of her exalted place in the world. The petty annoyances of the day would slip away, and she would consider the larger, wider perspective on her life. She was well provided for materially; she had friends, including a few close friends; she lived at what she believed to be ground zero for the best of what the world had to offer in culture, literature, and art; and if New York could make such a claim in rivalry to San Francisco, why, she had means to sojourn in New York for a season. She was challenged intellectually in her college curriculum. She was aware that over the course of the last three or four years, she had gained an increasing ability to interact in the sophisticated adult world with intelligence, depth, wit, and charm. And yet she maintained this self-perception in a reserved way. She exercised mental discipline. She divided her mind so that this awareness of her own manifold gifts would not turn inward, to effect a corruption of another set of gifts equally important to her—charity, benevolence, kindness, honesty, and a kind of innocence not kindred to naivete.

She was well-nurtured and well-tutored and well-positioned, and yet there was a sameness to it all that made her feel just a little frayed at the edges. Elise was conscious of being at the highest and best summit of all the world had to offer, and in that position, she would expect to be entirely fulfilled. If she had everything she could want, then she ought to feel complete. But she didn't. What she felt was not lack of gratitude, however. She was neither ungrateful for all she had, nor unmindful of it. Her lack of complete contentment arose not from lacking some identifiable thing in her life, but rather from being aware that if there was not contentment now, with all that she had at this moment in her life, could there ever be?

Far below, she saw a familiar figure striding up the sidewalk. *And Tino*, she thought. All this, and now Tino, too. Tino was recognizable even from this vantage point, from his self-confident bearing and that beautiful mane. Elise knew he would be some time with her father in his study. It was a pleasant evening in the loggia, even though it was November. Tino would soon come upstairs looking for her. Elise lingered, savoring the moments of anticipation.

Tino never presumed, and Elise found that endearing. Elise was not a person to be pulled hither and thither by the passions of the moment or the tyranny of the urgent, and Tino was sensitive to this. If she was asked for her company a day or more in advance, she would fill her time in-between in her own way, at her own pace, and under her own control, and in addition have the pleasure of anticipation. She felt an undeniable attraction to Tino. She enjoyed the anticipation of a pleasant evening with him nearly as much as the event itself.

Walking down the street a half-hour later, Tino held Elise's hand. What a sweet, old-fashioned thing. She seldom saw that anymore. It made her think back to a little boyfriend she had when she was ten. She'd held hands with him, too, but then it was a momentary frisson followed by a panic of self-consciousness—hands rigidly joined, eyes straight ahead, not sure what to do next. Elise had that memory to contrast to Tino's warm, natural affection, taking her hand without embarrassment or affectation, and then releasing it only to embrace her with one arm as they walked, and then releasing her again until she seized his upper arm and clung to him, leaving him free to gesture as he talked.

"A beautiful night, a beautiful woman. Intelligence, wit, charm. Everything is perfect," he said, looking around the city as they walked.

"It's getting foggy."

"Ah! So you agree about the beauty, intelligence, and charm."

"No, silly. Where are we going?"

"Have you been to Queensland Grill?"

"Once. It's very nice. You know we could go somewhere not so expensive."

"Every date with you feels like a reason to celebrate."

Elise noted Tino's expansive mood but was not inclined to comment on it. Tino was unusually expressive this night. She said, "That's impossible."

"Not with you."

Elise felt this was as good a time as any to gain some insight, if she could, about what she was to him. "If every date is a celebration, then we should have fewer of them."

Tino laughed. "Okay, help me here. It's good, so we should do it less?"

"No, no, you can't get away with that. 'Celebrate' implies an unusual and special occasion. 'Good' can apply to anything."

"Oh, where to start," Tino said in a voice tinged with sarcasm. "First of all, Elise Brinkley is not an everyday, routine thing."

"True," Elise responded, as though magnanimously conceding the point.

"Second—" Tino left off the thought and voiced mock exasperation. "Why do you vex me, female? Did you learn to argue this way from your old man?"

"Speaking of my old man," she began.

"Revered patriarch," he amended.

"Speaking of my revered patriarch, what do you two scheme about every time you come over?"

"Deep philosophy. City politics. Business."

"Elise."

"Elise," he confirmed. "Most perplexing, though, Elise is."

"He lectures you about neurophilosophy."

"I like your dad. We talk about a lot of things. He's gone out of his way for me, and I appreciate it. He's a good man."

"Seriously, are you working for him? What are you doing?"

"I told you, I'm a consultant for some companies doing business with the district supervisors."

"But what do you consult about? And what's my dad's connection?"

"Your dad doesn't have a connection, except he seems to know everyone in the city, and his friends hooked me up. Here's the restaurant."

Tino held open the door for Elise. There was a lull in the conversation as they took in their surroundings and were shown to a table. The atmosphere made Elise think of Tino's repeated extravagances. When they sat down, she returned to her question before Tino might run off in a different direction. "So do you work for a consulting firm of some sort?"

"Independent. This isn't really very interesting, but I'll tell you anything you want to know."

"Are you a lobbyist?"

"Not exactly. You know, there's a lot going on in this city. It's a very progressive place, no secret there. The city government is very, very hands-on about what happens in San Francisco. It's not an old-school municipality where they run the police and the fire department and that's it. There are lots of competing interests. Lots of feathers to unruffle. Lots of delicate negotiation." Tino made a gesture with his shoulders as if he were maneuvering through a crowd. Then he focused on his menu.

"Pays well, though, I guess," Elise said.

"I'm really lucky to have fallen into it." Tino suddenly looked up from his menu, as if considering for the first time what might be going through Elise's mind. "But I wasn't destitute when I got here, so…" His voice trailed off. He looked back down at his menu.

"Oh, Tino, I'm sorry to pry. I was just curious." The smallest crease in Tino's brow had caused Elise some regret that she might be the cause of it. "I care about you. I just want to know more about you."

Tino sat back a little, and his face took on a satisfied grin. "Wait, say that again. You *care* about me?" He drew out the word "care."

"Don't make fun of me."

"I am not, at all, making fun of you. I just want to savor the moment. I think maybe, after all, you're not merely tolerating me."

"Humph," Elise responded, making a show of studying her menu. But then she decided a better retort should follow, so she said, coquettishly, "We'll say no more about that."

"No," Tino said, his voice suddenly passionate. He'd dropped his menu and had reached across for Elise's hands, causing her to let her menu drop, too.

"Yes, do say more, Elise. Do. I care about you. You know I do. I just want to know I'm not in it alone. Tell me. Don't be ironic or coy. Tell me."

Elise closed her eyes, a moment longer than a blink, and opened them to the table before her, though her face was uplifted to Tino's. Then she looked up at him. She could feel that her cheeks were hot, and that every emotion she'd felt about Tino was there on her face for him to see, no matter what she said. She just nodded her head yes, just so slightly, seeing his eyes transfixed on hers. She felt him gently squeeze her hands, in reply, and then relax. A waiter had approached but had paused several feet from the table. Elise glanced over at the waiter, and then back to Tino, as they withdrew their hands from the tabletop. Elise felt no embarrassment at this display, but instead felt liberated. A feeling she would ponder later.

For the rest of their time at the restaurant, Elise felt as though she were watching the two of them there at the table from another vantage point. They laughed. They talked frankly. They talked in conspiratorial asides. They spoke with gesture and inflection and with shared understanding and to each other only. The evening was a pastiche of Tino's eyes on her, his candlelit face, the clink of silverware, Tino's hand on hers, the low murmur of the crowd in the restaurant.

This continued, this feeling of observing while participating, on the walk home. They went the long way. Now they walked side by side, facing forward, rather than sitting still and facing each other as they had in the restaurant, and it struck Elise that this posture was emblematic, or symbolic, perhaps—a short season of being absorbed each with the other, and then a longer one of walking together through the world, looking outward, but with frequent turning of their attention each to the other, and throughout the walk, arm in arm or hand in hand.

Elise's nature was not like Tino's, she knew. Tino was spontaneous. He wore his heart on his sleeve. She was more reserved. It could make for an interesting and mutually helpful combination. The walk home was a continuation of their exchange, but, as at the restaurant, Elise continued to experience it almost secondhand, storing up memory to recall later the feeling, and to turn over in her mind the nuance and shades of meaning to all he said, and how he said it, and what he must have been thinking as he responded to her. The whole evening, she knew, would replay itself for her in parts, in her mind, until it had settled into an emotionally coherent whole, becoming part of her. She experienced a shared consciousness with Tino that seemed to live and breathe on its own.

They walked through Walton Park, and to a spot next to the water. They looked out toward Treasure Island and watched the reflection of light on the water of the bay. They walked along the Embarcadero, past the spot where the farmer's market was sometimes set up, and stopped again to look out over the water. The words they exchanged seemed less important than the new quality of the space between them in which they were exchanged.

Now, though, Elise felt she was returned to reality. A breeze had sprung up, and it was chillier. They turned away from the waterfront to go back out to the main road via a gap between buildings. Even at this hour, there were a few people milling about. A small, thin woman stood on the walkway, midway between the two buildings, looking at them. Wide-eyed, it seemed to Elise. She was not one of the drug-addled wraiths that sometimes glided by, but a woman in late middle-age, dressed in a common-sense style suggesting a provincial home far from San Francisco. Elise's arm was curled inside of Tino's. She felt him tense up. The wind gusted. Elise looked around, up the sidewalk along the bay in each direction. She thought she heard Tino's name, not enunciated clearly, but with a quiet sigh, instead. And then she heard the sound of the breeze against the corner of the building and thought it must be the wind, gusting off the water and making itself heard in its sweeps through the edifices alongside the quay.

Chapter Six

David stood at the door to the school with a handful of flyers that served as programs for the morning's service. He had dedicated a half-hour that morning to praying for the success of the Twin Peaks Galilean Church, a daughter church to the Berkeley congregation. David had attained an unusual level of concentration, in his prayer, and of God's presence, praying specifically for each person involved in bringing about this opening day. He had prayed for people as yet unknown in the areas of Twin Peaks, Eureka Valley, Cole Valley, and the Castro. He had gone past his thirty minutes, and when he stood to get ready for the day, he resolved to maintain an attitude of prayerfulness as best he could. He drove and stopped to pick up Joy. He was a bit distracted, but Joy was patient. He was grateful she understood his preoccupation with the success of the church plant.

Joy parted from David at the door of the little classroom building and was instantly engrossed in conversation with some of the members of their church in Berkeley and others they saw less frequently at their sister church in Oakland. The members of those churches had come this day to salt the proceedings, providing an inviting crowd-let calculated to put genuine newcomers at ease.

David passed out a number of the flyers, mostly to the Berkeley and Oakland church members, but there were a few he was unsure of—they might be from those churches or might be present from curiosity at something new. San Francisco was like that. Old-time religion was not received well, but San Franciscans like most people are ever in search of spiritual understanding and at least open-minded about what that might mean. Some, David knew, would think of the experience as just an hour or so of spiritual exercise, employing one familiar tradition of spiritual seeking. But others might hear the words and understand they had meaning apart from a general expression of spirituality.

David had prayed earnestly for his friend the pastor, Sung-ho Park, who was only a few years older than David. Earlier in the week, Sung had sent David an email that was immensely encouraging. It was a continuation of a discussion they'd started earlier. About words and reality. Do we speak words that correspond to reality? Or do we speak words that *constitute* reality? Do we use words to discuss the reality that is, or do we use them to construct our own subjective reality within our own mind? Sung wrote that God's reality was something to be discerned by them rather than created by them, but hearers of the message now might not receive it with that understanding. In the culture they were speaking into, someone might be exposed to the truth, yet feel he'd selected but one spiritual path from an array in front of him. How would that person respond to the words of Jesus, which David and Sung believed to be independently true? The danger, Sung pointed out, was that they might impute to the messenger the same way of using words that they employed for themselves—a construct for the speaker's subjective reality. How could they hope for penetration of the words of He who is "I Am"? The One whose very words were living waters rather than merely a personal choice? People have learned to think critically, Sung pointed out, but often they thought that meant being critical of the very idea of objective truth.

David stepped away from the door a few paces to greet Mark Hanigan. "Hanny. I hoped you'd be here. I prayed for you by name this morning."

"Thank you," Hanny replied tentatively. "How am I doing on time?" Hanigan fumbled for his phone while he looked quickly around at their surroundings. "I walked past and had to turn around."

"You're fine. Fifteen minutes to spare. Did I mess up the directions on my email?" David had a moment of anxiety. He'd sent Hanigan a cut-and-paste of the same directions he'd put on the flyers.

"No, the directions were fine," Hanigan said. "Second thoughts, I guess, and then I wasn't paying attention and walked right past the street. Should have looked up." The school building they had rented was on what amounted to a wide cul-de-sac high on a shoulder of Twin Peaks.

"You're here, though. And you said before, you want what's real and what's true. Do you know Christ? Or are you seeking?"

"Come with me, Hanny, I'm rescuing you," a bright voice said. It was Joy, who had materialized beside them. "David is a little overeager."

David realized his error immediately. He had lapsed into a stock procedure for old-school evangelism, as if Hanny were a bumpkin who had never considered spiritual or any other truth and would hear the Good News through David's pressing and be instantly transformed. "Sorry," he muttered and gestured to acknowledge he was out of bounds. Joy walked with Hanny out into the yard in front of the little school building, where others were congregating. David self-consciously throttled back his enthusiasm, but resumed his post.

After the service, David stood with Joy in the yard of the school building again. It was a fine day, sunny and bright. They were trying to greet as many as they could among people who appeared to be true visitors. David was feeling a glow of success. "It couldn't have gone better," he said to Joy.

"I love you."

David lowered his voice to speak an aside to her. "No time for that, flirt." Then he turned a bit in the other direction to speak to a young man who was blinking from his exit into bright sunshine. David saw Joy slip away to connect with a middle-aged woman and a girl who was about Joy's own age, possibly the older woman's daughter. The young man David greeted had an air of bemusement at the proceedings. David wanted to query him about how he'd heard of the church—had the flyers been effective, had he been personally invited, had he just wandered by—but, chastened from his encounter with Hanigan earlier, he held back. Even setting himself up as an established member might be taken the wrong way, so David ended the encounter by saying only, "I hope to see you here next week."

David turned to see Hanigan just stepping through the door and was gratified to see he was apparently not in a hurry to run off. Right behind Hanigan was Sung-ho, speaking animatedly. They parted, and Hanigan walked toward David.

"How was your Thanksgiving?" Hanigan asked.

"Great. Yours? Did you stay in town?"

"Yeah, my brother and sister-in-law came up from San Jose."

"When's the next show?"

"Coming up. In a month or so."

"We'll be there if we can. We're still on the email list, right?"

"Absolutely," Hanigan said.

"We parked at the bottom of the hill. Do you want a ride?"

"No, thanks, my place isn't far."

Joy approached. "Is he behaving?" she asked Hanigan.

Hanigan just chuckled. They fell into step together, taking the steep hill slowly. Hanigan asked David, "How's work?"

"Pretty interesting, actually. To me, anyway. Have my own project. Having to learn some local politics to execute it."

"Good luck with that." Hanigan's tone suggested the task might be overwhelming.

"Do you follow local politics?" Joy asked of Hanigan.

"I more or less keep up with it. I sometimes have a hard time tracking the principle behind decisions that get made. I mean, I understand what they do and the reasons they give for it, but no one seems to be asking what's an appropriate thing for the Board of Supervisors to be involved with in the first place."

"The welfare of the city, I guess they'd say."

"Right, but that could mean anything. Aren't there some kinds of things that are proper for the city to take on, and some kinds of things that are just private?"

"Like the vacation house thing," Joy said. She was between them and a half-step behind.

"Sure, that's a good example," Hanigan answered, turning slightly toward her as he walked.

"That's one of the things I'm working on," David said.

"What are you doing with it?"

"I'm taking some workflow software and specializing it for local government. Starting with San Francisco."

"So you want to track legislation about vacation rentals?"

"All kinds of legislation, but vacation rentals is a hot topic in San Francisco politics right now. Still trying to get the whole thing up and running, but we're doing some off-line beta testing. They passed that ordinance, and we're backfilling data to show how the process fits it. We want to make it more scalable for all kinds of issues."

"The ordinance. The one that says you can't rent out your own place online? A lot of people are up in arms about it," Hanigan said, "but to me, even the state of the law before that was incomprehensible."

"What was that?" Joy asked.

They were now standing next to David's car. David knew better than to leave Joy to one side of the conversation, and she seemed to be interested in the subject. "Join us for lunch?" he asked Hanigan.

"Sure."

To Joy, David said, "Why don't we walk toward Hanny's and find a place to eat, and leave the car here?"

"Sure."

They proceeded north. Hanigan said to David, "Go ahead with the story. You probably know more about it than me."

"Well," David began, by way of instructing Joy, with Hanigan as an attentive audience, "for a long time, the law was you couldn't rent out places to stay unless you operated as a licensed hotel. You could rent out your apartment or house with a regular lease, but you couldn't rent for a few days or a week, like for vacation."

"Why shouldn't people be allowed to do what they want?" Joy asked.

David said, "Sorry, Joy here is an anarchist."

"I'm a *selective* anarchist," she said. "Continue."

"The law was intended to make hotel taxes enforceable and add to the character of the city, blah, blah, blah. Actually, it doesn't matter why. People will debate that sort of thing till the cows come home. I'll just say what it is and leave it at that."

"Wise policy when you're talking San Francisco politics," Hanigan said.

"Do cows take a long time to come home?" Joy asked.

"Moving along," David said, "they changed the law so people could do short-term rentals, but only if it was their own place, the place they lived a certain number of days out of the year."

"A step in the right direction," Hanigan said.

"Of course, that got people to thinking why there should be any restriction at all. Technology makes it feasible now. The big debate is about whether renting out places would change the character of the city, whether it would make it harder for locals to find some place affordable to live. Which is already a problem, as some of us know all too well."

Hanigan and Joy uttered emphatic assent.

"Hotels don't want the competition of people renting out their place here and there. Every stay in a private rent-out is one less hotel room sold. 'Hotelization,' it's called."

"Sounds like part of a time-honored tradition," Hanigan said. "Big business getting together with government to pass laws to keep out competition from small business. In this case, hotels against people who just want to rent out their own property."

"The backdrop here is that the city has traditionally controlled this sort of thing, but it wasn't that big of a deal. But then along came websites for private short-term rentals, and it came to be an accepted thing. The market for apartments and houses available for a day or a week just took off. It's not just a matter of opening up the market to private local renters. It's on a whole new scale, and it's a threat."

"To hotels," Joy said.

"And to the city. They have a concern with the taxes getting paid, but they also have a concern with housing availability for locals. They think there will be fewer places available for long-term rentals."

Hanigan said, "The city wants control."

"Sure," David said, "but they articulate a reason for it. It's a political issue whether it makes any sense or not. But because it's a political issue, it's just the kind of thing I want to try to measure."

"What's to measure?"

"I'm trying to correlate lobbying effort and money spent to political outcomes."

"Oh, now that could be really interesting."

Joy said, "David is a genius."

"So," Hanigan said, "the availability of instantly reliable information opens up a whole new market. Just like with the ride service apps. The hotel lobby wouldn't be so worried about mom-

and-pop renters, except that Mom and Pop are signing up with these websites."

"It's 'economically disruptive,' as they say."

"It just sounds like buggy-whip manufacturers trying to outlaw cars."

"Joy, I admire how you crystallize the issue," Hanigan said.

"Thank you," she said with an exaggerated bow of her head.

David continued, "The technology also makes it pretty irresistible for out-of-town or corporate owners to jump into hotelization, so I can appreciate the hotels' consternation, but—"

"That's what innovation does," Hanigan finished for him. "The hotels should adapt or die."

"Don't forget the taxes," Joy intoned.

"Yes, of course. The city's real interest. They have a big tax base with the hotels. They could go with the flow, and change how they tax—"

Joy interjected, "Or they can do what the City of San Francisco has a history of doing—try to control the private economy to fit it into the city's old way of thinking. I'm not seeing any restaurants."

"Oh, sorry," Hanigan said. "We have to go over a block, to Cole Street. Do you like Mexican?"

They settled in at a window table at Paquito's. After they had ordered, Hanigan was eager to resume the conversation. "About the hotel business. It seems to me the first question about anything ought to be 'who decides.' I'll give you a personal example. My building. Not far from here. When I was a teenager, we moved from Ohio, and my parents put everything they had into this run-down building. We lived there, and my parents worked to maintain it. When my mom died, she left the building to my brother and me. We get a little rent out of it, a very little bit after all the taxes, and of course, I live there. If I wanted to rent out one of the apartments or one of the rooms to vacation renters, technically I couldn't."

Joy said, "So you think you ought to decide, not the city."

"Crazy, right? My brother and I own the building."

"Well, it gets a little more complicated," David said.

"This is San Francisco," Hanigan wryly observed.

"It turns out the websites for short-term rentals don't all work the same. Some collect the taxes, and some leave it to the individual owners to collect the taxes."

"Nobody's going to do that if they don't have to," Hanigan said.

"And people have been renting places out for years, just FYI," Joy added.

"Right, but that just means there's a little more complexity to the project of how the government might continue to tax out-of-towners."

"There's no way the government is going to be agile enough to react to that," Joy said.

Hanigan said, "Joy, I want you to run as my district supervisor."

"Busy."

David said, "Let's deal with the reality of government as it is, not what we think it ought to be. There's a big battle brewing, and it's all brought on by this disruption. We're looking for a big showdown between the entrenched San Francisco hotels and the websites that would like to list short-term rentals in the city. Maybe individual property owners, too, if they can come together."

"I'm sorry to hear this affects you personally," Joy said to Hanigan.

"Well, it's a little more direct, for me, but you pay taxes, too. This affects everyone, ultimately. That's why the principle behind government action is more important than the individual actions. In my humble opinion, it would be nice to have the option to fix up the unoccupied apartments on my floor and rent them out on a short-term basis. I would have a little more revenue, but I wouldn't have to have neighbors in my workspace all the time. You hear these debates, and it's all abstract."

"Yeah. Until it's personal."

"Isn't it about freedom?" Joy said. "The city tells you what you can and can't do with your own property."

David said, "My project makes me realize there's a difference between general interests and special interests. Some companies are more affected by a rule than others, and they have an incentive to get in there and lobby for it or against it. But the rule that results is going to affect everyone's freedom."

"Special interests. Now there's a phrase you don't hear so much anymore," Hanigan said. "I remember when I was growing up, my dad used to go on all the time about special interests. He came along in the sixties and seventies. The idea used to be that government action was for general interests. If it affected special interests, then it was suspect."

"Because it opened the door to soft corruption," David said.

"Or hard corruption," Hanigan responded. "Back then, if you had winners and losers among the special interests, that would signal the government was reaching into something it shouldn't. Back then, lobbyists were thought to be kind of shady."

David considered that he might not have been engaged in this issue at all were it not for his work project. It occurred to him Hanigan was in a sense proselytizing, just as David had been earlier, overstepping himself in talking about Hanigan's relationship to God.

"What's funny?" Hanigan asked.

"Just thinking," David said, waving his hand a little to signify a private, and inconsequential, thought.

"Anyway," Hanigan said, "that's why I was going on about principle. We don't have to lobby about things we decide to do on our own."

Chapter Seven

Tino found the gate for his Austin flight and looked around for an out-of-the-way place to wait. He could spin a story about this trip on the spot, if necessary, but by longstanding habit, he preferred to keep his private affairs private. He carried himself as he always did—as if he owned the place. His usual sunny demeanor had not materially withered when he decided it was necessary to meet with his friend Roger. It was necessary, that's all, and he would make of it what he could. If life circumstances took him to a fair city to meet an old friend, what could be wrong with that?

And yet, Tino couldn't help a mild resentment, because he wouldn't have been visiting Roger in person if Roger were a little more on the ball. Tino wanted to be loved by all, and he wanted to enjoy his new life in San Francisco with the benefit of his carefully-laid plans. The unexpected appearance of his mother meant those plans had failed, and failed significantly. This called for more than a mere adjustment to plan with Roger over the phone. Tino could normally turn unexpected events somehow to his favor, but his mother had caught him by surprise. He'd had no time to plan a reaction. Moreover, the encounter was not a solo event that could be managed in isolation. His mother. Here. San Francisco. He had imagined she might show up in Austin, where Tino was supposed to be. Not here.

This might be a little awkward, but not more awkward than that night with Elise when he'd hurried her away from the Embarcadero, with as much an air of insouciance as he could muster. Elise was not only a love interest of Tino's, but she represented a connection to others he relied upon. When his mother had appeared in the windswept walkway alongside the quay, there had been on Tino's part the strained effort not to see, nor hear, in that compressed little moment when his eyes met hers and then slid down and away to the wet pavement ahead.

He had quickened the pace as much as he dared, for himself and Elise at his arm. It pained Tino to have to stroll by in that way. His whole life was charted by mechanisms for avoidance of pain. The moment threatened to stain the self-image he had built of himself and the one he had actively cultivated in others. He would have liked to think of it no further, but he was painfully aware of how it might be received, as if he'd turned his back on his own mother. It would be too hard to explain the longer, more complicated story. If necessary, he could try to work with an explanation having to do with the poor visibility in the fog and gloom of night. With Elise, that would strain plausibility, however. She was there. The atmosphere was not so murky that Tino might conceivably have glided by his own mother, insensible of her presence. And anyway, it would just pop open another problem. Hadn't he told Elise he had no family left?

Tino took a cab from the Austin airport and found he was only ten minutes or so from Roger's apartment. It was about three in the afternoon, but Roger sometimes kept odd hours. The apartment was hard by the Colorado River, part of it fronting on East Riverside Drive. The driver let Tino off, and he walked around a commercial strip to the apartments behind. The interior of the complex was accessible only by key-carded exterior gates, but Tino remembered a gate at one end that remained ajar all the time. He entered and walked straight to Roger's apartment. He knocked. No answer. He called Roger's number. No answer. Roger's place of work was a bank. He did some sort of data management there, so he worked at the bank's main office, downtown. Might as well try that. Tino had texted Roger a message from San Francisco that he was coming, and Roger had responded simply, "See you then," not responding further to inquiries about when, specifically, and where.

Tino felt a rising irritation at these events, doing war with his usual calm affability. He reminded himself he had free time in a hospitable city and, in his normal state of mind, would be readily received and among friends who were moments before strangers. He texted for a car and had a ride almost immediately. He was let off on Sixth Street. Tino was not a big drinker, but that seemed to be the draw for the area around Roger's work building. Tino decided to camp out nearby. He settled onto a bar stool in a trendy spot with large glass windows facing Roger's bank and ordered from a weirdly complex menu of local beers. He would take a sip, stare out the window, look at his phone, and repeat. Twice he was greeted by locals who turned out to be University of Texas students, one a leggy blonde clearly disappointed that Tino would not be detached from his perch.

An hour later, a text finally came back from Roger, suggesting they meet at Sock Hop. Another bar. He inquired of the bartender and was told to head uphill from where he was, the last spot before leaving the bar district. Tino walked briskly up the hill, finding that the only place it could be was not Sock Hop, but a bar called Illannoy. No other place around looked like a good candidate for a bar. Tino was now truly exasperated. He went in and inquired of the bartender where he might find Sock Hop. The bartender smirked and pointed to an interior door behind Tino. Tino looked back, and the bartender gestured confirmation. So Tino went through the door and found a windowless chamber that was a little bar within a bar, and at one end, seated at a little table with his back to the wall and facing the entrance, was Roger.

"Congratulations," he said, a little flatly it seemed, to Tino. "You passed the Austin test. You persevered."

"What are you talking about? What is this place?"

"Sock Hop, man," Roger said. "Secret bar. Seemed like just the place for our rendezvous."

"I can hardly hear," Tino said loudly over the old-style vinyl-playing stereo.

"What?" Roger yelled. Then he laughed. "Messing with you. C'mon, we can talk in the other room." Roger stood and stepped awkwardly around the little table. He'd put on weight since the last time Tino saw him. Roger had always been fond of beer. Tino wondered if he wasn't already somewhat inebriated. He assumed Roger had just left work, but perhaps not.

The noise level was only a little better in Illannoy proper, but they had a large booth walled in on three sides, and Tino decided it would have to do. He had come halfway across the continent to manage his own situation, not just to give Roger an earful. He might yet need assistance from Roger.

Albert Norton, Jr.

Roger ordered another beer as he sat down. "To what do I owe the honor, Tino?"

Tino gave what he intended to be an ingratiating smile. "Haven't seen you in a while, man. Thought I'd come see you in your natural habitat."

Roger smiled, his mouth in the right place, but not his eyes.

"I just wanted to hear from you directly what's going on," Tino said. "I was getting my mother's letters from you, and everything seemed fine."

Roger shrugged.

"So," continued Tino, "she always wrote me more than I wrote her, but then I heard less and less from her. Until lately."

"So why are you here, Tino? If you want to get in touch with her, go to New Albany."

"Well, that's not it, Roger. I had wanted to kind of keep up the charade for a while until I was more settled."

Roger shrugged again and signaled for the waitress. Tino was taken aback at how fast the last beer had gone. Then Roger said, "Yeah, I know, that was the story, I got it. But that was months ago, right? How long do you want me to pretend to your mother you're living in Austin? The whole thing doesn't seem right to me, Tino."

"It's complicated," Tino said.

"You know what, Tino? I don't think it is." Roger had let slip just a hint of...what? Irritation? Contempt, even? But then he looked up at Tino with more a look of almost pleading, as if it pained him to be involved and didn't want to think the worst of him. Roger sat looking at Tino. Even while he lifted his beer and upended it, he watched Tino all the while.

"She's my mom. You're not doing wrong by her," Tino finally said.

"Sure about that, Tino? Why are you here?" Roger spoke with a flat calmness at odds with the words he spoke.

Tino tried to read his expression.

Roger resumed, more assertive now. "Why did you come all the way from San Francisco? Just to hang with Rodge? What do you want me to do? Why not just say the charade is over? Tell your mom where you are. Pick up the phone and talk to her. Write her letters with your return address. Call her and say, 'Hey Mom, digging the West Coast, come on out and visit.' She may not do email, but the postal service still serves Indiana, far as I know."

"She knows," Tino said, solemnly, studying Roger. Enough with what he ought to do, he thought. Tino wanted to return Roger's attention to what Tino wanted his mother to know. How was it Roger's business what he chose to share with his own mother?

"Tino, I sent her letters on to you. I postmarked yours to her from Austin, just like you asked. She writes you a hell of a lot more than you write her, by the way. Why couldn't you just set her up with email, and leave me out of it? Then you could pretend to be anywhere."

"She's old-school that way. I told you. Talk to me, Roger."

Tino saw the color rise in Roger's face, but Roger said nothing. He just waved for the waitress again.

"You're going through those fast," Tino said. "Look, Roger, I'm sorry I even asked you to do this. I'm just trying to protect her, but I had to get away. Maybe I was wrong, but I thought I could take care of her and do what I felt I needed to do, and this would be an easy way to handle it. I never thought it would put you in an embarrassing position. It was just supposed to be an innocent ruse for a while."

"She knows you lied because she found you in San Francisco."

"Yeah, about that…"

"I told her."

Tino felt his forced smile fading. "Why?"

"Because she came here first, Tino." Tino felt a tightening in the stomach. A rare thing for him. He could see by the way Roger was responding that if she had appeared here in person, Roger would have quickly capitulated, not only telling her Tino was in San Francisco, but telling her it had been set up that way since before Tino slipped out of New Albany. His mother was trusting, and naïve, and innocent, but she wasn't stupid.

Roger resumed. "Did you use me, Tino?"

"What did she say?"

"She came here looking for you, Tino. How could you not see that coming? She cares about you. She sensed something was amiss. She's your mother. Mothers do that." Roger took a long swig of beer. His eyes were bleary. "She was worried about you. I couldn't sit here and lie to her face. I told her you had your own reasons for wanting to hide your real whereabouts." Roger was beginning to slur his speech. "And, buddy-roe, I even spun it in your favor. For whatever reason, you wanted to be on your own, but you couldn't quite cut her off completely, so you came up with this Austin story. 'Tino's out there finding himself.' You know what? She was still just worried about you. She wasn't even angry. She just wanted to know why for your own sake. She's a good woman."

Tino relaxed a little. Roger drank too much. He was becoming mawkish. He probably only wanted an end to relaying letters. But then Roger continued.

"I didn't know much about your dad."

Tino felt a tensing at the back of his neck.

"A hard worker, I gather," Roger continued. "Until he died, I mean. That was, what, a few months before you took off? Weeks?"

Tino shrugged, a gesture to hint this was irrelevant.

"When we were growing up, we did everything together. But I saw your dad what, a dozen times total? Always coming in from work or going off to work. How many jobs did he work?"

Tino looked back at Roger, trying to maintain a neutral expression.

"But your family lived modestly, just like mine. Your mother certainly respected your dad. He did well for you and your mom, even on a dockworker's pay."

"Yes."

"Quite well."

"I suppose."

"I think you know."

Tino tried to maintain a neutral look.

Roger turned the bottle up and drained the last little bit from it, trying not to look at Tino directly. He set the empty bottle back on the table between them. Then after a tremulous pause, he looked Tino in the eye and said, "Did you steal from your mother, Tino?"

Tino had another of those rare moments of inability to rise immediately to the occasion. What did Roger know? And for that matter, what could his mother know? But he ended up saying the only thing he felt he could say: "No."

Then Tino looked around and caught the eye of the waitress. Holding her attention for a second with uplifted finger, he asked Roger, "Do you want another beer?"

"No. Go back to San Francisco, Tino."

Tino landed in Oakland. Landing back in San Francisco that same day seemed distasteful to him, so he paid extra for the switch in airports, and from Oakland rented a car so he could go straight up along the East Bay and cross over to Marin County. He had it in mind to stop in to see Cassie, but it would be late by the time he arrived. He texted her that they should meet the next morning. Moments later, his phone pinged, and without picking it up from the seat next to him, Tino could see a string of yellow smiley-faced emoticons.

Tino found his patron's vacation rental and trudged inside with his bag. He slept in an upstairs room with the window open, and early the next morning awoke to the sound of gravel crunching under car tires. He knew without looking that it would be Cassie's truck. Sure enough, it was parked on the wide gravel park adjacent the house Tino had obtained for the weekend. He rolled out of bed and quickly brushed his teeth, and then greeted Cassie as she ascended the outside steps to the front door, with grocery bags in hand.

"Here, I got it. Is that all of them?"

"That's it," she said cheerfully, returning her keys to her straw purse now that her hands were free. "This place is great."

"Yeah, I thought you'd like it. Come look around." The apartment was the refurbished upstairs portion of what had once been a stand-alone garage. It apparently had been within the curtilage of the large house next door at one time. There was climbing ivy and exotic coastal flora around the grounds, overgrowing the brick wall surrounding the apartment. Inside, there was a living room, bedroom, bathroom, and a spacious kitchen with table and chairs. It was all painted white, with utilitarian but attractive carpet, and lots of light shining through the numerous windows.

Tino felt he'd awakened to a new day, with his life somewhat back in order, and it seemed fitting they greet the coolness of the new day with coffee in the warm kitchen. But that would have to wait, because Cassie was inclined to start it under warm covers in the bedroom, and Tino was persuaded to her point of view immediately.

Later, they did have coffee, and Cassie made toast for herself and an omelet for Tino. "Who's manning the store today?" Tino asked.

Cassie turned toward Tino, spatula in hand. "Oh, the market. My brother. Billy. What do you want to do today?"

Tino smirked.

"I mean, besides that."

They set out to walk down Mesa Road into Point Reyes Station. Cassie was all smiles, alive to the world around her. "It's wonderful. It's all so wonderful," she said.

"You live maybe five miles from here."

"I know, but it all looks so different today. Look!" Ahead of them, to the right of the road, was a pasture. A water basin and feeding stall were at the corner of the pasture close to the road. A grand-looking but old horse of maybe sixteen hands loitered there. He was slow but not doddering, enjoying his active retirement. Behind him, the pasture sloped down toward a treed bottom, and to wetlands, and eventually to a tributary to Lagunitas Creek farther in the distance. Low fog was burning off, and the mist gave way gradually, as one looked up, to pale blue sky above the mysterious gray. A pickup truck rolled past them, down the hill, coming to a stop in the middle of the road next to the horse's pen. As Tino and Cassie watched, an older, gray-bearded man of perhaps sixty stepped out, leaving the driver's door open. He wore a gray, floppy felt hat. He walked around behind his truck, hopped the little roadside ditch, and approached the imperious retiree with two apples. By the time Tino and Cassie caught up to this scene, the man had finished with what they took to be a daily stop for the animal. The man squinted toward them, giving a slight nod that caused the brim of his felt hat to dip and momentarily obstruct his eyes. Then he was turning toward his truck again. He drove downhill at the same trundling pace as before his stop, rounded the bend, and was then out of sight. Tino and Cassie paused next to the gray-withered, attentive horse.

"Enchanting," Cassie said.

They supped that night at Dmitry's in Inverness. Tino felt far removed from the painful Austin visit, and from the low-grade anxiety that might await him in San Francisco. He tried not to think of his mother's whereabouts and to concentrate instead on the here and now. Impossibly beautiful surroundings, starting with the fresh-faced girl who sat opposite him.

"You've barely touched your food," Tino said. "You don't like it?"

"It's very good, but that's all I can eat. I'll get a box."

"You're not sick, are you?"

"A little queasy. It'll go away."

"Maybe you should see a doctor."

"I have."

"And he says it'll go away?"

"Yes. Soon, probably. But definitely not more than six months."

Tino eyed Cassie uncertainly.

Cassie let her gaze break from Tino's. She tried to suppress a smile as she looked down to the table, and around the room, and then back to Tino. "We're going to have a baby," she said.

Chapter Eight

Joy and Elise walked along on the packed-dirt path that would take them all the way out to the northernmost tip of the Point Reyes peninsula, Tomales Point. Joy stopped and turned. "Mary, catch up!"

As Mary trotted up, Elise said, "Sorry, Mary, we can go slower."

"No, no, no, I'll keep up. I refuse to be the dead weight."

"We'll slow down a little, you speed up a little, and we'll rest more. How about that?" Joy suggested.

"Works for me," Mary said. "I will do my part. But this is a bachelorette thing. It ought to involve beautiful men in some way."

"I'm sure there will be beautiful men on this trail," Elise said.

"I was thinking of an abundance of beautiful men. An extravagance of them. Dressed in a sort of way, you know."

Joy laughed aloud.

"We're kind of remote for that, I guess," Elise said. "But we don't need men cluttering up the view, anyway."

"Says the girl with the Greek god," Mary observed. "*My* Greek god."

Before Elise could remonstrate, Mary added, "Poor Joy, no longer among the living after tomorrow. And for us, no more Joy. And Elise, you'll be next."

"I won't—"

"You'll be next. And then the Axis powers will be broken up. The sisterhood will be torn asunder."

Elise said, "Such drama—"

"What is that?" Joy asked. She had stopped dead in her tracks, and Mary, a half-step behind her, bumped into her.

"Shh."

"Why are you shushing me, Joy?" Mary said. "They know we're here."

"It's the tule elk we read about," Elise said. "Let's get a picture."

"Careful, Elise."

Elise moved quickly but at an angle she hoped the animals would not find threatening. Several females stopped their grazing and raised their heads to eye her better.

"Elise," Joy hissed. Several more elk raised their heads. One turned a step toward them. There were no trees here, nowhere to go should the elk take offense.

"Elise," Mary said, more loudly. As she did so, there became visible a huge set of antlers, looming up between bushes to one side of the fifteen or so females grazing or lying on the ground. As they watched, the impossibly wide antlers rose up higher and higher as the male took to his feet. He was a good seventy-five yards away, but even at this distance, he seemed huge.

They watched as Elise made a rapid retreat, jogging with arms down by her side in a posture that would have said to another person, "Don't mind me, moving out of the way," but of course this body language might be lost on a bull elk disturbed in his nap. Elise belatedly realized there was really nowhere to go. The open path was no safe ground. It was just as open to the elk. The girls walked briskly along it, looking over their shoulders, hoping the male would stay put and not approach.

Fifty yards on, they felt safe enough to giggle over the near misadventure. They slowed down, exhilarated by the excitement and more sensitive now to the natural beauty around them, in part as a result of the unfenced proximity of the bull elk. They paused for one of their breaks with Mary, sitting on path-side boulders, when Elise spotted a dog walking without an owner. Or what she thought was a dog. As it drew nearer, they saw it was a coyote, entirely focused on some smaller prey in the straw grass a few yards from the path. It ignored the young women just a few yards away. They all sat quietly, fascinated that they should be so studiously ignored by this animal that ought to be afraid of them. And, it occurred to Elise, perhaps they should be afraid of it.

They walked along the crest of the land that sloped off to the east and to the west. The Pacific was sometimes visible to their left, and sometimes not. Several times they left the path to stand closer to the shoulder of the ridgetop and take in the vast expanse of blue, 180 degrees from northeast to southwest. Partway into their hike, Tomales Bay came into sight beyond the slope of the ridge to their right.

ROUGH WATER BAPTISM

The hike was longer than they had expected, but as they drew closer to the point, they felt compelled to go on. The atmosphere was changing. It was foggier at the point than it had been the whole way out, and the wind whipped them first from the northwest, and then from the southwest. One moment there was tentative sunlight, and the next, they were in ground-scraping clouds. They crept up stealthily to the edge of high cliffs, hundreds of feet up from rocks that disturbed the water as it flowed in, leaving fascinating patterns of churned surf. Elise peeked over the edge but quickly crept back. This was wild land.

The highest cliffs were a hundred yards or so from the point, so they descended to get to the farthest point north. They walked carefully, not trying to talk over the wind and the sound of incalculable volumes of surging water close by. They descended quite a bit down the crooked path, to the land's end at Tomales Point, and looked on with awe at the dynamics of wind and water. They stood briefly at a vantage point they realized was separated from the top edge of more cliffs only by a hedge of vegetation that looked substantial but was actually a false barrier to the danger. They moved a few yards over, to a more level place. Ahead of them, to the north of the point, were massive rocks, some standing high above the surface of the water, and some shaped like massive rough tabletops that were inundated and then exposed, over and over, as walls of water swept in.

The spot was awesome. The din effectively walled them off, each from the others. Elise was alone with her thoughts. She had the impression the massive waves must have gathered across the entire wide Pacific to deliver one blow after another on the solid rocks. At the point they landed, the waves were twenty and thirty feet high. Elise watched for waves impacting at just the right point in the massive swell so that explosive jets of ocean foam and muscular torrents of water would be sent high into the air to be followed by a gathering of ocean swell flooding around the rocks, swallowing them and removing them from sight.

She thought of a poem she'd memorized for a class earlier in the year, Matthew Arnold's *Dover Beach*, in which the words so clearly evoked the sound of the approaching and retreating sea. She listened for and felt she heard the "tremulous cadence slow" of the waves, and realized that, just as in the poem, they brought "the eternal sadness in." She imagined the sea before her as the Sea of Faith of the poem, and as she did so, she felt she heard

>Its melancholy, long, withdrawing roar,
>
>Retreating, to the breath
>
>Of the night-wind, down the vast edges drear
>
>And naked shingles of the world.

Elise shivered, feeling suddenly alone. The noise of the wind and waves isolated her in these ruminations, even though she was in the company of her two best friends. She considered the only solace offered in the poem, the presence of a lover, in the face of irretrievable loss:

>Ah, love, let us be true
>
>To one another! for the world, which seems
>
>To lie before us like a land of dreams
>
>So various, so beautiful, so new,
>
>Hath really neither joy, nor love, nor light,
>
>Nor certitude, nor peace, nor help for pain;
>
>And we are here as on a darkling plain
>
>Swept with confused alarms of struggle and flight,
>
>Where ignorant armies clash by night.

After some time alone in this reverie, Elise felt a nudge and saw her companions on their feet, inquiring with their eyes why she lingered so long. They were ready to trudge back up to the peak overlooking this wind- and water-swept place of majestic violence.

They walked back mostly in silence, content to bear their fatigue in isolation, settling into a rhythmic beating back of the miles. There was no trace of cloud now, and the sun was brilliant. They were tired. Ready to sit for a while. At the trailhead, they found a place to rest near preserved farm buildings no longer in use, other than by the park service as an outdoor museum of sorts. They spread a blanket and dug into the elaborate picnic stored in the trunk of Joy's car, all part of the girls' day out Joy had requested. In short order, their spirits were restored, and they sat back on the grass talking, Elise and Mary returning to the theme that Joy would be too tired to get married the next day.

After much rest, Joy convinced her companions the day's plans had not been too ambitious after all. They drove in a leisurely way to the south end of Point Reyes, to another walking trail leading to the outermost point of Drake's Bay on the Point Reyes headlands. Once there, though, Mary begged off a walk all the way out to the end, and Elise refused to be a swing vote. They compromised on a shorter walk to see the elephant seals regularly camped out on a section of the beach of Drake's Bay.

"They're just ahead, I think," Joy said, pointing with excitement.

"Where?"

"Straight ahead. In the shadow of the cliffs there."

"They're kind of far-off," Elise said.

"We'll get closer."

They did get closer, but only to an observation deck still quite a distance from the elephant seals.

"Look how they move," Joy said. "They kind of shuffle along." One of the bigger animals was scooting from the base of the cliff to a spot closer to the water, where other seals lay like shapeless sacks.

"They look like giant slugs," Mary said.

"They do," Elise agreed.

"No, they're not slugs," Joy said. "They're beautiful. Look at that big one chasing off the two little ones."

"Another bossy male," said Mary.

"I wish we could get closer. I wonder why this trail stops here."

"If it were closer, it would disturb the slugs, I imagine," Mary said.

"Plus, you don't want to get too close to those guys. They can be ferocious," Joy added.

"They don't look ferocious."

"But they can be," Joy assured Elise. "They'll attack if you invade their territory."

Elise imagined herself on the beach with the seals, trying to fix in her mind the scale—how big the beasts would be compared to her if she were right next to them.

It was the middle of the afternoon when they headed back toward San Francisco. Even Joy had a little less than her usual bounce.

"I'm so glad we did the rehearsal earlier," Mary said. "I'm going straight home to bed."

"We're just getting started," Elise said. "Time now for beautiful men. An extravagance of beautiful men."

"Too tired," Mary said.

"Joy will sleep tonight."

"Yes," Joy said emphatically. "To be honest, that's a big reason I wanted to do this instead of something more conventional."

"We'll still be the Axis powers, girl," Mary assured her. "You call us if that boy is mean to you."

Joy smiled at the schoolyard image. "Thank you. It's good to have my girls backing me up." She reached over and patted Mary on the shoulder and put her hand back between the seats to clasp hands with Elise.

"Well, if you're both crashing early," Elise said, "then for once, I'll outlast you both."

Elise had second thoughts about dinner with Tino after the day's activities, but then decided she could call it a night early if she chose. Tino would be understanding. He usually picked her up, but this time she was meeting him at a nearby restaurant. She was glad they wouldn't be delayed by his usual tete-a-tete with her father. The restaurant was a casual place. She had time to put on a simple dress, so she did.

"What's the matter, Tino, you don't look your usual effervescent self," Elise said, teasingly, once they were seated.

"Sorry. Just work. A lot going on." Elise could see her comment had recalled him to himself, and she knew he would for the rest of the evening be the suave and clever Tino she usually knew him to be. Elise felt a pang of regret that she'd spoken as she had. Perhaps it would have been better to commiserate, rather than rebuke. He might bring her into this more twilight part of his world. She desired to know something of the man Tino was in all seasons, and she wanted to give of herself to the man she was learning to care for.

"Tell me about it," she said, taking his hand.

Tino brought her hand to his lips, leaving a light kiss, and when he returned her hand to the table, he was smiling with his whole face. The kind of smile that seemed to exclude everything around them. It caused Elise to sit up with both feet flat on the floor, as though to steady herself.

"It would bore us both, telling you all about it," he eventually said.

"Well, just grit your teeth and tell me a little bitty bit," she said, making a cute gesture with her hand to specify how little. "I just want to be part of your world."

"My darling Elise. Stay in your world. It is so much more noble and pure, and interesting besides."

"Okay, I'll just have to quiz you," Elise said. "How do you like navigating San Francisco politics?"

Tino made a show of faux exasperation, capitulating to her request. "I don't know if anyone in the history of the world would say they 'like' navigating San Francisco politics, but sometimes it's a little intriguing. Watching all the gamesmanship. It really is like playing chess, I'm learning. It's all about thinking several moves ahead."

"I took some political science classes early on. I have the sense they're pretty irrelevant to the real world."

"What did you learn? Theories of government? Statesmanship?"

"Plato. Aristotle. Locke. Burke. Rousseau. History. The polis, the changes brought about by religion. The rise of the nation-state."

"Impressive."

"And nothing to do with local politics, I bet," Elise said before Tino could make the observation for her.

"Absolutely nothing. It's all personal. Everything. No one debates first principles in the hallway."

"Maybe just because it's San Francisco. Everyone is progressive."

"Probably right. Not much of a spectrum to work with. Maybe I should get a job in—"

"Jackson, Mississippi."

"Oh, my, too much the other way," Tino said, laughing.

"Charleston, South Carolina. Louisville, Kentucky."

Tino's laugh faded.

"What's wrong, Tino?"

"Nothing," Tino said, recovering quickly. "You just make me realize everything's relative. I've got it pretty good, I really do. I don't wish for another job, or for this job in some other place."

"Or any other friend," she said.

"Friends. Friends? Elise, friends?"

Elise tried to look neutral but felt her face might be flushed.

"Oh, we're not friends, you and I." Tino almost growled the words, but it was a sound of assertiveness, not anger, and it sent a thrill through Elise.

Elise had her hands in her lap, where she had been fiddling with her napkin, and now she brought it up above the line of her dress, and below her chin. Then she looked away and returned her hands to her lap.

"Elise."

She hesitated.

"Over here, Elise."

Elise returned his gaze, but for only the briefest moment before looking down. "I don't know what to make of you, Mr. Crocetti."

Tino shrugged, as if to say nothing could be simpler.

"I feel like you read me like a book. It's unfair."

There were a few moments of quiet between them, and this time Elise was in no hurry to return the conversation to the lightness that earlier prevailed. What was she to Tino? She wondered this to herself while she thought about how she might put this to him. She even had a sense of—resentment was too strong a word, of course—but what? Why would she be off-balance like this with him? She couldn't wait to be with him, and then when she was, she felt like she needed to be alone to process her feelings. He was an enigma in some ways, but he cared for her. He was thoughtful. Clever. Passionate. Mysterious. And he was beautiful, she thought and chuckled aloud.

"Private jokes now?" the enigma asked. "Now that's unfair."

"I'm sorry. You make me feel girly."

"You are girly. I like girly."

"What am I to you, Tino?" Elise folded her hands delicately in front of her on the table. She sat up and looked Tino in the eye, feeling her next move might be to stand gracefully and walk with head up to the door, and then go through it, never seeing him again. He might dodge the question, and in so doing answer it in the most emphatic way possible.

Tino looked at her plaintively. For just a moment, he looked lost, adrift, and Elise fought an impulse to rush over and comfort him, like she might a lost puppy. But then his usual self-confident bearing re-emerged, though in a way mixed with humility that was more endearing even than the lost puppy. A diffident smile spread across his face. "My future?" he said.

Chapter Nine

Elise felt nervous for her friend. The procession down the aisle was stately, but not stiff. There were candles. Maroon and lilac bunting was suspended on the ends of the pews. Above them were massive cantilevered beams of dark, aged wood, which lent solemnity and gravitas to the proceedings, even as the delicate colors of the dresses and decorations and flowers lent life. The church as a whole felt like a joinder of gaiety and seriousness, frivolity and high purpose, celebration and sober contemplation. The visual contrasts suggested all these differences, each calling out to its complement, like male to female, and wife to husband, just as the occasion warranted.

Elise wondered if Joy had intuited that it would all come together in just this way, or whether the transcendent feel to the whole thing was as much a surprise for her. Joy was aglow, in part because all her precautions of the day before had not prevented some burnishing as an effect of the sun and wind. But it was a healthy look. Joy was more vibrant and alive-seeming than ever, though this time not in her usual electric, almost jumpy way. Instead, Joy radiated a serene and contained happiness, more suited to the life-altering event. In a way Elise could not articulate, Joy's countenance seemed fitting to the contrasts of darkness and light, and permanence and transience, contained in the atmosphere of this old Berkeley church building.

Elise stole a glance at David, who was at his station up front awaiting Joy. Delight was in his eyes, but Elise felt there was more, too. It was as if he had absorbed the same impressions from the ceremony thus far as had Elise. The ceremony went long for a wedding, it seemed to Elise, but it did not tip over into tedium. The preacher, a young Korean man, spoke of an episode in the Bible Elise was but vaguely familiar with—Christ's teaching that His followers were to eat of His body and drink of His blood, and about how this teaching was off-putting to many, then and now, resulting in many of those curious about Jesus leaving Him. It struck Elise at first as a stark and even gruesome story for a wedding, but his point, Elise gathered, was that a spiritual union with Christ was somehow more binding even than the physical joining of food to the body, and that marriage, too, was a spiritual union, and so similarly indefeasibly binding.

Elise wondered, not for the first time, why intelligent but seriously religious people like David and Joy would have truck with such earthy and even bloody imagery. The preacher could have given all kinds of nice, marriage-appropriate messages. Why fixate on something like this? On the other hand, Elise guessed Joy would find this kind of message fitting, and not ask that it be otherwise. And truthfully, there was an attraction. Life so often presented contrasts of love and cruelty, pain and delight, good and evil, even rationality and absurdity. Why would it not be acknowledged even on an occasion like this? Perhaps especially on an occasion like this?

Elise was not immune to all the symbolism. She had an understanding of how the ceremony was rooted in patriarchy. Not that she found it offensive, necessarily, but it was interesting that it persisted so well against a pervasive background of feminism. Why was Joy presented to David, and not the other way around? Why did Joy appear veiled, or symbolically veiled? And why the aisle, to be walked? Elise thought of the bloody covenant—an animal separated into parts, and promises made over the carcass. Old Testament tribalism. Covenants, not mere promises, always harkening back to that covenant God was supposed to have made with Abraham. Now, thousands of years later, the happiest of occasions still harkening back to that bloody mystery.

This was Joy's and David's God. Why? Elise had asked that of Joy, once, and then realized that opening the door to a real believer, with a question like "why" might subject her to a sermon. But Joy had been gracious. At least it wasn't something Joy swallowed whole because her parents fed it to her. And there was hope associated with it, if otherwise somewhat science-fiction-y in its particulars. Certainly, it offered an ethical system, though that seemed beyond many of the individual Christians who supposedly subscribed to it. Elise wondered about that. And this dying God myth—a "real myth," Joy said on that occasion. Elise knew from her study of classics not to dismiss it lightly. But it seemed in this age such an anachronism.

Joy never preached but had asked Elise, "What do you believe?" The question resurfaced in Elise's mind from time to time. Elise was more conscious of what she didn't believe, or rather, what she had been taught was false and not so much what she did believe and what was true. Her father's off-the-cuff remarks about religion conveyed more of his attitude about it than of its merits in contrast to his materialism. Elise's beliefs—his beliefs—had been about the absence of something, not the facts of reality. There could be a pragmatic social consequence, she understood, to the absence of tribal gods or totems or even systematic beliefs about an invisible supreme God. So as time went along, Elise came to think of her default view of reality as somewhat spare, even bleak. She nonetheless felt instinctively that she should resist the particulars of this currently dominant god story. She shared her father's insistence on truth alone.

And yet the whole ceremony spoke to Elise of something real beyond the event of Joy's marriage, as significant as that was. She imagined Joy would say it was celebration of something bigger than both of them. Bigger than the institution of marriage itself, even. Elise listened and observed attentively, wanting to capture such ephemeral essence as would reveal a deeper reality behind all this. What if it were all true? Or if not all true, true in some basic instinctive way. An actual God. Not a demiurge like Zeus, but a necessary God, like the Greek philosophers imagined. Her father had once railed about Plato's Euthyphro discourse. Are the commands of the gods good because they are the gods' commands, or are they the gods' commands because they are good? It proves there is no God at all, he said. What we imagine is approved by the gods is so only by our own definition. Even as he had said it, however, Elise doubted. She had just studied it. If we conceive of God as the Hebrews did, then this question would be meaningless, and she thought perhaps that was even Plato's point.

And now here she was. Her best friend's wedding. It was drenched in the symbolism of ideas claimed to be true almost four thousand years before. Elise was reminded of the relevance, even the immediacy, of these cultural memories. Faulkner was right, she thought. "The past is never dead. It isn't even past."

Chapter Ten

"I'm sorry, I have to move again," David said. He was lying on the couch, entangled with Joy. He couldn't quite maneuver both his laptop and a printout of data.

"You love that computer more than you love me," Joy said.

David stood with the computer and then sat on the floor, positioning his laptop on the battered coffee table. He flipped through several charts on the screen and then looked back through his printout.

"I want to go back to the Grand Canyon," Joy said, resting her hand on David's shoulder.

"Right now?"

"Yes, right now. And Sedona. And the Indian reservations. And Jerome."

"You want to replay our honeymoon." David could feel Joy shifting her weight on the couch, behind him.

"And I don't want to go to work on a Saturday."

"Someone has to. And I bet right now there's some newly-married couple in Arizona wishing they could come back to San Francisco to relive their honeymoon."

"What's so fascinating about those charts?"

"What's so fascinating is what's not in them. I expected to see some correlations here, but I don't."

"Sometimes what's important is what's not there, instead of what is there. Medical records are like that sometimes."

"Do you know that if you're a lobbyist in San Francisco, you have to register your name, client, how much money the client spends, how many contacts you have with supervisors, what you're trying to accomplish? All this data is public. I thought it would be easy to import and find correlations with outcomes."

"Well, that's not fair. The average person doesn't have a lobbyist."

"Well, that's—"

"Who's the lobbyist for the average person who's just going about his life?"

"Joy, darling, you don't have to convince me, but that's not even where I was going with this."

Joy adopted an ironic, supercilious lilt to her voice. "Sorry. Carry on."

"I was trying to track the relationship between all that lobbying activity and various actions of the Board of Supervisors. You can't help but get into this, it turns out, when you're trying to trace government workflows, because there's more interaction with outside sources like lobbyists than I realized at first. So I was trying to do this side project that would fit with the government workflow software, but it's not really even a side project. A lot of the drafting and legwork and feasibility studies and action plans and so on are provided from outside, by the advocates for different laws, so that obviously affects the workflow of the government, but it's uneven. It all depends on what the issue is."

"You have to follow the money."

"Well, yeah, but it's hard to fix on criteria to code in, even at that. You can't just say x amount of lobbying yields y result."

"But what's the missing data?"

"I've been working with different models for correlating government activity and lobbying, and I picked this hotelization issue to test it out. Remember Hanny talked about it that day we had Mexican after church?"

"Of course."

"What's missing is the money. I expected huge torrents of cash from the hotels, on one side, and then from the vacation rental websites, on the other."

"And?"

"There was some at first. Then it declines. I would expect a lot more lobbying activity than there is."

"But it's been a big issue in the news. Maybe they're just playing by the rules."

"Well, there aren't really any rules. Not that there should be. There's no rule saying you can spend only x dollars in lobbying. Free speech, and all that."

"You're turning into a politico, David."

"I'm just trying to make the code work. It should be a simple matter of figuring out whose interests are at stake. On one side are the people who want to go back to the old law, so you have to be basically in the hotel business exclusively to rent out rooms. On the other side are the people who want to throw it wide open so that anyone can do short-term rentals all they want. The middle ground we have now doesn't make anyone happy."

"More freedom is better than less. Don't you think it would all work itself out if the city didn't try to control the market?"

"Maybe," David said, turning back to his computer. "That's the laissez-faire point of view. But that's not really my issue. I'm just trying to make the patterns emerge from the data. Maybe politics is just too messy for that."

"I have a hard time seeing anything wrong with renting out a place you own."

"Me, too."

"If I were from out of town, I wouldn't like it at all," Joy said.

"Out-of-towners don't vote for San Francisco politicians."

Joy was quiet.

"Too boring?" David asked, again without turning around to face Joy.

"No, I was just thinking. I thought the old rule was in place so more housing would be available to permanent residents."

"It was, but the demand for short-term rentals was so strong that people blew it off. A lot of owners rent out places year-round, despite the law. It's basically the same thing as a hotel. But depending on the website involved, the city may not get the hotel tax, and people who want to live here have less housing available."

"Not if they pay what the short-term renters are asking."

"Right, but a hotel costs more than an apartment."

"It does now," Joy said, "but if you throw it all open, maybe the short-term rentals come down."

"And maybe apartments go up even more."

"Maybe, but there are short-term rentals all over the place anyway. The city can't just control private transactions any way they like. Maybe if the rents are allowed to go up, developers will find it worthwhile to build more."

"And change the character of the city. That's the concern."

"Oh," Joy said fiercely and punched David in the back of the shoulder. She had no patience for artsy aesthetics ahead of real human need.

David turned, straining to see Joy behind him. "You're punching me over it?"

"If people are so concerned about the character of the city, they can patronize developments that maintain that character. These rules that try to control honest behavior just turn everyone into a criminal. People do normal everyday things, and they go around the law if the law is stupid and too hard and unfair."

"You really are an anarchist."

"Well, I think people like Hanigan ought to be able to do what they want with their own property. Especially since it's good for everyone. And people looking for a place to live shouldn't have to pay more just because the government has monkeyed with the market. Hanigan can't rent his extra space out to anyone under the old law or the new one."

"My reading between the lines is that he can't fix it up without money, anyway, and he can't make money without fixing it up, and he really doesn't want people wandering around his sanctuary anyway. But that's Hanny. If the city was hands-off, don't you think we'd end up paying more for this place?"

"I bet not, but the city should be hands-off regardless." Joy swung her feet over the edge of the couch. "I have to get ready for work. Don't forget I'm working a twelve. I won't get off until midnight."

"Midnight. We've only been married a month. Can't you schedule regular shifts?"

Joy walked back over to David, and putting one knee on the couch, bent over so her lips were next to his ear. "We've talked about this," she whispered. "If we have a little monster, I can take the time off then."

"I know, I know," David said as though resigned to some sort of hardship. He was pleased, though, and it came through in his voice. "I'll pick you up at midnight."

"You don't have to. I'll be fine."

"I'll be on your floor at midnight."

Joy was walking to the bedroom to change. "I'll text you if I'm going to be held over."

David had in mind digging deeper into this project while Joy was working so many hours, but an hour after she was gone, the apartment seemed too quiet. In all the years he'd been single and on his own, he had never experienced this. When they were apart, it was as if Joy left a hollowed-out place in his surroundings. That empty space didn't exist before she was part of his life. David pondered this, as he was wont to do. Before Joy, his life was just fine. He was a different person now compared to then. Expanded emotionally in both directions. More delight, more vulnerability to pain. He wondered how it would be if they realized their hope of having a child. Could he move to yet another level? Might his range be widened yet further?

David decided to get some air. He needed to come at his work project with some fresh perspective. He walked over to the window and peered down the street. It looked like it might still be raining, a fine mist. David preferred a hooded, knee-length raincoat to umbrellas that would break or turn inside-out at inopportune times. He set out from the apartment in Fillmore, heading west, in the general direction of Golden Gate Park. He had it in mind to take a turn in the park and then head back, a little ahead of the evening fog that would in all likelihood follow the drizzle. Maybe after an hour of brisk walking, his mind would be clearer. David was dogged in pursuing an answer to the puzzle in his mind, but he knew he could be too dogged. He'd learned from some of his religious discussions over the years that it was good to step back and get the largest picture possible, and try to look at abstract questions from the point of view of someone who didn't accept the same assumptions he did. This mental discipline often helped with programming logic. Usually, the difficulties came not with how to elegantly direct a process in code, but rather in sorting through the human inputs on the front end. Garbage in yielded garbage out. In this short-term rental situation, for example, if it were possible to render meaningful correlation between non-government inputs and government outputs, he would have to, for starters, at least recognize all of the actual inputs.

David had walked this way before, so for variety, he headed south a couple of blocks and turned west again on Fulton, taking him to the corner of the park. But he'd entered the park near the northeast corner a few times before, so this time he turned left on Stanyan and walked down the street along the sidewalk next to the eastern border of the park. He glanced over in the direction of a grocery store just off Stanyan, when he thought he heard his name called out. The rain was light, but the fog was now heavy. A bearded man waved to him from the front entrance of a coffeehouse called Soul Cycle. David thought it might be Mark Hanigan. Awaiting a break in the traffic, he jogged over.

"I haven't seen you since the wedding," Hanigan said. "Congratulations again. Where's your bride?"

"Working. How are you doing?"

"I was going in for coffee. Join me?"

David's first thought was that this was supposed to be a one-hour jaunt, but he quickly discarded that hesitation. It was the middle of a Saturday afternoon, and other than puzzling through work, he had nothing to do until midnight, when he'd walk over to St. Francis and then walk back with Joy.

"Sure," he said.

"I'm not interrupting something important?" Hanigan asked as they sat down.

"Not only are you not interrupting, but it occurs to me you're just the person I ought to see."

"I can't imagine what I'm uniquely qualified for, but go ahead."

"I went out for a walk to get this out of my head, but instead I just keep going round and round. Do you remember that talk we had after church a few weeks ago? Your first time at Twin Peaks Galilean?"

"We were talking city politics, I think."

"We were talking about short-term vacation rentals. You know, those websites where you can rent out a place for a few days at a time."

"Oh yes. We veered off into general government meddling, as I recall."

"I'm trying to work through a programming project, but I'm banging my head against the wall." David went on to explain his dilemma—his unexplained absence of data.

Hanigan began, "I can't speak to the computer project, and whether it's even possible statistically to get to meaningful correlations, but it sure seems odd that the money trail isn't bigger, given what's at stake and how big an issue it's been. The players on all sides of this have money."

"I'm doing something wrong. I just don't know what it is. I should be able to track workflows from government to private interests back to government. It makes sense to me that this tracking can measure the influence of private interests. So if I have an issue that doesn't come close to fitting like I expect, I worry that it wrecks the whole model."

"Maybe your working theory is right, but you're just missing a piece of data."

They were both quiet a few moments, taking first sips of their drinks.

"I'm sorry, Hanny. I get my mind on something and can't let it go. Tell me what's going on with you. I saw you at church but couldn't get over to catch up."

"You were surrounded by well-wishers, so it's all good. Actually, I've only been to Twin Peaks a couple of times in the last month anyway."

"Losing interest?"

"No, but I've been visiting around. I've been reading a lot about the calling of the magisterial in the 'high churches' so-called."

"Something to that, I'm sure. I suppose for some people, God seems more real when He's represented in the surroundings and the ceremony and the solemnity. Maybe we miss out on something in churches like Twin Peaks and Berkeley Galilean. But the downside is you can get caught up in the institution and the building and the ceremony and miss that it's all about relationship with Christ."

"I was in Antigua once. Not the island, but an old, old colonial city in the Guatemala highlands. It was disorienting, in a way. I felt like it could have been today or 400 years ago, or anytime in-between."

"Sounds like an interesting place."

"I was out one day, walking around town. No mistaking me for a local, that's for sure. I was admiring the architecture of the city, taking pictures, doing a lot of sketching. Spent some time in the markets, trying to sketch some of the people without being intrusive. Anyway. Point of the story. I wandered up to a yellow-stuccoed church that was quite impressive from the outside, but when I went in, I was just blown away. I'm used to seeing the grand old gothic cathedrals like that in a preserved state, like a bug in amber. This church in Antigua was grand, like those European cathedrals, but it felt completely different. It was impressive, but it was well-worn. I don't mean threadbare, but it was used. It was part of the fabric of life in the town. It felt like prayers hung in the very air. There were candles burning for various saints, in little reliquaries off to the side. I didn't think they did that anywhere, anymore. I tried to move around with some respect. I walked up toward the front—there was no service going on—and over to one side was a young man on his knees. On the stone floor. Praying for all he was worth, crying, facing a statue of some saint. I wanted to go, but I wanted to stay. I felt like there was something there. I had to stop and think about what day it was. It was a Monday afternoon. There weren't a lot of people in the church, but it was obviously in regular use. Continuous use. Like it wouldn't close just because it wasn't time for service. I imagine it as the place people might come to for actual refuge."

David said, "You'd like to experience that kind of physical presence of God."

"Yeah. But I take your point, too. I can see how it could be an impediment to the kind of intimacy I understand the New Testament talks about. God in you rather than God out there high above."

"You really think about it. That's good."

"How could we not?"

"A lot of churchgoers seem to think that God is real because they had an emotional experience, or it's self-evident there's a God because look at what He created. Most believers aren't master theologians."

"People might be unreflective about these big ideas, but that doesn't make them true or untrue," Hanigan said.

"True. But what about you?"

"Well, I'll tell you this one thing. I've come around to the view that we live inside an illusion if we think we can be neutral about it. If it's not true, then it's not true, and it's just a subject of interesting sociological study about why people would be so devoted to a lie."

"But if it's true..."

"If it's true, then it's perilous to ignore it, to say the least. And I've gotten past the sense of resentment about being beaten over the head with dire consequences if I don't buckle under. There's a promise there, too, and it's much more profound in a positive way, if it's true, than the negative is negative. Does that make sense?"

"It does." David looked outside at the gauzy fog. "Hey, I haven't heard about any new show. Have I missed it?"

"I'm putting something together. Professor Brinkley is going to come to my aid again, I think. But can I tell you a secret?"

"Sure."

"Seriously. I'm not sure I want this out there yet."

"Well, if you confess to a murder, I'm going to report it."

Hanigan chuckled. "I take myself too seriously. I did have a show, a couple of weeks ago. With a couple of other artists. It was up in San Anselmo. Do you know where that is?"

"Yeah, but if your show was a crime, you ought to go further away. That's just up in Marin County, right?"

"I got a commission from it, and some more interest. Pretty exciting."

"Do abstract artists get commissions?"

"Well, yes, but this wasn't abstract."

"Oh. Is that the secret?"

"Yes. For some reason, I've been drawn to faces, wanting to find in them some spark of something to see if I can draw it out."

"So add them to your show here."

"Mm, not sure about that," Hanigan said. "It's San Francisco. We love art, but that sort of work is looked down on in a lot of circles. Some artsy people think it's passé. Overtaken by expressions of ethereal spirit or human longing—things that are not tangible but felt. So I'm not sure it's a good move to combine the styles if I want to sell my stuff."

"So you'll be a different artist to a different audience."

"Feels deceitful," Hanigan said.

"Not to me. For what it's worth."

"That's gratifying to hear. So I'm free to be devious for good old marketing reasons. Speaking of which, who else has an interest in keeping short-term rentals from catching on in San Francisco?"

"Just the hotels."

"Are you sure? Who would be interested in seeing the San Francisco short-term rental market regulated out of existence? How about unit owners in Oakland? Berkeley? If I came here from Cincinnati, just to pick my actual home town, I'd stay in some idyllic Marin County hideaway on the other side of the Golden Gate Bridge."

"So," David said, "I'm looking for corrupt or negligent politicians and quiet collusion among business interests that ought to be competing."

"The heart is deceitful above all things, and desperately wicked."

"Jeremiah."

"I still remember something from Sunday School."

Chapter Eleven

Tino discerned that though Teague was an older man, he enjoyed his walks on the demanding hills of the city. When Teague called, Tino had the presence of mind to suggest their meeting take place on foot so there would be no need for self-consciousness about who might be around to overhear.

"Tino, I commend you. You have good presence, but you keep your cool. You keep the end game in sight. Well done, young man."

"Thank you, Mr. Teague."

"Gerald. Call me Gerald." Teague clapped Tino lightly on the shoulder. "I need to talk to you about something substantive, Tino. You're doing well with the money. No criticism at all. But I think we need to be more proactive on the city side. We don't want the supervisors to go wobbly on us."

"Completely agree."

"We can get some money back to them, or to some of them, anyway. I can help with that. It won't take much."

"It would require some subtlety and indirection."

They were passing an art gallery, and Teague stopped in front of the window. "What do you think of that?" he asked, pointing to two framed pictures on elaborate easels. They consisted of sunset colors against a deep blue background, in roughly horizontal swipes of color.

"Not a big pull for me, truthfully."

"You needn't be so tactful, Tino. They're awful. I wouldn't give you a dollar for both of them. Nice frames, though."

"Knowing you, this is part of a plan."

"Yes. Someone will give a lot more than a dollar for this excrescence. Imagine large sums going into a box, and small sums trickling out the other end."

"The money goes for art."

"Yes."

"But the artist doesn't keep it all. We'd have to recruit artists who understand the rules."

"Of course we need artists, but they don't have to know the whole program. We can set up a consortium of sorts. Our clients can pay for the art—too much, of course—and the artists get less than the full amount because the consortium has 'expenses.'"

"Why would the artists go for that?"

"One, because they're making sales they wouldn't otherwise. Two, because big prices beget big prices. It's the strange world of marketing art."

"That's money in, but how to get money out? The consortium could have a city connection."

"That's good thinking, but if it's a quasi-government entity, it's too open to scrutiny. As a private association, we can expense out pretty much whatever we want. Exhibition halls and the like. The money will end up where it needs to go, but it'll be indirect."

Later that week, Tino met Hanigan at vacant commercial space on the edge of the Mission District. It was a corner building with windows along two streets. The main door was somewhat recessed, angled to cut off the corner. Tino fumbled with the keys. "What do you think so far?" he asked.

"Perfect. How long has it been empty?"

"I'm not sure," Tino said absentmindedly, concentrating on methodically trying the keys. The next one slipped into the keyhole raggedly, but he kept at it, and it worked. The door swung open, and they both stepped in.

"Oh, yes. This will do nicely," Hanigan said.

"Yeah, the place seems to be in good shape."

"So it's a restaurant going in here?" Hanigan asked.

"That's what I'm told. They need to do some work in the kitchen area—I assume it's through those doors back there—but the front here is nice and open. They'll get a little for subbing out for the art show while they're working in the back." Tino went on to explain to Hanigan where the "coming soon" announcements would be, and how prominent, and how displayed, in an effort to work out an accommodation that would create the right atmosphere for a short-term show, followed by a front-of-the-house build-out for the restaurant.

"Well, the key is location," Hanigan said. "The duration is just right. The location couldn't be better. I'm even on the Market side of the Mission District. "Why is Brinkley coming to the rescue again?"

"I guess he likes you," Tino said.

"Even though I ditched his program. He's a good man. As are you, Tino."

"I'm just a go-fer today."

"Professor Brinkley had me to his club for dinner a couple of weeks ago. He suggested this little escapade for an art show, and the next thing I know, Tino's in the picture."

"Tino's seeing the old man's daughter," Tino said.

"Marry the girl, Tino."

"The thought occurred to me."

"You'd get the elder Brinkley in the bargain. How would that work for you?"

"A good father-in-law to have."

"He's certainly generous. And he seems to have his fingers in everything."

Tino made a gesture as though to indicate Hanigan didn't know the half of it, as he flipped around to find the right key again. "Maybe you'd be interested in an art consortium of some sort. Have you ever thought about it?"

"I don't know what you mean."

"I thought it might be a known thing in the art world. A guild of artists working together?"

"I don't see that taking off, Tino."

"I don't mean working together as in doing art together. I mean presenting together, sharing some costs and some benefits. You might make sales you otherwise wouldn't."

"I've heard about different programs from time to time. To whom would the art be presented?"

"Oh, offices, restaurants. Businesses with a little bit of art discernment."

"I don't have time for my art projects as it is."

"Oh, you wouldn't be knocking on doors yourself. In fact, that's part of the idea behind it. Someone would do that for you."

"For part of the proceeds."

"Well, of course. But I think you might come out well. Some good exposure. Just think about it."

"Sure. Oh, can you wait just a minute," Hanigan said. "Sorry. Just a few measurements." He dug out a small tape measure from his pocket, and Tino held the zero end while Hanigan moved about, making notes in a little spiral-bound notebook. "I don't want to spend half a day messing around with the layout once I'm here."

"Understood," Tino said absentmindedly. He said it with an insouciant gesture to convey he had all the time in the world.

"Over here, please," Hanigan said, and Tino stepped up to the spot with his end of the tape. Tino's phone buzzed in his pocket, and he casually took it out to see who it was.

Hanigan pulled the tape out to a distance of about twelve feet, made a note, moved in an arc pivoting around Tino's position, and made another note. "What's the matter?" he asked.

Tino knew the number that showed up on his phone, and it shook him. He had turned a little, quickly, to hide any hint of surprise, but his turn caught Hanigan's attention anyway. "I'm fine," he said. "Just trying to see around the glare from the window. I'll call them back later."

"Go ahead. I'm in no hurry."

"Really. Not important."

"I've almost got what I need." Hanigan made another note and then pocketed his notebook and tape measure. "I didn't see you park," he said, as they made their way to the door. Tino fumbled with keys. "I walked. Hardly seemed worth getting the car out for."

"Me too. That's why I love this city. I walk almost everywhere. I can go with you a few blocks if you're going north."

"Great."

"I wonder if Brinkley thinks I'll be able to help him out in some way. I don't see how."

"Don't worry about it. I imagine he just likes patronizing the arts."

"He doesn't let go of people easily, that's to his credit. Even after I told him I was exploring spiritual things."

"What did he have to say about that?"

"He said I was engaged in 'tergiversation.' I had to go look it up. Apparently, I'm an apostate to the faith."

"What faith? You'd be an apostate to apostasy."

"Exactly. Anyway, 'spirituality' is a pretty loose word. Even atheists in Brinkley's camp use it, though I haven't figured out why."

"Brinkley can be pretty strident about this sort of thing. Elise has to rein him in sometimes. People don't like to be on the front lines of that debate."

"No, indeed. You need to get that?" Tino's phone was buzzing again.

"I guess I should."

"I need to turn off anyway. Thanks for everything, Tino."

"You bet," Tino said, smiling thinly as Hanigan turned toward his building near Haight Street. He glanced down at the 812 area code for New Albany, and then again over his shoulder at Hanigan's quickly-receding figure. Instead of answering his phone, Tino quickened his pace and turned to walk parallel to Market, toward the Embarcadero. He regretted now not having brought the car. When he set out that morning, he had envisioned a leisurely stroll out to the farmer's market there, and a late lunch with Cassie. A good bit of walking, but he had expected a light day of work all the way around, in which the exercise would be agreeable. He had no clandestine trips to make out to Marin County, nor one of those meetings with Gerald. Instead, his day was supposed to start out with just a little jaunt to help out his friend Hanigan, at the behest of their mutual benefactor Brinkley.

But now this. When had she gotten his number? Now her voicemail resided on that little box in his pocket, and he dreaded playing it. She had reappeared out of nowhere since he'd seen her as a shadowy figure in the yellow fog of deep night along the San Francisco quay, in a scene like an overacted melodrama. For days afterward, Tino had lived an unsettled existence, wary that she could reappear, ghostlike, and possibly at an inopportune time for the liaisons he'd made in San Francisco. He'd even let Elise believe his mother was no longer alive. He reproached himself now for that short-sightedness.

In all of this, Tino was chagrined that his plans had developed a kink, but he was not burdened with thinking his conduct amounted to denial of his mother. The passage of time since that quay-side appearance caused the memory of it to fade, and in Tino's self-serving imagination, so even the reality of it. To have the event recalled vividly to his mind was exasperating. Tino wanted this smoothed over. He desired to be free of his past and any claim it might make upon him.

"Tino," the well-recognized voice pled on the recording. "It's… It's your mother, Tino. Call me." There was a pause. Tino expected more. There was background buzz that told him she yet held the phone. He wondered if she meant to say more but held back. He could almost hear her disappointment in the silence. Then there was the click of her hanging up. Then another message. No words the second time, just the click as soon as the call rolled to Tino's voicemail. Tino debated within himself as he walked along. Call her back? Pin down her whereabouts, at least? The temptation was strong. He could have some peace of mind if she was in New Albany where she belonged. But on the other hand, if she was here in San Francisco, what would he say? He'd have to ponder this. He kept churning along up Mission Street at a pace to match his unsettled thoughts. He held his phone in his hand as he walked, a tangible reminder of the need for decision.

Within sight of the farmer's market, Tino realized he had walked many blocks at a strong pace and was now overheated. He thought of Cassie in her usual spot inside the crowd of vendors and paused to collect himself. Cassie was his island. A respite from all the unfair intrusions into Tino's equanimity—the furtive assignations of Brinkley's network, Gerald's concern about the inconvenient timing of Joy's husband's software project, the distasteful cutting off of his boyhood friendship with Roger, the appearance of his mother and not knowing what she knew and didn't know about his father's inheritance.

Perhaps he worried too much. Worry was a new thing for Tino. Events usually fell out his way. The overcast skies seemed to lighten as he came in sight of the park opposite the Ferry Building. Perhaps the sun would peek through. He resumed his progress toward the farmer's market, now at a more leisurely glide. He decided to believe it would all work out, and he would act on that belief, on faith. The ongoing work for Brinkley was just a job. The software project would not raise suspicion where human minds had not. Roger was turning into an alcoholic, and maybe there was something Tino could do for him. Later. His mother was surely safely ensconced in New Albany. And she hadn't known the extent of his father's estate anyway.

Tino paused to loiter a moment in the park, letting the internal turmoil subside before seeing Cassie. He desired to leave his troubles at the doorstep, wiping his feet of them before stepping into her world. Not to spare Cassie, but to preserve his own sanctuary. He then crossed the street and made his way through the vendors. She was there, as promised, with a bright, animated smile, selling two loaves of bread to a middle-aged couple. She was still smiling as she turned to Tino. It took a moment for his presence to register. When it did, her countenance was incandescent. Shining eyes, raised eyebrows, her mouth a cute "o" shape as if she were surprised to see him. Then she quickly finished her transaction as Tino closed the distance to her booth.

"You're here," she said, pulling the front of his shirt toward herself. She kissed him.

"I've been looking forward to seeing you all day," Tino said.

"Me too."

"There's still a pretty good crowd. Don't you need to stay open?"

"No. I want to spend time with you." She had a pouty look as she said it. She intended the gesture to be fetching, and it was.

They had loaded her truck when it occurred to Tino for the first time that lunch with Cassie here would breach his usual rule of confining his relationship with her to Marin County. Too late to do anything about it now, he decided, as he slid the last box into the bed of the truck.

"Pretty soon I won't be able to do this by myself," Cassie said.

"Why not?"

For answer, Cassie placed her hands on her stomach and widened her eyes at Tino.

"Oh, of course. I can hardly tell, though, so far."

"But you can tell."

"Well, if I'm thinking about it, I suppose, but you're not showing much."

"I feel like I'm wide as a doorway."

"There's a place right down the street that looks good."

"I don't care where we go. I just want to be with you."

They had that kind of exchange, as they walked, unique to lovers—the meanings of their words would not be apparent to someone overhearing. When they sat down at the table, however, Cassie said, "Tino, we'll have lunch, and then I'll go back, and then I'll just wait around until I see you again." She said it with a tone in keeping with the theme she'd already established, a pout intended to beguile because it was premised on desire for him.

"I come out every week, plus weekends."

"I know, but come live there. Be with me every night." Cassie was seated adjacent to Tino at a small table, and she wrapped herself around his arm as she had done when they strolled along the sidewalk.

"Cassie, my dear, if we had all the money in the world, I'd want nothing else. But I've told you. It's too far to commute. I have to keep my place in the city."

Cassie was quiet. Tino knew what she was thinking. Why not move in here with him? He relied on her reluctance to say it. It would go beyond the unspoken boundaries established so far. Tino had set Cassie up in an apartment in Point Reyes Station. Instead of a weekend in this charming spot or that one, he had an alternative "home" he could dip into when it suited him. From Tino's perspective, this was the way it must be. Certainly, securing a nest for the two of them suggested some element of continuity to their relationship, but it was indefinite, still, and open-ended. The unexpected pregnancy was a reason for more distance, not less. Tino was not so crass as to suggest terminating the pregnancy outright, but he made sure Cassie knew it was her decision whether to continue with it or not. And so far, the child was just an idea, not a pressing need for definite plans, on a definite schedule. This fit Tino's way of thinking. Tino's life thus far had not been marked by careful goal-setting and planning. Instead, opportunities swam toward him, as if they were his birthright. It would all work out, with Cassie, one way or another.

The afternoon was well along when Cassie slipped her truck into the traffic headed toward the Golden Gate Bridge. Tino turned in the direction of his own apartment, but at this hour, it made little sense to go all the way there when he was due at Elise's before long. Ten minutes later, he called Elise.

"Tino?" Elise said, having recognized his number.

"Beg permission to be a little early, madam."

"Of course. When should I look for you?"

"It depends. Are you in the loggia?"

"Yes, as a matter of fact."

"Well, then look down, on the bay side."

"Oh, you goofball," she said. "Come on up. But I'm not ready."

"Your dad home?"

"Yes, yes, yes. I think you just tolerate me to see my dad. I'll meet you at the ground floor."

Tino smiled up at Elise as he pocketed his phone and walked around the house to the main entrance.

Tino was greeted by Elise, but Brinkley rolled up right behind her. "Master Tino," he said. "Come in the house. So pleased to see you. We should catch up."

Tino looked inquiringly at Elise.

"Just come up when you finish. Knock on my door, or go on up to the loggia."

"Perfect," Tino said.

Elise turned toward the stair, and Tino made a point of watching her go, holding an appreciative look on his face, not minding that Brinkley saw this. Then he fell in beside Brinkley, who turned his chair and began wheeling it toward his study.

"She likes you, you know," Brinkley said.

"I hope so, Dr. Brinkley."

"Young man, this 'Dr. Brinkley' stuff won't do."

"I can't very well call you Potter."

"Well, you can, but if it feels strange, we'll come up with something else. How about Peter?"

"Why Peter?"

"Well, that's my name, sport. Why not?"

"I've just never heard it."

"Close those doors, will you?"

Tino turned to close the double doors to Brinkley's oversized study. The doorway was wide and was at an angle to an open central area of the house, so when the doors were closed, the study seemed much smaller. Still large and ornate, with plenty of room to navigate in a wheelchair to the numerous wheelchair-high bookshelves, but now it seemed less a grand section of this floor of the house, and more a largish room within it.

"Peter is my name. Obviously, I didn't choose it. Too Biblical. Peter, Petrus, the rock."

"And Potter?"

"Well, just a corruption of Peter, obviously, but I like the connotation. A contra-Biblical connotation. You know, all that in the Bible about the potter and the clay. The clay doesn't get to tell the potter what he can and can't do with the clay. It's all there, in the folklore. I thought Potter fit the bill. I'm certainly not the clay."

"Ingenious. But you don't want to take on a distasteful label for my sake, do you?"

"Ah, good for you, Tino. See, that's why you're worthy. You understand me. I don't hate the name Peter. I just avoided it in my youthful zeal. It's not really offensive. In fact, I intend it as an intimate name. Better than Doctor or Mister something. For you, I mean, Tino."

"I am honored. And so Peter it will be." Tino was conscious of having crossed a threshold. He'd spent a lot of time with Brinkley, in this study, over many weeks. Only now was there to be a change in appellation, a change to greater familiarity. It was due to more, Tino realized, than the working relationship. Something at the heart of this old man was involved. This was about Elise.

"Peter, Peter. I'm practicing." Tino sat down on the plush guest chair next to Brinkley's desk.

"Ha. You'll get used to it. Tell me, Tino," Brinkley narrowed his gaze on Tino's, "tell me about your meetings with Gerald. Instructive?"

"Quite."

"Gerald says you're a quick study. You're doing well, Tino. I think you're doing a great service for the City of San Francisco, and mark you," here Brinkley paused, to cast a meaningful look at Tino, "San Francisco is a cultural center. I'd say 'the' cultural center— maybe yes, maybe no—but what we do here matters beyond local city politics. 'We are the makers of manners, Kate.'"

"*Henry the Fifth*."

Brinkley loosed a satisfied chortle. "You're a man after my own heart."

Tino smiled his most endearing smile at the man whose influence he stood to inherit.

"I think I just uttered a Biblical turn of phrase," Brinkley continued. "See? You can't escape it. About King David. After God's own heart, allegedly. But I digress. Here's what I want to tell you, my young friend. It's never about politics, or voting, or any of that sort of thing. It's about culture. Culture alone matters. I don't mean formal—"

"I understand. Not high culture. Not opera or painting."

"Well, that's important, too—it filters down. But yes, I mean something else. What people think is right and wrong about what they do, something apart from law. What do people expect? What's the norm?"

"Where does it come from?"

"Well, we teach it to them, Tino." At this, Brinkley displayed a somewhat disconcerting skull's grin. "We decide. That's the short answer. That's what we're about here."

"What I'm spending my effort on right now..." Tino trailed off. He was conscious of the need to tread lightly. There was a level of specificity he might have in conversation with Gerald, but he understood that his exchanges with Brinkley—Peter—were to be at the highest level of abstraction. "I feel like I'm only at the outermost edge of all that. Affecting culture. I feel like it's more about seeing one little political issue get resolved one particular way based on one particular set of interests."

"Sometimes it seems like it's not about high principle."

"Exactly."

"And yet it can be. What do you suppose is the big principle in your project?"

"If it's not about grabbing power, directly, then it's about who should have the power."

"I don't want you to think you're just flailing away for nothing. The hardline conservatives would have us believe that everything is about competing interests. Everyone's at war, all the time. But it's the wrong paradigm. Probably comes from the man/god/devil perspective. But there is no God. Man desires peace. We can say there are different 'interests,' but that only means that different people, with different jobs, and different functions consistent with those jobs, look at a situation from different perspectives."

"Like the children's story of people standing around an elephant and seeing something entirely different from the others."

"Exactly. It doesn't mean they're not all trying in good faith to come to a consensus about what they're seeing. The solution is adopting the same perspective, not fighting about the differences. And that's what's going on here. The city is coming at it from one perspective, and that's the consensus perspective—what's good for us as an entire city."

"Understood."

"But the hotels, the various websites, the conglomerates that want to sell temporary rooms—they're all capitalists."

"They all want their own interests, and it's not about what's best for everyone."

"Exactly, Tino."

"So one group wants resolution through the interplay of competing interests, and another group wants resolution through the working-out of a consensus conversation."

"I couldn't have said it better myself. But," Brinkley paused and shook his head, doubtfully, "I'm not sure it would come up that way. This debate, frankly, is never going to happen. And that's as it should be. We don't want the debate—we want our point of view to prevail. If we can do that without debating it, better to skip the debate. And that's the way it always is. Debates. Arguments. Political disagreements. These are all sideshows. We engage in them only as a means to an end, not as a process to find the answer."

Tino bowed his head in a gesture that might have ambiguously meant "just so" or "what else do you have to say?" These were deep waters.

"The city slipped up with this rule change. We had a balance. The hotels paid the taxes, and the city controlled the availability of housing for residents. Then we let the camel put his nose under the tent. People were allowed to rent their own places, and they want to do it all the time."

"It's one segment of a housing market," Tino said.

"But of course it's never just that, is it? It's never just the immediate issue. It's the principle. The principle of keeping control, of doing what's best for everyone."

"They were doing it anyway," Tino said in a neutral tone. He'd not had such a specific conversation with Brinkley before, about his main work project.

"Yes, but we could keep an eye on that. The new rule gives people ideas. They want to rent their places and move out themselves. Or go into competition with the hotels, but using housing that could go to residents. Now it threatens to become the Wild West. All this talk of individual freedom—what is it for? To turn the city into a playground for tourists, with the residents having nowhere to live?"

Tino said, "The larger principle, then, is that we should have unity on this. What we want is for people to buy into the notion that the city should be in charge to keep this in balance."

"Let the city speak for the people collectively. And why not? More social cohesion, and what's the cost? 'Individual choice' is just shorthand for accumulation of capital in the hands of the 'haves.'"

Tino nodded, communicating appreciation for Brinkley's pronouncement. His instinct was that this conversation was best left at the level of Brinkley's masterminding of ideas, rather than getting into gritty details of their execution. Tino could cynically say there was accumulation of capital even with their involvement and, on top of that, corruption among keepers of the public weal. But maybe Brinkley was right. Maybe a higher purpose was served, for San Francisco if not for outlying areas like Marin County. Money flowed from hotels, to vacation websites, to official gatekeepers of San Francisco, with a sizeable bit landing in his own pockets. Tino knew this because he facilitated the transactions, using his manifold gifts of discretion. It wouldn't happen if the hotels didn't see their payments as an expense that would yield return. But it all worked out. The flow of funds kept San Francisco's restrictions on vacation rentals in place, in turn keeping hotels full and the vacation rental business vibrant in places like Marin County. The city government thereby maintained control over its housing supply, and control was Brinkley's interest. Tino knew this was just the way of the world.

Chapter Twelve

Elise saw the fog outside her bedroom window. It was dense even by San Francisco standards. It was not all the same consistency, however, and as a result, Elise could see its movement past her window. She went up to the loggia and experienced the otherworldliness of it, drifting past her stance atop the house. She imagined it stationary, with the house itself moving instead, like a ship drifting rapidly but soundlessly over calm water. Elise was so caught up in this illusion that she began to find it unsettling—the idea of moving at speed with no perception of the perils which might lie ahead. It took some mental effort to return the sensation of movement to the fog, rather than the loggia-turned-ship's-prow of her imagination.

An hour later, she bade her father farewell. She had on a light fleece under a nylon shell and carried in her left hand a knit cap, holding it from the inside. As was her custom, she gave her father a quick hug by leaning over the back of his chair as he sat at his desk. As was his custom, he leaned into the hug and then reached across to pat the hand resting on his right shoulder, half-turning to look up at her.

"Where are you skipping off to now, my dear?"

"Joy's."

"Ah. How is the young couple?"

"Well, I'll soon find out. Do you need anything before I go?"

Brinkley was already turning his attention back to his desk. "I'm fine, dear. I'll see you later on then?"

"Noon-ish. I'm going to the grocery store on the way back."

"Okay, dear," he said, already engrossed in his reading. Elise doubted he'd registered her last remark, not that it really mattered. She'd found him to be less and less energetic lately, but she put the observation on a back burner in her mind.

The fog was much lighter by this time and had cleared out almost entirely on her walk to Joy's. She had to remind herself Joy was no longer in the old place but in an apartment new to both she and David. It was a quaint thing, this refusal to live together before the wedding. Elise could not think of another couple among her friends who hadn't, once their relationship had progressed to a stage of presumed permanence. In some cases, it was because there was no thought of marrying at all, but that seemed a different situation in her mind. Living together first was the norm, even among those who pictured themselves marrying in the future. And what would she, Elise, do? She had not considered it before this moment. Her initial giddiness at Tino's proposal had given way almost immediately to guarded caution, and then to exhilaration, and then to fear. Back and forth. While she was swept up in the immediacy of his presence, all was right, as if she were suffused in golden light. Joining with Tino in life seemed to be the most natural and right thing. Their conversations had developed closer and closer to this idea, over time, and when she was with him, she felt no reservations. Apart from him, she construed her reservations as merely a desire to be with him at the moment. This was the way of the world, she had decided. Why should she not be swept up with him, at the threshold of adventure, in the springtime of her life?

Elise stood on Joy's welcome mat, staring at the door. She started to ring the bell, but paused. She thought of Joy and David's wedding. The deep mystery of it, transcending the party atmosphere of the occasion.

The door swung open, and Joy's thousand-watt smile greeted her.

"I didn't even ring!" Elise said, feeling a rush of joy in her friend's presence. She flung herself on Joy's neck, a display of emotion uncharacteristic for Elise. "I'm so happy to see you."

"It's been weeks! I missed you."

Elise had stepped over the threshold. Now she held both of Joy's hands in hers and stepped back to look at her, as if seeing her anew.

"It's still me, Elise."

"I have to be sure."

"Marriage doesn't make you a pod-person."

"I'm afraid it does. I want my friend back."

"You'll have to settle for me," Joy said as she led Elise into the apartment.

"David's at work?"

"Just for a meeting."

"Are you back on nights?"

"Second shift, for now."

"Well, that's no good. The two of you will be working opposite shifts, and you're newlyweds!"

"It'll work out. I swing back to day shifts in a few days. Coffee?"

"Yes. This is nice," Elise said, swiveling around on a bar stool to take in the kitchen/living room combination.

"We lucked out. Rents are insane, if you can find a place at all. You take it with the works, right?"

"Right."

"Good. Live life at maximum volume," Joy said. She placed Elise's mug in front of her on the little bar that separated the kitchen from the living room. Elise placed her hands side by side on the counter.

"Elise?"

"Yes?" Elise said, trying for nonchalance. An uplift in her voice gave her away.

"This. Is. Unbelievable." The two young women came together at the end of the little bar, hugging again, this time for another reason altogether.

"When?" Joy asked.

Elise shrugged. "Working on that. This just happened last night."

"The ring is beautiful."

Elise basked in the warm glow of her friendship with Joy. The talk was helping her to bring the future into better focus. Before this meeting, it had all seemed mysterious and adventurous. But there were practical considerations. Where they would live. What she would do. What about children? At first, Elise resisted these practicalities. The last thing she wanted to do was think about pots and pans. But as the conversation with Joy flowed, Elise began to feel there would be more mystery and more adventure, if of a different kind. Thinking of the incidents of a household and a life together did not have to mean the adventure would recede and be replaced by bourgeois domesticity. Elise began to feel that some of her inevitable misgivings were the result of forgetting she wasn't simply moving into a phase of married life, a phase that would have restrictions on the freedom she presently enjoyed. She was forgetting Tino. Joy assured her she was not marrying a cardboard cutout, but a flesh and blood man with all the complexities and expectations and hopes and desires that she, Elise, had. Here was the adventure.

"Have you thought about the ceremony?" Joy asked.

"I have not even begun."

There was context to this innocent exchange. They had talked about spirituality in the abstract, and Elise knew Joy took her comments on the subject to be vague. They had something of a tacit détente on the subject. Joy might imagine an entire dimension beyond the here and now, and somehow it was tied up in that medieval story of pain and torture and blood and grit and sin and sacrifice. But the nice picture of it, the wedding picture, one could accept. It would seem in keeping with the universal spirituality that even Elise bought into. Then she thought of her father, more conversant with all the Christian symbolism. If she opted for a traditional ceremony, he'd have a conniption fit.

"What's funny?" Joy asked.

"Oh, you know, the ceremony. I was thinking about my dad."

"No escorting you down the aisle, then."

"He'd disown me first. Too much patriarchal ownership implied there, not to mention all the stuff symbolized by that kind of ceremony. It would be simpler if he didn't know all about it. Anyway, Tino said let's skip the nonsense and just do it."

"Ooh. Elope!"

"You wouldn't be disappointed if we didn't lay on a big to-do?"

"Of course not," Joy said, gently squeezing Elise's forearm. "It's an important step, but it's not about the ceremony."

"I'm really glad I came. You've helped me get my head on straight. And I don't want to go, but I have to," Elise said.

"You just got here."

"I have a rendezvous with Tino."

"Can I tell everyone I know?"

"Oh my goodness, no, I'm so glad you said that. I haven't even told my dad. I hid my ring this morning when I left."

"Elise!"

"I haven't gotten used to the idea myself. I'm going to talk to him today."

"But he likes Tino, right?"

"Oh yes. And this won't be a total surprise to him."

"It's more of a surprise to you."

"Kind of. You know me better than I know myself. But I have to go. Tino is meeting me to go grocery shopping. See how domestic we are?"

"Go, then. And tell me when I can spill the beans."

"Okay. Bye."

"Soon."

"Yes, soon, mother. Good-bye."

Elise floated along the sidewalk in something of a dream world. It wasn't exactly elation she felt, but rather a sense of peace, in contrast to the vague sense of unease she had before seeing Joy. She replayed in her mind the events of the previous night. She felt then like she and Tino were inside that golden bubble, separated from the world around them, and all seemed right. His suggestion of marriage, and her acceptance, were the last of a series of small steps leading inevitably to that culmination. He had walked her home, as on so many other occasions. They had agreed to hold their news, for now, until Elise could have a heart-to-heart with her father the next day. When they arrived home, her father was still up, and Tino exchanged small talk with him. Elise listened, wondering if it would even be possible for Tino not to blurt it out. He didn't. In fact, Elise was impressed at how calm and matter-of-fact he was. One would never know they were on the brink of a grand precipice, ready to jump off together. Elise excused herself from her father's presence the moment Tino was out the door. She could never have suppressed her heightened emotional state from her father, as had Tino.

That morning, before taking in the moving fog, Elise had lain in bed awake. She was contemplating her future, feeling neither exhilaration nor fear, but instead thinking about her own life as if she were on the outside of it, looking in. She had not been aware of the moment of having awakened, as if this thought process were going on even before she opened her eyes. It had been fully dark outside. Possibly an hour or even two before she would normally arise. She had made a point of not looking over at her clock. Elise had no trepidation about talking to her father. He would approve of Tino. She felt sure he would have little reservation about marriage in general. As to him, her thoughts began and ended with imparting this in a way to make him feel included.

Now, walking to the grocery store, Elise's deeper thoughts were for her own future. So often she had wished for adventure, and purpose, and to experience the abundance life had to offer. Those were vague feelings, however, and her life experience to this point had taught her marriage was not necessarily the vehicle to answer those yearnings. But wasn't it so that young men and women had for thousands of years done just this? Become enamored one with another, yearning after the mysterious Other that was yet an Other like me? Interest running to infatuation running to deep, mutual identification each with the other? Love?

And this was not about an idea, but about Tino. Elise smiled, and realized she was smiling. This drew her momentarily out of her internal dialogue, and she was again actively conscious of her surroundings. She noticed a bent-over, older Asian man with a drooping moustache and eyebrows to match. He was holding two leashes, each with a tiny, nervous dog at the end. They looked up at Elise at the same time the old man did, to comical effect. This gave Elise more reason to smile, and she gave in to it, unconcerned about how her internal musings played out on her face for passersby. Tino. Tino's eyes drew her in, made her feel she was wandering around inside his mind, experiencing a place of mystery. Tino was soft-spoken and gentle, but there was a hard edge there, too, which she took for manly resolve. It was a hard edge that he would never use against her, but she was drawn to the fact that it existed in the background. He was unafraid of the future. He was open to what life might bring. He was a little bit dangerous.

Still. Marriage? That staid old bourgeois enslaving institution? Elise's circle of friends outside of the Axis included many young women who would describe it just that way. Always, Elise noted, outside the earshot of young men they might care about. Elise retained enough sense of intrigue about the opposite sex to associate still that touch of magic, to romance—magic that could make it a forever proposition. That "they twain shall be one flesh" was more than an aspiration. It was a phrase from the Bible, but that didn't make it untrue. Tino gave no sign of resisting commitment exclusively to Elise, and in fact attended to her touchingly, endearingly, gently. Marriage in the abstract might be suspect. Marriage to Tino would not be.

Still on autopilot as she approached the grocery store, Elise's thoughts dissolved into the reality of her surroundings, but Tino's face did not. And then he smiled. Elise was shaken by an instant of suspension between the picture in her mind and the reality in front of her: Tino standing near the entrance to the store. She associated with him that frequent sense of unsteadiness, as though his magnetism was so strong as to throw off her own sense of direction. Now it was as if he were breaching the very wall between Elise's subjective consciousness and the reality of what was there. Elise found herself unsettled, like in that half-moment after a minor earthquake, when one realizes what just happened.

"What's the matter?" the apparition said.

"Oh. Too little sleep, I think," she said.

"You've changed your mind. You can't go through with it."

Elise laughed. Her charming enigma was back, firmly placed in the real world outside her thoughts, where he belonged.

"Don't be silly."

They turned and went through the automatic doors. Tino turned to Elise and cocked an eyebrow. "Your dad?"

Elise drew in a deep breath, pressed her lips together, and looked at Tino as if preparing to appraise his reaction. "He was already at work when I went downstairs. I felt like his mind would be elsewhere. Anyway, I didn't feel ready yet. I don't know why. And I hope you don't mind, but I told Joy."

"I don't mind, but if it gets around to your dad before you tell him yourself…"

"Oh, don't worry, Joy will be a sealed vault. I trust her completely. And she would completely understand—I told her I haven't said anything to him yet. I love my dad, but he's—" Elise paused.

"Not your bff," Tino finished.

Elise nodded her approval. "He'll be home this afternoon, so I'm going to make him lunch, and then we'll talk."

"So I won't go in with you. I'll carry groceries and leave you at the sidewalk. You can call me with the verdict. If you text me to run, I'll leave town with just the clothes on my back." Tino was acting out the melodrama, there in the store's aisle. "If you text me the coast is clear, I'll come to dinner."

"Here," Elise said, laughing, handing Tino a bottle to put in the cart. "Better get his favorite wine."

"It might be a hard pill to swallow. Better get two."

"You know he likes you more than me."

Tino took Elise's hand and looked her in the eye. "That is true of literally no one in the world, Elise, and certainly not your dad."

Elise looked down, delighted.

Chapter Thirteen

"I could see it coming a mile away, couldn't you?" David asked.

"Well. Yes. No." Joy woggled her head in ambivalence. "I guess I could, but I'm not sure if it's the best thing."

"Tino's a good man, isn't he?"

"I guess so. He speaks well. He's mannerly. He seems to care for Elise."

"But?"

"But, but—" Joy's voice trailed off, uncharacteristically for her.

"Maybe this will be the thing that nudges Elise over to God. And Tino."

Joy looked over at David as if to get a better explanation from his facial expression, but he was looking down, peering into the lunch bag Joy had brought. The noontime light was peculiar. It was not so much fog they were surrounded by as just unusually low clouds. There was no diffuse fuzziness close to the ground, and the light filtering through the low cloud cover was neither flat nor sharply shadowed.

"Roast beef? Yes, roast beef," he said.

"With the hot mustard you like."

David looked up at her and smiled. Joy sensed his delight was not so much in the roast beef and mustard as in her thoughtfulness in preparing it for him and meeting him with it here in the park between their apartment and his office. David bobbed his head in appreciation, going at the sandwich like it was a Christmas present, and he a ten-year-old boy.

"Are you glad you married me?"

"Mmph," David said into the sandwich.

Joy surveyed the park around them as David was engrossed in the sandwich. The odd light didn't seem oppressive to her at all. Instead, it seemed magical. She loved San Francisco for its changing weather. The erratic atmospherics of the city seemed to represent all the possibility and all the wonder that the world beyond this world meant to her. God was in every breeze, every raindrop, every bird twitter. Before David, she had often felt ungrounded, pulled along by so much love and possibility, but, she realized, with not as much practicality as she might. David was earthbound. He approached everything with a weighing of the options and probabilities and pros and cons, methodical and thorough. She imagined herself as a helium balloon on a string that David held in his hand. She smiled at him now.

David covered his mouth with his hand and, still chewing, gave a muffled "What?"

"Nothing." Joy knew he was genuinely perplexed by her sometimes, and she relished this feeling. She liked it that David seemed never to know what she would come up with next. She didn't fully understand David, nor, she surmised, did he fully understand her. She thought her own behavior was fairly straightforward—it was an immediate response to the electric excitement in the air all the time. David, on the other hand, would internalize some impression or thought or offense or emotion and chew on it in private, long after Joy had completely forgotten about it. He'd resume a conversation from the previous week as if they'd left off seconds ago. Joy smiled at the thought that they would have all their lives together to puzzle over these unshared idiosyncrasies.

"What are you working on today?" she asked.

"Same old government thing."

"Not excited? That doesn't sound like you. I thought this was going to be the next big thing."

"Yeah, it's still interesting, but I'm kind of stuck. I need to take a time-out on programming and do a little sleuthing, I think."

"Ooh, intrigue. Mystery. That sounds exciting!"

"I like being a software developer."

"Oh, David, stop it. Get out and follow footprints or whatever. Solve a crime. Get away from the computer screen. It's for your job, anyway."

David looked over at Joy with a smirk on his face.

"I'm serious. Don't look at me like that."

"Actually, I've already started, I'll have you know. Mostly by sitting right at my computer screen and talking on the phone. And I've been down to city hall a couple of times to look at details of documents that are only summarized online. Lots of researching companies."

"Companies doing business with the city?"

"No, actually. Companies that are impacted by the laws the city passes. But located elsewhere."

Joy had just been making conversation with her husband, about his work, but at this she had to inquire further, to keep up. "What does that have to do with it?"

"I wasn't getting data to trend the way I expected. The lobbying activity and money wouldn't track with what's at stake, compared to other issues of this magnitude. So I kept trying to reconcile it. And finally, I decided it wasn't a problem with the analysis or the algorithm or the code. The problem is out there in the world. Something squirrelly going on in San Francisco politics."

"What's the connection to businesses outside of San Francisco?"

"Just an idea. Hanny helped me with this. On one side, you have the hotels and the 'limit short-term rentals' lobbyists. You see some money coming in and lobbying efforts, but not really like you'd expect. You'd think they'd be more keen to preserve the law as it is, or even better, roll it back to the day when no one, not even individual owners, could rent out their places short-term."

"I read about this fight in the paper all the time."

"Oh, there's a big public show, that's for sure. In fact, that's why I was so puzzled there wasn't more money and more lobbying to show for it. It's like both sides want to be perceived as fighting tooth-and-nail over it, but they're really not."

Joy scooted closer. David put his arm around her and pulled at her collar a little, as though to pull her jacket tighter around her. She nestled into his embrace, putting her feet up on the bench, and her arms around her knees.

"If the hotel interests aren't battling to roll back to the old rules, why? And if the websites and property owners aren't trying to roll back to no rules, why? I think they're in cahoots."

"Ooh. Conspiracy!"

"If the hotels came together on this issue, they could buy off the new form of competition. And if necessary, the public officials, too. Meanwhile, the websites and larger property owners can beef up their interests outside of the city if the hotels cooperate. If vacation rentals are outlawed in San Francisco, the tourists coming in will fill up the hotels, which can keep prices up, but they also have other options. They can go out to where the vacation rentals are allowed. Other places in the Bay Area."

"But they want to experience San Francisco."

"But put yourself in the shoes of someone just visiting. There are fantastic places to stay within an easy drive of San Francisco. Like all the towns around the bay. Up Highway 1. Or Point Reyes, where you went with the Axis."

Joy smiled at his reference to the Axis. Then she lit up. "We should go stay the weekend up there!"

David hung his head, but with an indulgent smile. "Okay. We'll pick a weekend."

"I'm sorry. Finish your tale of intrigue."

David took a deep breath. "If we assume that money talks..."

"They're soulless corporations."

"The vacation rental places are going to be okay with the law, even though it closes out a market, because the law also closes out the competition. At the same time, it builds up another market in another place, where they don't have to compete with the hotels. Marin, Napa, Berkeley, even Oakland. What could be happening is that the hotels and the vacation rental places are just tacitly agreeing to dominate different areas."

"What about the people in San Francisco who just want to rent out their own property in San Francisco?"

"Well, they'd be the only people going against the law."

"But how are they supposed to have their say?"

David shrugged.

"Once again, the people are left in the cold by the government that is supposed to look out for the general interest. People like Hanny. And the big boys split up the pie. Isn't this the 'crony capitalism' you always hear about?"

"It's a changing world. I don't think people realize. All the markets are smaller. Even the markets for something like short-term rentals. It's not a strictly local thing anymore."

"Well, that's good. But it's bad if the city just capitalizes on people's ignorance about it. Somebody somewhere is making a boatload of money, I bet."

"Mm."

"Thank you, David, for this depressing lunch."

"'Course, this is all just my theory. But I don't think I'm missing anything in the data."

"There's more to life than money." Joy gathered the lunch debris and walked over to a trash can and back.

David followed a few steps behind, absentmindedly.

"Maybe the press should investigate. How about all the website journalist investigators?"

"That . . ." David made a nodding gesture. Joy could see he thought the idea had merit. "It would also have the effect of leveraging my effort."

"You could stick to what you're a genius at. Are you glad you married me?"

"You only get to ask me that once a day." David stepped forward to encircle her waist, but Joy stepped lightly back.

"Go to work," she said.

"I just want a smooch."

She feigned shock. "David! We're in a public park."

"I'll walk partway back with you."

"Sure." They turned in the direction of the apartment, walking slowly, with Joy hanging on David's arm.

"I'm sorry I went on and on about work."

"I'm always interested."

"No," David interrupted her, "I meant to talk about what's really on my mind, and I got going about the stupid project instead. Easier than talking about things that matter."

Joy looked down at the ground as she walked. "No," she said softly. "Not yet."

"Well, it's okay. We're doing fine. I don't want you to be upset by this. It's perfectly normal. It hasn't even been three months."

"Four, but you're right. God's in charge."

They paused at the edge of the park.

"David, I'm fine. I just don't want you to be disappointed."

"No, no, no," David hastened to say. "We're just being impatient. People go years before having a baby."

Joy smiled and nodded, uncharacteristically pensive. She reached for the edge of David's jacket and curled her hand into it, stepping forward into his space. David thought she might look up to kiss him, but instead, she touched her forehead to his chest. He pressed his cheek against the top of her head.

"You really should go to work," she said.

"I'll see you at midnight."

"You don't have to."

"I'll see you at midnight."

David returned to his office but was not of a mind to pick up where he left off before lunch. Nor was he in the mood to distract his team members with idle chit-chat or play ping-pong in the corner rec room. He sat at his desk, but with his chair turned so he could look down the aisle and out the expanse of glass window at the end. There was the familiar cityscape, across the top of the building on the other side of Market, and then away to the north uphill. With the cross-sectioning of streets, the view was of little bits and pieces of many buildings, a varied if somewhat static tableau. The hillside caused the buildings to seem to rise up from Market Street so that his view included only a sliver of sky.

He imagined all those offices and apartments before him, and all those hundreds, perhaps thousands, of people hurrying to and fro inside them, either working or, like Joy at this moment, getting ready for work. But that wouldn't be all of them, surely. Inside all those windows visible from his vantage point would be many who entertained no thoughts of work. He might even now be looking at the exterior of abodes where people indulged their worst appetites, for drugs or alcohol, perhaps—any means of altering reality from inside their own minds. Or perhaps in those same rooms, some were engaged in illicit sexual encounters—liaisons formed in a vain attempt to bring life to an empty husk, calling upon a half-remembered spark of enchantment to descend again upon them. Perhaps many were unconventional pairings in which the melding of personality was no longer even the pretended object. This was San Francisco, after all. Inside many of those rooms would be men seeking fulfillment with men, or women with women, eschewing a complementary relationship built on unbridgeable difference. In all this array of buildings representing the humanity behind their walls, David wondered at the despair, frustration, anger, and pain lived out just in front of him. So many souls in torment, and within easy reach of the truth which would free them from it and reconcile them to the inevitable disappointments.

On the other hand, not all of those visual gateways before him would lead into the lives of people so weighted down and struggling. Inside them would also be children, well-loved and spontaneously joyful, and mothers and fathers, pacing the floor with toddlers at the chest, laying them gently to sleep on pallets for afternoon naps. And old couples, reading each other's minds and helping each other to navigate the hard places of a world that has grown past them. And adults of all ages, some of whom have an ability to see past the hustle and churn of daily commitments and live with an awareness of the longer view — the goals and aspirations and purposes of an entire lifetime, however long it might last. David considered the population of those many behind all those closed doors and open windows. People dart here and there and don't seem to pause and consider why. What is the purpose to a whole lifetime? And if a person has adopted an ingrained pattern of seeing only the next obstacle or task, can they nonetheless recoup an ability to stop? And wonder? And see their lived life from start to finish, considering the net good that has come of it? This was a blessing, he thought, that he should desire for all of them, and as he considered this, he decided to pray for all those people in all those buildings in front of him, feeling a little foolish but doing it anyway, praying that they might have the awareness of life to see past the tyranny of the moment. Perhaps in doing so, they would consider the Author of that life, and He who is vitally concerned with how it is lived.

David turned back to his desk, re-energized, his big-picture break concluded. Seconds later, he was finding contacts for local online journalists who might take an interest in the puzzling non-battle over San Francisco vacation rentals.

Chapter Fourteen

Marriage had certainly not been on the radar screen when Tino arrived in San Francisco. But now, a few months later, it seemed like a natural next step. Elise would be an asset to him. She was graceful. Charming. Beautiful. Tino was not unconscious of the fact that as a couple, they made more of an impression than he alone might make. The manner of their wedding seemed to have added an aura of mystery to the already-popular couple. It was not news in their circle that they were seriously seeing each other, but to so suddenly visit the county clerk and then disappear to Europe for two weeks caught their friends by surprise. There had been no build-up, no period of public affiance. Once they returned to San Francisco, Tino had the impression their actions were regarded as a spirited bit of derring-do. A romantic sense of urgency and passion was imputed to them. Their reception on returning to town suggested there was a certain cachet attached to them, owing to the way they had jumped in. On all sides were keen well-wishers, and a desire to overlap social circles with Tino and Elise. The marriage to Brinkley's refined and adored daughter had proven to elevate Tino's status. And on top of that, he found her all the more charming, seeing that she was eager to please him and build a new edifice on this new foundation for life. Tino was drawn into the changed nature of their relationship more than he had imagined he would be. He found himself unexpectedly more flirtatious and flattering and flowery with Elise than ever. This transition was proving quite agreeable to Tino.

"Tino mio," Brinkley said, one morning soon after the wedding trip.

"Peter?"

"How are these arrangements working out for you? You know you're free to move on if you like, I'll not insist you stay here with me."

"I think it's perfect. I have no desire to go elsewhere."

"And Elise? What does she say when I'm not around to hear?"

"She wouldn't have it any other way, Peter. I've told you it was one of the first things we talked about when we decided to do the deed. She wanted to be here for you."

"I don't deserve that girl, Tino."

"Nor do I, but truly, the house is fine. Separate access to the kitchen, the whole upstairs floor. Plus the loggia, of course. I'd have a hard time duplicating something like that for Elise."

"She loves you, Tino, not the loggia."

"Yes, but it makes me happy to make her happy. I know she loves the loggia, and she wants to remain close to you."

"I can easily get help for getting around and getting meals and so on."

"I know that, and Elise does, too, but she wants to do it. She's sincere. And so am I. Set your mind at ease, Peter. But thank you for bringing it up."

"And let's hear no more about it," Elise said. Both Potter and Tino turned to see that she had appeared in the hallway leading to the kitchen. Tino gave her one of his knowing smiles, one that hinted at perplexity that she would have consented to him. It had the desired effect. She seemed to lose her concentration on the partial conversation she had overheard.

"Well, I'm not a third wheel here—I'm more like the third through seventh wheel," Potter said, referring to his wheelchair.

"Oh, stop it," Elise said. "You're not a third wheel. Tino is distracting me."

"Lot of that going on," Potter said.

"Daddy!"

"I'll just be going to my study," Potter said, cackling. He reached to the side of his chair, but Tino stepped over and began the turn for him, slowly at first to make sure his hands were clear of the push ring.

Tino returned to find Elise in the kitchen. "He's going to rest after that little exchange," she said. "I think he's getting weaker, a little more every day."

"Age."

"Well, age, and the illness that put him in the wheelchair, but he's declining quickly. I can see it. But he gets a kick out of making comments like that."

"And you get a kick out of pretending to be shocked," Tino answered. He sidled over to put an arm around Elise's waist, and then, not forcefully and even a bit diffidently, leaned forward to place the most delicate kiss on Elise's willing cheek. He sensed her subtle tremble.

"Tino, what have we done?"

"We jumped, darling. We stood at the edge and leapt."

Elise smiled and put her arms around his neck.

"Hey, I've got to get back to work one of these days," Tino said.

"I think Daddy understands."

"I don't just work for your Daddy, love. We'll have a lifelong honeymoon, but I've got to work once in a while."

"All right," Elise said, putting on her best pouty voice. "I guess I need to work on my grad school papers anyway."

Tino had an invigorating uphill walk to his office, where he stopped at least once a day, if only for an hour, to catch up on emails and phone messages. He sometimes bought a copy of the *Chronicle* or *Examiner* on his way, because his work didn't allow for languishing in front of the computer for long periods of time. He found that as he became more invested in San Francisco, he felt a greater affinity for its comings and goings in the news, and reading the paper newspapers made him feel more a part of it. He glanced over the headlines as he walked. Once inside his office, he paused to read the local political blurbs before firing up his computer. Nothing of note that would affect him.

Tino carried on in this way all during the week, dutifully hiking up the hill to his office before setting out to see what he referred to as "clients." He was beginning to feel a bit like the man in the gray flannel suit he'd once joked about with Elise and her friends. He was married now and visiting the office and clients every day. But he was also quite popular among many in the city who admired him and were positioned to push him along to greater things.

On Friday morning of the first full week back at work, Tino settled into his oversized leather chair and took the keyboard down from the desktop, setting it across the tops of his thighs. He had skipped the paper-paper that morning and was settling in to one of the local online journals he regularly visited. There was an intriguing headline—"Vacation Rentals: A Mellow Fight." Tino sat up suddenly and swung his feet down off a low stool he used when he had his keyboard in his lap. Just then his phone rang. He looked at the phone, buzzing on the desktop, then back at the computer screen, then back to the phone.

He grabbed the phone without looking at the incoming number. "Hello?"

"It's you. Tino, are you okay? I haven't heard from you in so long. Didn't you get my messages?"

Tino took a deep breath and forced himself to turn away from the article on the screen. He knew it wouldn't do to try to read and deal with this call at the same time. Focus.

"I'm sorry. Remember I told you I was going out of town on business. And then I was buried when I got back. I'm sorry, darling."

"I forgive you. I just worry about you. When am I going to see you again? I have a lot to catch you up on."

At this point, Tino had shifted to his other world in his mind. With the computer screen out of sight over his right shoulder, he looked out his window at the upper branches of the ginkgoes that grew across the street from his office.

"And I'm missing out," Tino said. "I miss you."

"I *know*," came the voice on the other end. It was almost a whine, but an acceptable whine. An *I miss you too* whine.

"I can come see you today, but I have to get back by evening. I have a work thing."

"Tino," came the plaintive voice, "Billy is taking me to the doctor's in Novato today."

"Is everything okay?"

"Sure. Everything's just like it's supposed to be. I go every three or four weeks now, remember? But today's my appointment."

"Okay, then. Not today. I just miss you," Tino said as he thought about the demands on his time over the coming weekend.

"Tomorrow?"

"Hey," Tino said, "let's go to the farmer's market in Point Reyes Station and make a nice breakfast tomorrow. How about that?"

"You can stay over!"

"No, I only have the morning. I have to be heading back in the early afternoon."

There was a pause on the other end. "I understand. But let's talk when you're here."

Tino understood Cassie perfectly. The "let's talk" would mean talk about being together more. She probably spent more time at her parents' in Olema than she did at the little stand-alone apartment Tino had gotten her in Point Reyes Station.

"Sure, we can talk. Nine?"

"I'll be waiting for you," came the smiley voice on the other end.

Tino pressed the "end" button and tossed the phone so that it clattered across the desktop. He sat ruminating for a moment about the lives he had going simultaneously and the need to compartmentalize them, just as he did his business ventures. He turned back to his computer to get messages and saw the headline and remembered.

There wasn't much to the article. It just cited some facts about the level of lobbying activity and money spent for it, relating to the law on vacation rentals. Not too much controversial in the article itself. It was more the headline that bothered Tino, along with the fact that the online paper thought it worthwhile to print the lobbying facts in the first place. He sat for a moment in thought. All this effort to keep the profile of this debate down, and now the very fact of the low profile was the newsworthy item. He went online to see if there was anything else on this subject, but apparently, he'd already seen the leading edge of it. Or, he hoped, the one-off story.

After a few minutes of returning emails, Tino glanced again at his calendar and noted he was supposed to meet Hanny in half an hour. His car was in the garage across the street from Brinkley's. He calculated it would be nearly as easy to walk as to go back to the house, get the car, and find a place to park once he arrived at the show venue. Tino decided to chance rain and set out on foot. He was generally a stranger to any sense of foreboding, but this article sparked in him a feeling of unease. He disliked the feeling intensely. A good walk might help dispel it.

But then, as he walked along, came a call from Teague. "Did you see it?" Teague asked.

"I did. 'A mellow fight.'"

"Can you meet me?"

"I'm headed to the Mission District on an errand for Dr. Brinkley. I can come by later."

"Are you walking? Where are you?"

"Golden Gate and Franklin."

"Hold up for me? I'll walk with you."

Five minutes later, Teague came marching down Golden Gate Avenue and turned south on Franklin. Tino fell into step with him.

"It started with some computer simulations for lobbying," Teague said. "I don't see how something like that could capture all the variables."

"I happen to know the guy who did it."

"Can you send me his information?"

"Sure, I'll text it to you."

"Use snail mail."

Tino found the words alarming. Why use snail mail? What next, carrier pigeons? Should he really be concerned about electronic surveillance? He said, "If you think that's best."

"I do. Listen, Tino, there's something you should know. This will make the hotel group nervous. And the website group. They've watched us pretty close, the whole time."

"I pretty much expected that. But they've got no reason to complain. Everything flows the way it's supposed to flow."

"But you're going to be the focal point. If things were to get out of hand, you're one person who can finger everyone involved. Watch your back."

"It wouldn't make sense for them to interfere with me if I'm not cheating them, would it?"

"No, but it's a two-way street. If this thing gets traction, you're the one with all the answers."

"Okay, I hear you."

"Maybe we moved too slow on the consortium. How's that coming?"

"Slow. My two weeks off to get married didn't help—"

"Oh, that's right. Congratulations."

"Thanks. But I'll move ahead on this as best I can. The 'mellow fight' thing will die away, I'm sure. I'm going to see Mark Hanigan right now. I'll bring it up with him. Remember that was his gig where I first met you and Potter."

"Yes, of course. I'll peel off here, then. Be careful, Tino."

Tino turned and beamed his most confident smile at Teague. "It'll all work out, Gerald."

Hanigan was in front of the space talking to a Hispanic man at the rear of a white cargo van. Inside the van, Tino could see a wooden structure divided into padded vertical sections. He deduced they were for paintings to be moved, and as he looked closer could see that several paintings were already in place.

"Uh oh, we have to hurry, Javier," Hanigan said upon seeing Tino. "This man is here to evict us."

Tino again smiled his confident, man-about-town smile. "I'm only the bearer of keys, you know that," he said.

"My friend Javier," Hanigan said.

Javier shook hands with Tino. "Dias," he said.

"Buenos dias."

Hanigan said, "I should have called you, Tino. The restaurant guys are in the alley at the back bringing in some equipment already. I hope that's okay."

"Fine with me. Are they in your way, though?"

"No. I'm taking my stuff out the front."

"Looks like you're making good progress."

"Well, yes, but I've got more than I started with because I stored some paintings here a couple of weeks ago."

"Aren't you having to move them twice?"

"I was staging it for one big move. This way I can get Javier to move all of it in time for a three-week gig starting tomorrow."

"Tomorrow! Congratulations, Hanny. You're getting to be quite popular. Where do you go from here?"

"Branching out a bit. Headed up to Marin County. Art show in San Anselmo. Second one, actually."

"So you're giving the city a rest for a bit. Similar theme to this one?"

"I'm impressed you would even understand there's a theme."

"Too busy to think about the consortium idea?"

"Not ready to pull the trigger on that."

"Do you have misgivings about the concept? I think it makes good sense, but I need a critical mass to move forward. What does it take for someone in your position to consider it seriously? Is there something about the artistic temperament I'm not appreciating?"

"I guess I'm skeptical. The idea is that our work would bring in much more than it would standing alone, but I don't see how that's viable for the buyers. I don't want to end up in the wrong tier of the art market. I want to be careful what my work is associated with. But I'm open-minded about it. Don't count me out just yet."

"Do you have time to show me some of your work for the next show? In case I can't get up to San Anselmo before it's over?"

"Sure. I'll make it quick. I know you need to see me out and the restaurant people in."

They went inside. Javier had already resumed his task. It was clear he understood the imperatives of handling original art. There were pads on the floor along the display walls, for temporarily positioning art being moved. Hanigan took advantage of the pads to show Tino a few pieces from a small storage room behind the display room.

"Hanny, I'm impressed," Tino said when the first few pieces were set out.

"Now you're privy to my secret. I'm living a double life."

Tino looked at Hanigan, feeling momentarily disoriented.

"What's wrong?" Hanigan asked.

"Oh," Tino said, recovering. "The portraits, you mean?"

"'Portraits,' I guess you could say, but I'm not trying to do portraits *per se*. I'm painting realism in the expressions of people. I hope you're not disappointed in me?"

"What are you talking about, Hanny? Why would I be disappointed?"

"I feel weird about it. Like I'm stepping back from the cutting edge of the San Francisco art scene, and back to the hard earth of gritty, human experience. Like I'm not a real artist."

"Honestly, Hanny, I like this as well as your abstract work. It's almost the opposite. You had this idealistic impression going, and now I'm looking into the faces of real people who are just trying to make it through the day. Different. But good."

"I do feel a little schizophrenic because I like them both. It's a big switch from one extreme to the other. Let me show you a couple of more. I promise I won't trot out my whole show."

Hanigan jumped up and disappeared around the wall into the storeroom. Behind him, Tino saw that Javier was moving toward the truck at a deliberate pace with one of the larger abstract paintings, carefully wrapped.

"I'll go ahead and just set this here, but there are two more that go with it. Look at it just superficially."

Tino smiled. How does one look at something superficially? Must be an artist thing. Hanigan was excited like a little schoolboy as he disappeared around the wall again. Tino glanced at the picture, wondering if he should wait until the other two appeared, but his glance told him much more than art appreciation alone might have. He recognized the person depicted there.

Hanigan strode quickly forth with the next painting, and then with a third.

Tino stood looking at all three, carefully, and thought perhaps he could impress Hanigan with his sincerity by taking to one knee to better observe, since the paintings were just resting on the floor.

"I know that man," Tino said, gesturing toward the first picture.

Hanigan was on one knee, too, right next to him. Tino could sense Hanigan's quizzical look without seeing it. "Really? Small world."

"I've seen him, I should say. I don't really know him."

"It changes the experience, I suppose, if you actually know the person. If you don't know the model, the picture is still somewhat abstract, in a way. You're reading a face and body expression, not bringing to the observation a whole history of knowledge of the subject."

"So," Tino said, "if you paint a landscape, you may get a feeling that the picture is pretty, or even emotionally or intellectually evocative, but it's going to mean something completely different to someone who has experienced that place in some way."

"And, of course, different people would experience a place in a different way."

"I'm learning from you, Hanny. If you do a portrait for someone, perhaps his family, you do a likeness, and the family provides the significance."

"Boom."

"Don't be hip, Hanny, it's unnerving."

Hanigan chuckled.

Tino said, "We talked about this before, how people bring meaning to the art."

"Well, it's an element of consciousness, I think. I'm not turning my work over to be interpreted any old way someone wants to interpret it. I do mean something by it when I present it. On the other hand, I recognize that the whole enterprise is undertaken for the benefit of the person viewing it. So I'm appealing to their consciousness when I put something down on canvas."

"The consciousness of the viewer. Someone you don't know."

"Right. So if I paint a picture of a person who is not known to the viewer, I'm saying something about people, not a person. And I'm intending something by what I paint, knowing the viewer brings an intentionality of their own to the experience of viewing it."

"Do you think that's what happens when people just talk face to face?"

"I'm sure it is. That's why I think of my painting as a form of communication. A subject-to-subject experience. Mutual consciousness each of the other."

"But they're not even together," Tino observed. "If I go look at the Mona Lisa, then da Vinci and I are communicating?"

"Exactly. Separated by time and space, yet communicating. It's time travel. Astral projection. Still a mutual consciousness between him and you. It's meaningless to talk of this consciousness as being bounded by space or time."

"This guy," Tino said, waving toward the picture of the man in the gray felt hat. "What about him? Does he participate in this? What it is he communicating?"

"That's a good question. I think no more than a landscape does, in the sense we're speaking of it. I saw him in a café in San Anselmo, when I had my first show up there, and he agreed to let me paint him. I sketched it out on the spot. He was just talking to some friends, but I was taken by the intensity of his expression around the eyes, and the way he looked out from under that hat."

"I see it."

"He was communicating to the other two people at his table, at the time, and I suppose when he got up that morning, he put on that hat and those clothes and carried himself a certain way, in part to communicate something of himself to the wider world, just like we all do. But he wasn't using the painting for that. He just sat relatively still for a few minutes, for my benefit."

"Probably felt complimented to be sketched and painted."

"I never have trouble finding models. I would say he's no more communicating through the medium of paint than a landscape would, because I'm the one communicating, not him. Just like God may communicate to us with a landscape, but it's God's consciousness in play, not the landscape's."

"If there is a God. Otherwise, it's just your consciousness, bouncing off the stuff in the world around you."

Hanigan rose to his feet, and Tino did, too. "That's what your new father-in-law would say, no doubt," Hanigan said. "I just…" Hanigan looked about him in the room, as if expecting to see the far-off horizon. "That just can't be right."

"So you're communicating in this way," Tino said, to draw Hanigan back to earth.

"Yes. These pictures, for example, are pictures of what I thought were compelling facial expressions, getting at something deep in the human condition and otherwise difficult to express. I want them to be universal. I'm not trying to say something about the individual person."

Tino gave Hanigan his full-attention look, nodding appreciatively. He was aware of his own instinctive ability to identify a person's passion and draw them out on it, as with Hanigan now. It would make him all the more invested in Tino. This was one of the ways Tino inspired loyalty, and trust, and confidence, even if on his side there was an unexpressed emotional distance. "So if I happen to know who this person is," Tino said, "that might actually get in the way of what you're trying to say."

"I suppose that's right. But you said you'd seen him before. How do you know him?"

"Well, I only met him once. And I didn't really meet him. The brim of the gray hat in the picture tipped me off, and then I recognized the face. So your rendition even of the hat is a compliment to you, maestro. I saw him one morning in west Marin, on Mesa Road in Point Reyes Station. He was feeding an apple to a horse. Early in the morning. He parked his truck in the middle of the road and walked over and fed the horse over the fence. This made me think it wasn't his horse, but I had the impression it was a regular event."

Hanigan stood with arms crossed, looking at his own paintings.

"These are good, Hanny."

"Thank you, Tino." Hanigan picked up two of the pictures to deliver to the front of the shop where Javier was loading. Tino reached for the remaining picture, the one of the gray-bearded and gray-hatted man.

"What is he telling you, Tino?"

"It's strange. I saw just a glimpse of his eyes before, under the hat brim. But there's no mistaking this is the same guy. You caught the look."

"And?"

"Eh, don't know if this is what you were going for, but mysterious? Not in a good way, but like he's hiding something. Maybe even sinister. Secrets. He's got a past, and there's a violent edge."

"Interesting. Even though you saw him in circumstances suggesting a gentle nature."

"Maybe especially so."

"Just set it here. Javier's an expert at packing them in."

Chapter Fifteen

It would be chilly in the loggia. Elise felt it all the more because it was summertime, but she needed just these few minutes to herself before going down to care for her father. His need for care had been increasing at an alarming rate, and Tino's work seemed to keep him away more than she had imagined it would. When she did see him, Tino seemed a little on edge, not his usual unruffled self. To be expected, she thought, that reality would settle in after months on a cloud during their courtship and marriage. After the impromptu wedding, Tino had just moved in with her and her father, so her routine was not so unsettled as it might have been. Elise was grateful that Tino had not insisted on their own place, given her father's declining condition, but it occurred to her she was looking out at the bay from the loggia in just the way she did before that magical time building up to the marriage. She could imagine the marriage had not taken place at all, if she chose.

Elise checked her phone for the time. She would need to get her father's medication in a moment. Perhaps her uncharacteristic pang of melancholy had to do with him and not with Tino's frequent absences. She faced facts bluntly. Her father was not doing well. He didn't complain, but he was often silent, and worse, no longer seriously working at all. He had always kept his visits to the doctor minimal, even after taking to the wheelchair. Now the doctor visits were frequent. He looked pasty, wan. The doctors couldn't or wouldn't put a name to his condition, but instead talked all around the symptoms and bloodwork results and diet and mental stimulation. Elise knew she was just witnessing age, though her father had friends of the same age more spry than he. It seemed unfair.

Downstairs she found him in the small living room opposite the entrance to his study, looking out the window. From his vantage point in his chair, she knew he could not see the street itself, but only the upper-floor windows of the houses across the street and across the intersection at the corner. Elise approached him with the pills and water she had picked up in the kitchen.

"Time for your medicine," she said brightly.

There was no movement at first, but then her father turned slowly toward her, leaning left as he looked up and to the right, as was his habit. Elise noted his waxy, yellowed complexion and dull eyes but had prepared herself not to let him see concern in her eyes.

"I'll miss you," he said.

"What do you mean, Daddy?" she asked, as if he had been joking. "Where are you going?" Even as she said this, Elise knew he was expressing a premonition of death. His decline had been too fast not to be quite noticeable. Perhaps even more noticeable given the height from which he was falling. His deep but nimble intelligence had been the signal feature of his existence for all of Elise's life. Now he was fading. And what could he mean by missing her, if he was referring to his own mortality? According to his view of reality, upon death, he would simply be no more. No consciousness at all to do the missing, unless for all his dogmatic materialism he intuited a consciousness that would yet survive.

Potter half-smiled and nodded to one side, a gesture a little like a shrug, and reaching to his shoulder, he covered Elise's hand with his own. He didn't answer her, but instead said, "I feel like I'm leaving something undone."

Elise said, "You ought to take it easy today anyway," but she knew he was thinking of his life's work, not this day's. She added, "Don't think that way. You've done so much. There's a time to work, and a time to rest."

Potter took the little paper cup she held toward him and downed the pills it contained. Then, somewhat unsteadily, the glass of water. Elise thought about how often they had repeated this little rite, and how this time it seemed to take longer.

After this, she spent some time trying to engage her father in small talk. There were sparks here and there of his former self, but for stretches of time, he would just look out the window. He might be deep in thought as he stared out over the tops of the buildings. But was he? Did he still have the capacity? Elise waited patiently at his elbow during some of these stretches, engaged in her own internal reverie. He would miss her? His convictions precluded an existence within which to do the missing. What if those convictions were off the mark? His life's work—lectures, academic papers, two books plus a textbook on neuroscience—had all been centered on his conviction that the processes of the brain were the seat of all that makes us human. When it dies, therefore, the human dies with it, returning to the oblivion from whence he arrived. Her father had scoffed at the idea there might be something more to one's existence than the neuronal sparks of the brain—the countless responses to stimuli, from event to event, word to word, emotion to emotion, from birth to last breath. His teaching and even casual conversation had, for as long as Elise could remember, been liberally seasoned with faith in the unity of brain and mind and soul. Alternative words for the same thing.

What if he was wrong? As she looked on her father in his late-life fatigue, she wondered whether he now had self-doubt on this subject. Elise had acquired some insight into the point of view that the mind and the soul might be different kinds of things altogether. This acquaintanceship with the opposing view left her with doubts. Her faith was not complete. How could the twists and turns of conscious thought and conscious awareness of another be entirely—and only—the product of electricity and chemical in the brain?

Elise turned her gaze from the window back to her father. He seemed on the verge of nodding off.

"A little rest, Daddy?" she said softly.

Potter started, then nodded faintly. Elise rose to help him to his room.

Moments later, Elise was on the sidewalk, eager for movement. She walked at a vigorous pace, agitated. She was having a crisis of faith, and at the same time, a feeling of deep loneliness, even though her father only slept, at the moment, and Tino was only at work. Seeing her father's decline shook her more than she had expected. He would go. Life would end. There would be no more. The enormity of this tragic and complete finality was borne in upon her. Implicit in her father's credo was that we must stand stoic against the harshness of that truth, because the truth is the truth. Elise had always considered herself strong enough to embrace that reality, not only for her father, but for herself. We all die. If oblivion follows, it follows for all of us.

Her crisis now did not result from the harshness of the truth she had learned, however. It resulted from her doubt about it being true in the first place. She was conscious of herself now walking along, shoulders hunched, rubbing her upper arms with her hands as she walked, despite the heavy sweater she wore. And of the mild burn in her legs as she purposely chose the steepest of the hills away from her house. And of the fog and the steely coolness it brought with it. And of the utter pointlessness of it all, if her father's faith were true. How could she be conscious of all of this, even as she experienced it, as if she were watching herself engaged in this activity and thinking these thoughts — and watching herself watching herself, in an infinite regress. How could she exist? Not just the contingency of her existence — the result of her parents' union, and their parents', and so on, again in an infinite regress — but the first Existence, the first uncaused-cause that begat all the subsequent causes, to the effect that Elise was here, at this moment, not merely existing, but conscious of it. How could there not be a vaster, greater consciousness that begat all this, within which she and every other conscious being rested?

Elise passed a duet of ginkgo trees and realized they looked familiar. Across the street was Tino's office. She could see through the street-facing window. To the left was the little anteroom, and to the right was the larger room with Tino's desk and a conference table surrounded by maps and other city information. From this vantage point, Elise could see the ceiling and not much else. The light was off. This reminder of Tino, and of life, buoyed her spirits. She needed him. She stepped lightly across the street.

Tino's building had long ago been renovated to include several sets of office suites. On the second floor were two, each a mirror image of the other. They had exterior doors, facing each other but perpendicular to the street, opening onto a small landing. Wrought-iron steps connected the landing to the sidewalk on the uphill end of the building. Elise stepped up and tried the door to Tino's office, but as expected, it was locked. She stood in front of the door, uncertainly, still steadying her emotions, and turned to face the street again. As she paused at the landing's handrail, she heard a jangle of keys behind her. She spun around, hoping it might be Tino, but it was a smiling young man, tall and lanky, securing the door to the suite opposite Tino's, an office that advertised real estate services.

"Oh, well, hello there," he said familiarly.

"Oh, hi, I was just going to drop in on my husband, but he's not in," Elise said with a futile gesture toward Tino's office door.

"Right, right. It's Elise, isn't it?"

"Oh, I..." Elise felt momentary embarrassment. They had met, at one point, but she couldn't remember his name.

"Tom. Widener. You wouldn't remember. We met at a thing sometime back."

"I'm sorry."

"It's perfectly fine. We talked for maybe two minutes. It was noisy. Plus, I have the advantage. I see Tino coming and going here. Gives me a mental association."

"You're very gracious."

"I haven't seen him today, though."

"He wasn't expecting me. Actually, I just sort of ended up here without thinking about it, so I thought I'd drop by."

"I'll let you in."

"You have a key?" Elise asked, surprised.

"Sure. We traded backup keys."

"I guess so. Since I'm here."

Moments later, Tom had given Elise directions on where to leave the backup key and had gone on his way. Elise sat in Tino's chair and spun around in it, looking about absentmindedly. She had only been in this office once before. It was utilitarian, but not without some interesting old-city touches.

Elise felt herself relax from the tensions that had accompanied her on the strenuous walk up to the office. She imagined Tino close by, his office serving as proxy for the moment. Perhaps he would even come by, though she knew he spent more time out of the office than in it. If he did show up, she would surprise him. She would make him take her to lunch. Elise picked up a day-old newspaper, glanced through the headline stories, and then set it down again. She realized Tino might not be there that day at all, and it seemed frivolous to call him just to hear his voice. Especially if the real reason was just a difficult-to-describe emotional uneasiness. Calling him randomly at work was something she had resolved not to do, anyway. Theirs was not to be that kind of marriage, and she would not be that kind of needy wife. Elise decided to write him a clever note instead, and she looked around for a notepad. In her work space at home, she kept a stack of legal pads in the same spot all the time. Searching for something so mundane should not take up a moment of life. Evidently, Tino didn't think the same way. In how many other ways were they different? There was no blank paper in the desk drawer, nor in the cabinet drawers behind the desk, nor on the shelf under the window. Elise walked over to the end of the room opposite the window. Along one wall were more file cabinets, so she looked in there. There were hanging file folders in one, and in the next more rolled-up oversized papers. She thought it likely that one of these drawers would have general office supplies because she'd seen none elsewhere. In the next drawer she opened, there was a stack of envelopes, hand-addressed to Tino. A feminine hand. Elise paused over them. Closed the drawer. Hesitated.

Then Elise slowly opened the drawer again and stood for a time staring down at the envelopes. There was a loose stack that had fallen over, so she could see there were several from the same person. She picked up the part of the stack that had fallen over, perhaps a dozen separate opened envelopes, addressed to Tino at the office address. Below were more, in the same hand, but she noticed they were addressed not to the office address, but to Tino at an Austin, Texas address. Elise tried to discern the name of the sender in the return address space, but no name was provided, just the address. On the top one, she could not even make out the address, only the zip code—47150. Elise looked around furtively and then felt foolish. It was not like her to slink around. She had lived her whole life determined not to carry around the stain of guilt that seemed so often to oppress people. Her solution was to live in such a way as to have no embarrassment for anything.

ROUGH WATER BAPTISM

She thought of tossing the letters back in and closing the file cabinet, but paused in the act of doing so, the letters not quite slipping out of her hand. The postmark on the top letter was only a few days old. She had known Tino almost from the time he arrived in San Francisco. Where was 47150? Giving in to her curiosity, Elise scooped up some more letters and walked over to the window, where she could see outside should anyone—meaning Tino—approach. Apart from the numbers in the return address, she had trouble with the hasty writing, but she had several samples. She finally determined that the return location was New Albany. The two letters for the state were not clear, but by comparing several, she decided they were IN—Indiana.

This could be anything, Elise thought. Someone in Indiana doing some sort of business with Tino. She had never been entirely clear on the scope of his work anyway. On the other hand, Tino grew up in Indiana before moving on to Austin and San Francisco. The Indiana connection was almost all she knew about his childhood. He had no more family there. Maybe he still had friends from there he hadn't mentioned? Elise thought about how little she really knew of the man she married.

Though it was distasteful to Elise to play the suspicious wife, she knew this would nag at her if she didn't find out more while the letters were still in her hand. She opened the topmost one, setting the others on the corner of Tino's desk.

> *Tino, Tino, come back to me. You stay in San Francisco. Or Austin, as you must. But come back to me in your heart. I don't stay upset about the money. Please call me. Would you write to Roger? He calls. I love you. Mama.*

"Mama?" Elise said aloud. Tino's mother was dead. Maybe this was a nickname? An odd nickname, if so. Elise turned the page over. Nothing there. Nothing else in the envelope. She carefully refolded the letter into the envelope and picked up the next one.

Dearest Tino, I don't scold you about San Francisco. I see you want me to stay from there, and I will. I only miss you. I miss your father. Roger is in Texas. Do you know his mother died? I have my circle at Our Lady, I have the ladies on the street, they are nosy as ever. But they are not my child. I miss you, Tino. I love you, Mama.

"'My child,'" Elise said aloud. She felt an odd mixture of emotions. The letters weren't from a concealed lover, past or present. But there was no mistaking they were from his mother, and quite recent. Why would Tino deny her? Was he embarrassed? He would not be the first person to go to the big city and feel embarrassment about relations left behind. But Tino hadn't seemed like that kind of person. And it was his mother! And she his wife! Elise thought about the brevity of the two letters she'd read. No chatting, just an appeal for a response. These were words borne of heartbreak.

Elise went back to the file drawer and began to flip through more letters. They were all the same on the outside, but on some of the earliest, she found three lines for the return address, not just two. These were in the same tiny and nearly indecipherable hand, but by comparing several, Elise was able to come up with a first name, Theresa. The last name was not legible at all, except she could make out a "C" to begin, and on some a dot above the line near the end of the last name. Of course. Crocetti. The name Elise herself would now have if she had taken Tino's name in the old-school way. Theresa Crocetti.

Under the stack of letter envelopes was another stack, this one of larger manila envelopes. The top one had a man's handwriting. As did the others. Elise thought these were probably unrelated, but then, if it was for business, why would the sender scrawl out an address and a return address by hand, in this day of easy laser-print labels? These were personal letters, too, probably. But so what? How did she, Elise, have any business going through Tino's letters, whether personal or not? On the other hand, all appearances were that Tino's mother was alive, after all, and how could he lie to her about such a thing? What other secrets might there be? Elise picked up the topmost manila envelope and shook out its contents on the conference room table. Inside were just two more letter-sized envelopes, also from Theresa. Tino's *mother*, Theresa. She thought fleetingly of how it might be to have a mother, something lost to her except for the vaguest of early-childhood memories. Elise looked again at the outside of the manila envelope. This writing was quite legible. It was from a Roger Williams in Austin, Texas. She looked inside and saw there was still a single sheet of lined paper inside. It read:

Tino—More from Mrs. Crocetti. Call her, Tino. I really don't want to do this anymore. Roger.

Terse. Not much more revealing than the two letters from Theresa. From Tino's mother. And do what anymore? Elise pulled a chair back from the conference room table, positioning it between the table and the file cabinet. She could use a little more light, this far from the window. She looked up at the dark light fixture and made her decision. She walked over to the switch by the door, flipped it on, walked back to the file cabinet, and settled into the chair.

Chapter Sixteen

"Here," David said, shaking the umbrella open and holding it so it covered Joy and partially covered himself.

"Thanks," Joy said, though she seemed otherwise insensible to David's efforts.

They descended the stone steps and turned uphill.

"Did that go like you expected?" David asked.

They walked several more steps in silence. The rain did not plunk onto the taut umbrella but instead delivered a calming susurration. It was a fine San Francisco mist, against which the umbrella was not very effective below shoulder level. Still, it provided a little cocoon for the couple's quiet exchange. Any hint of despondency on Joy's part weighed heavily on David.

Joy then perked up as though a switch had been flipped. "Yes, actually. Pretty much."

"We said it would take time. It takes time."

"I think they think we're jumping the gun."

"We kind of are."

"I know."

"And maybe their priority is for people who specifically want to adopt, rather than people who adopt because they—" David hesitated. He didn't want to say *can't have their own child*.

"We want adopted *and* our own," Joy answered.

David didn't respond right away. When he did, he said, "You know, God's in charge of all this."

"I know."

"So we have to trust—"

"David, I trust God. I'm not mad at God. I don't think God is punishing us. I just want a baby right now."

David chuckled.

"Right now," Joy repeated, this time with a smile behind it.

"Yeah, I get it. Right now. Right now. Shouldn't we wait to get home first?"

Joy smacked the arm holding the umbrella, sending a pattering of accumulated mist down on their heads. "We're talking about two different things."

"No," David said, drawing out the syllable, "I don't think we are."

Joy seemed her usual self again.

"You know, Joy, people adopt and then they have a baby. Happens all the time."

"David. Adoption doesn't cause pregnancy."

"I know what causes pregnancy. See, we are talking about the same thing."

"It will all be okay," Joy said, to put finality to that strand of conversation.

The following Sunday, David and Joy set out for church, well before start time. They had resolved to walk, thinking the weather only a bit cloudy, but as soon as they hit the sidewalk, they saw that it was a San Francisco cloudy—the clouds themselves scraped the earth, and the pair walked through it, becoming damper as they went.

"We can turn back, if you want—take the car," David said.

"I'm fine," Joy answered. "I want to walk."

They rounded the corner at Soul Cycle, and there was Hanigan, as planned. He stood expectantly under a little overhang at the coffee shop's Stanyan Street entrance.

"True San Franciscans. You braved the fog," Hanigan said.

"Good morning," Joy chirped.

"I can quickly get you a go-cup for the rest of the walk."

David looked at Joy. "I think we're good," he said.

Hanigan bounced down the steps and took up beside Joy and David.

"Today's a special day, you know."

"Why is that, Hanny?"

"It's just special. For me, anyway. You'll see."

"I'm glad you ended up coming back to Twin Peaks. You've been pretty steady lately. How many weeks straight? Four?"

"Six. I'm joining."

"You're saying—" David hesitated.

"I'm joining Twin Peaks. And the church universal. I'm being baptized."

David and Joy burbled their congratulations simultaneously.

"Big step," David said.

"It is, but I'm tired of wrestling with God. I went from skeptic to theist, but I never thought I would go all the way. Walking on water. Virgin birth."

"Resurrection," David added.

"All in," Hanigan affirmed.

"Next you'll be hootin' and hollerin' and falling out in the aisles," David suggested.

"David, stop," Joy admonished.

"Well, it's funny to think about. Someone like Hanny. Most thoughtful person I've ever known to embrace the faith. If anyone can articulate the intellectual path, it's you, Hanny."

"Intellectual is one thing. Belief is another. I had to cross over."

"You got past the problem you talked about—'knowing versus believing,' I think you described it as."

"Yeah. I had this epiphany the other day. I guess I shouldn't say 'epiphany' in this context. Strong mental impression, let's say. I was painting. One of my realist paintings. A little girl's face. I was caught up in it. Hours went by. I thought about how hard I was working to freeze something in two dimensions, to render this certain expression you might see flit across a child's face in just a twinkling of an eye—so fast. One little moment in a stream of continuous moments—one cast of light, one instant of emotional content, one pinpoint of inner beauty in this child. But God does this all the time, in four dimensions, not my two, continuously, and He does it on an infinite number of canvases simultaneously."

"That's beautiful, Hanny," Joy said.

"Another way to think about art," David said. "So is that the epiphany that crossed you over?"

"No. Death was."

"How's that?"

"I always held it against God that there's evil in the world. You know, skeptics say that if God is omnipotent but doesn't eliminate evil, then He's not good. And if He's not good, He's not God. But we're looking at evil in the world in the abstract, or we hear about this event or that one, and we shake our heads and say there's no God. But I think we're overlooking something."

"It's a fallen world," David offered.

"No. Well, yes, but what I mean is the evil and the awfulness and the pain are really kind of worse than we think they are. I mean, come on, we're dying."

"Just a minute ago, you were all happy," Joy protested.

"I'm still happy. But not mindless happy. We all die. We're all in the process of dying. But no one ever complains about that. Your favorite grandma breaks a hip and dies at eighty—well, it was her time. It's just what seems normal to us. A child dies—we say that's evil. But the child was going to die anyway. He just died earlier than we think is somehow right. So when we talk about evil in the world, we're talking about sad stories we hear, or unfairness, or starving children, or whatever. And we don't reflect on our own death. The corruption has to be so much deeper and so much more defining of reality than we realize. We can't just say man is fallen—another line in the catechism—and move on. We're dying. If we're not going to be mad at God about that, then it's stupid to be mad at Him about any of this other stuff."

"That's profound, Hanny," David said, thoughtfully.

"I don't know if it's profound. But I know the all-is-material point of view, and I finally concluded it's indefensible. Everyone thinks of it as just not-God-ism, and right now it's hip to throw over religion. But people don't think through the implications. People reject God but don't think about what they're embracing in His place, really. They just think of it in the negative. It's not God, period. But on its own, it doesn't make any sense."

"Well, you of all people would know the other side of it," David said.

"Systematic non-theology. A new field of study, maybe," Hanigan said.

"And today you're being baptized!" Joy added.

"Hey. What have you heard from Tino and Elise lately?" Hanigan asked.

David looked over at Hanigan, past Joy, and noted the pained expression on Joy's face. Joy had hinted there was trouble in paradise but hadn't wanted to go further, and David had let it lie.

Hanigan noticed her expression, too. "Joy?"

"It's not all bliss over there."

"I was wondering. Tino and I get together sometimes. He's distracted."

Joy made a face to express that this was very much an understatement. "I don't want to gossip," she said, "but they're having a hard time."

"Well, I don't want to gossip, either, but I also don't want to abandon Tino. He's more than kept up his side of our friendship. I don't know if he's got anyone to talk to about something like that."

"He's got plenty of friends," Joy said, "but I know what you mean. My impression is they're not so much friends as—"

"Strategic?" David offered.

"Sounds kind of cold, saying it right out loud," Hanigan said. "But maybe so."

"Mr. Tino keeps his own counsel too well," Joy added.

"Maybe I've let him down."

"I don't think so, for what it's worth," David said. "Tino's a pretty self-sufficient character. If he gave off a signal of wanting to talk about what's going on in his life, I imagine you'd pick it up."

"Maybe. He's very sociable, but not easy to really know. So maybe I should try harder." Hanigan shifted his attention to Joy. "Can you tell me anything that might help?"

"I don't want—"

Hanigan hastened to add, "I don't want you to compromise your confidences with Elise, I assure you, but if I had some idea, maybe I'd better spot the opening when it arises, with Tino."

Joy thought for a moment. "Tino has secrets. Being mysterious can be alluring, but it can also be—"

"Just secretive," Hanigan finished.

"Yes," Joy confirmed. "I guess I should just tell you this. I don't know how it could not be known anyway. Tino's mother is alive."

"Well, if that's some sort of shock, then I take it Elise thought otherwise."

"Yes."

"That's—" Hanigan's voice trailed off.

"How could Elise–" David began.

"I know, I know," Joy said. "That's why Elise is so upset about it. How could she not know that? What else is there about Tino that she doesn't know? She's been pretty tough on herself. She's thinking, who is this guy I married?"

"Has she been in touch with Tino's mother?"

"When I talked to her yesterday, she had not. She wanted to talk again to Tino about it, but the first time she tried, it didn't go well. He kept saying it was complicated, and then he was just gone for several days."

"So she didn't know what to do."

"Elise is frightened by the whole thing. If that's something you didn't know, you have to wonder what else there is. She thinks there's more to it."

"Probably is," David said.

"I'm pretty sure Elise knows more about it than she cares to explain."

"I'm sorry to hear all this," Hanigan said. "Maybe it will help if I talk to Tino."

"Well, be circumspect. Tino of all people wouldn't want to feel like everyone's talking about his business. You know how he is."

"Oh, I know. He does guard his privacy."

The misty fog had not abated at all during this exchange, and the trio fetched up at Twin Peaks Galilean, stepping inside to the large fluorescent-lit former school cafeteria that served as their church's main sanctuary. They had been inside only seconds when Sung Park materialized, shaking Hanigan's hand.

"You're wet," Sung said. "Like you've already been baptized. You don't need me."

"You joke, but that gives me an interesting analogy," Hanigan said.

"Oh, here we go," Sung said, smiling over to David and Joy.

"I know. I overthink everything. But I could've gone along thinking I was sort-of-baptized just by living, absorbing the atmosphere. Like this short life was all the spirituality there is."

"But you didn't," David said. "You were called out."

"And it occurs to me that what brought me to this day was good old atheist materialism," Hanigan said. "If I hadn't been in that camp, I don't think I would have come over to this one."

"And seen the other camp for what it was," Sung said.

"You'd just be idling in neutral," David suggested.

"But there's no such thing," Hanigan said. "That's the lie."

"I'll just make the announcement, and you come up," Sung said to Hanigan.

Hanigan nodded his understanding to Sung Park as Sung took leave to go to the front of the room.

Chapter Seventeen

"Billy, how is she?"

"Tino, where are you?"

"I'm on my way."

"Well, she's fine. Disappointed you didn't make it, I think." There was reproach in Billy's voice.

"Didn't make it? She's already—"

"It's a boy. Congratulations." Tino could tell Billy was trying to bend his tone from reproachful to genuinely congratulatory, all in the space of a few words. They were related, now, after a fashion. Tino sensed that Billy's concern for his sister's happiness would outweigh a desire to indulge ill will against Tino.

Tino was stuck in traffic on Highway 101, on the bay side. His usual route was Highway 1 along the coast, to the place he kept for himself and Cassie in Point Reyes Station. He had stayed straight at the turnoff so he could continue north on 101 to the hospital where his son had just been born. His son. Tino was not displeased, certainly, but the warm fatherly emotion that was supposed to kick in just hadn't, yet. Perhaps it would when he actually held the infant. He would have to think through in advance how he would react, once he arrived, and how to interact with Cassie's parents, who had a more conventional view of how things ought to be. They might hint at marriage between him and Cassie, for example, and so he would have to deflect skillfully. Tino was used to having his own way, but never by confrontation.

Tino was not normally stressed by heavy traffic, even when it was more than a little inconvenient, as it was now. This time was different, but not because of how his being late would affect Cassie. She seemed to think Tino could do no wrong, and Tino relied on that. In fact, Tino, in essence, saw it the same way, thus seconding Cassie's opinion of him, in a manner of speaking. So Tino's stress at the traffic was not borne of impatience at seeing his son, or of being late to support Cassie emotionally. Not being there for the birth might contribute to awkwardness with her parents, but Tino realized that wasn't the thing eating at him, either. It was so rare for Tino to feel anxiety that he had to engage in a bit of introspection, sitting there in traffic, to figure out why he felt it now. Once he began his mental list, it quickly grew longer, making Tino wince at the unfairness. The baby would mean his dual life with Cassie and with Elise would be harder to maintain. He had known this, of course, but now there was an actual child, not a theoretical one. Tino felt regret, not for the first time, that Cassie hadn't chosen to take care of the matter early on.

This turn to being a father didn't by itself explain the angst finding articulation in this traffic jam, however. Brinkley was dying. They could no longer deny it. Tino was not brokenhearted about his friendship with the old man but was, rather, concerned for what this would mean for Tino. Brinkley had been more than Tino's patron. He was enough of a power broker in San Francisco that he could run interference for Tino if it was needed. And now, just when it was needed, Brinkley was checking out. Again, Tino felt a pang of resentment at the unfairness of it all. As if the stars had suddenly aligned against him. Every day now, there were local news items online, doggedly pursuing questions about the city's regulation of rentals. Tino had hoped it would all blow over, but there was enough momentum on this question to cause some close scrutiny of the warring factions in the lobbying efforts. Then there was that correlation study Joy's husband David was responsible for. Too many questions, as far as Tino was concerned. Very powerful people could be in jeopardy over this. Gerald Teague explicitly warned Tino that it could bring the wrong kind of attention to him. Tino knew he was right. His activities actually went far beyond just the vacation rental question. He had become a sought-after, discreet presence at city hall. The money that went through his hands on a whole host of matters far exceeded the bought-and-paid-for rental regulations.

And then, if all that weren't enough, there were Elise's questions about his mother. She had started innocently enough, and so caught Tino by surprise. She asked about his mother abstractly, out of the blue. What was she like? How was her relationship with Tino's father? What had she died of? Tino had taken the questions at face value. It seemed harmless to double-down on the story that his mother was no longer alive—even to add a few details, suggesting she'd died of cancer. But then Elise's questioning hardened, and Tino realized she knew. No doubt his meddling mother had come back to San Francisco after promising she wouldn't. She had probably found Elise and bent her ear. What pained Tino was the look in Elise's eyes the last time he'd seen her. He'd fled to his haven with Cassie. Tino had stayed away from Elise since, even after returning from Marin.

Chapter Eighteen

While Tino was sitting in traffic imagining his mother contacting Elise, Elise was contacting his mother, speaking to Theresa for the first time.

"Mrs. Crocetti?"

"Yes?"

Elise switched the phone to her other ear. "My name is Elise. Elise Brinkley." It occurred to Elise that Theresa might know more than Elise supposed. But the lady said nothing, right away. "I'm calling…" Elise had thought to say "to introduce myself," but that didn't seem the right place to start. "I'm calling about Tino," she said.

"Is he all right?"

"Oh, yes, he's fine," Elise hastened to say.

Silence on the other end.

"I wonder if Tino has said anything to you about me?"

"No." Theresa didn't seem shocked or even unduly curious about this question. Elise realized how hurtful this conversation was going to be. She was Tino's wife, calling Tino's mother to speak with her for the first time. It would be obvious, no matter how Elise delivered it, that Tino had denied she even lived. From the letters, it was obvious they had not been estranged, at least not on Theresa's side. If Elise had known Theresa was alive, how could there have been no contact between them at all, until now?

Theresa broke the awkward pause. "Are you and he dating?"

"Yes. Well. Actually, we're married." It couldn't be put off, Elise realized, and there was probably no strategy to make this less painful for Tino's mother.

"I see."

Two words. But such pain underneath. Elise knew all about the exchanges between Theresa and Tino. Or rather, her one-sided entreaties. She had delayed calling Theresa because she had wanted Tino to talk to her. To show Elise there was more to it than it appeared. But now, Elise realized she had also been putting it off because of this difficult moment.

"Mrs. Crocetti, I'm sorry. I made a mistake. I assumed Tino had no family left. Or else I would have called you before now."

"That's generous of you to say, dear, but..." Theresa's voice trailed off.

"Can I come see you?"

"Of course, dear. But it's a long way. I live in New Albany, Indiana."

"I know," Elise said before thinking whether she gave away too much. But this lady had endured enough dishonesty. Elise resolved to be truthful no matter what. Theresa's feelings could hardly become more bruised than they already were.

That night Elise packed a bag for her flight out the next day. Tino was still not home. She went downstairs to sit with her father. He had a caretaker now, and this gave Elise some peace of mind. Her father's condition had become too much for her alone.

"Elise," the caretaker said, "he asked for you, but I think he's asleep now."

"Thank you, Jolie. I'm just going to check on him." Her father was sitting in his chair, in front of the window, but was napping rather soundly. His pattern now was to sleep like this intermittently through the day. He would likely be awake again before going to bed for the night, but for now, he remained asleep when Elise sat next to him. Elise watched him, his head slightly bowed. There was just the barest movement about the shoulders as he breathed. He had been such a force, for so long, and now he was winding down, like a soft breeze following a tropical storm. He seemed childlike at the moment. Elise wondered whether, between naps, he had second thoughts about the oblivion he maintained would come next. He must surely know, now, that he would never return to health.

Elise returned to the kitchen. "Jolie, I need to leave tomorrow, just for one night. Can you make sure the agency has him covered?"

"I'll do it now," Jolie said, taking out her phone.

"Great. Listen, I need to step out for a bit, but I should be back before nine."

"When he wakes up, I'll tell him. I expect he'll be up when you get back."

Elise was pressing along the sidewalk, single-mindedly, so much so that she didn't notice at first when Mary fell into step beside her.

"Good timing," Elise said.

"I had to park on the next block."

They arrived at Joy's and were greeted at the door by David.

"Ladies," he said, nodding a welcome.

"David," Mary said, holding up her fist and giving him a warning glare. It was their standing joke that he was to be nice to Joy or face Mary's wrath.

They greeted Joy and were soon seated. David had disappeared to the bedroom and now returned with his computer and a jacket.

"We don't mean to run you off, David," Elise said.

"I know, but it's okay. You have a good talk. I'd like to get some air anyway. Hanigan's going to meet me at Soul Cycle."

Now that Elise was sitting with her two best friends, in this very intentionally-arranged meeting, she found herself tongue-tied. Where to begin?

"Tino?" Mary started for her.

Elise nodded her head, but ambiguously.

"Your father?" Joy said, taking Elise's hand.

Elise nodded her head again. And then, to her chagrin, tears began to fall, but she was in the embrace of her friends, figuratively and literally.

An hour and a half later, they heard David's keys jangling in the door, and he stepped inside.

"You haven't moved since I left you," he said. "Should I extend my walk a little?"

"No, David, you're very considerate. But I have to go anyway," Elise said. "How's Hanny?"

"He's on top of the world. He couldn't stay long. He had to get ready for another show."

"I'm glad he's doing well. I've always liked Hanny," Elise said.

"And he's seeing someone."

"Good for him," Elise said.

"I thought he just stayed up there and painted and kept to himself," Mary said. "Where did he meet the girl?"

"Church," Joy said.

"You dragged him to church?"

"We didn't have to drag him. He came on his own. And then he joined. He was baptized a few weeks ago."

"What would your dad say, Elise?" Mary said.

Elise just rolled her eyes. This old conversation. God or no God. It hadn't seemed to matter one way or another, until now, with her father in his condition. He had lived all his adult life adamant that God was no more real than a leprechaun. Now he was dying. Her father, that is, not God. God didn't exist, she'd been taught. Only, her father hated that expression, that God "doesn't exist." "It's like saying the God who exists does not exist," Potter had said. "Instead just say there is no God." Soon her father would not exist. Her husband was a ghost—in and out, with no accounting to Elise. Life would roll on, for Elise, but to what end?

Joy said, "You should both come with us Sunday. If you get nothing else from it, you'll see Hanigan there."

"Are the guys good-looking?" Mary asked.

"Well, yeah," David said, gesturing to himself.

Joy said, "Hanigan met his girlfriend there."

"That's right. How'd you know?" David asked Joy.

Mary said flatly, "Girl power, David. Don't question it."

"Elise, let's all three go," Joy said.

It had been some time since Joy had brought up the subject. Elise was actually drawn to the idea this time, in part because of the turmoil over her marriage. It had eroded her self-confidence. She felt a little lost at sea. On the other hand, it would feel disloyal to her father, in a way, and especially now with his illness. "Not right now. Sometime, maybe." It was the most openness to things spiritual Elise had ever expressed.

Because of her trip the next day, Elise was especially eager to have some time to visit with her father before he was put to bed for the night. But it was not to be. Jolie said he slept longer than usual after Elise left, so she thought he would be up later. But he'd only wakened for an hour or so, then had some soup and tried to read, but he didn't have the energy to wait up for Elise. He was already in bed when she returned home.

Disappointed, Elise saw Jolie to the door, peeked in on her father, and then ascended to hers and Tino's apartment above. It was quiet. She wondered where Tino might be at this moment. She wondered, for the hundredth time, how she would bring up the subject of his mother again, and why he disappeared for such stretches. What had she done wrong? What explanation would Tino give for declaring his mother dead? She realized she had been living with the tension of not wanting to think poorly of Tino despite the evidence. Was there some noble reason for his distancing himself from his mother? For his secrecy? Perhaps this was like the grand plot of a certain kind of novel, where the protagonist's virtue is doubted but then shines through. Perhaps he would be her Darcy after all, and she his Elizabeth.

Elise mounted the steps to the loggia, took her flannel coat from the hook, and put it on as she walked out into the air. The bay in the distance was illuminated all around the edge, as always, and the lights reflected across the water, as always. The air felt harsh against her face. She wrapped the flannel more tightly around her. She looked out on the lights of the bay and on the tired, rusting tankers anchored there. They were emblems of the workaday world, no longer romantic in her imagination. They were features of her existence in this spot, and if she lived somewhere else, there would be recurring features of that place, too, neither significant on their own.

Elise felt that her world had constricted around her. The sense of mystery had ebbed. She thought to revive that sense of mystery by remembering the surge of mighty waters at Tomales Point, and doing so caused her to remember the poem she had recited to herself when she was there with Mary and Joy, the day before Joy's wedding. She imagined the "tremulous cadence slow" of the waves in the bay, breaking up the reflections from the lights on the boats and at water's edge. The waves brought "the eternal sadness in," just like in the poem. She felt "the breath/of the night-wind, down the vast edges drear/And naked shingles of the world." Elise shivered.

In the poem, the sense of irretrievable loss was to be assuaged by lovers being true to one another. That solace would be lost to her now.

It no longer seemed that there was a great big world out there for her to find adventure in. Life was indeed an accident, and all the variables of time and space from the beginning of everything brought her to this one instant and this particular realization—that it was all pointless. Life was not without fleeting moments in which we might stand on a platform of human dignity and see far into the distance, but it was all ultimately pointless. Beauty, mystery, and purpose were just feelings.

Elise thought about a night when she stood here on this very spot, looking out at this very view of the bay, when fireworks were suddenly and unexpectedly sent up from the Giants' stadium to bring magic to the night sky. That seemed so long ago, but it had been less than a year. Elise looked at the sky, yearning for it to suddenly come alive again with color and vitality as it had on that other night. It remained dark. Elise shook her head, thinking how foolish it was to try to wish the display back into existence.

Chapter Nineteen

David was stunned. He'd sensed there was something afoot, but he hadn't anticipated this. He'd been a star. Now he was shown the door. It was late in the morning when he'd been called into his boss's office. There was stammering. Foot-shuffling. Fleeting eye contact. It apparently took the morning to muster the courage to officially push David out. David sat looking out the window, a view much like that at the end of his line of cubicles. Sitting there in his boss's office, he imagined he heard the traffic out on the street to match what he was seeing, but then realized it was only his imagination. It was actually utterly quiet in the office. He looked up at his boss's sheepish, questioning look. There was a question hanging in the air, evidently, but David hadn't heard it.

"I'll get my things. I don't have much personal stuff on my computer. I'll email it to myself."

"It's taken care of David. Don't worry about it."

David looked at the closed door of the office. "While I've been in here?"

David walked down the hall, accompanied by two men he'd never seen before. They passed his corner cubicle. It was stripped bare of any remnant of David's presence. He kept walking past, without breaking stride, to the elevators, and then to the lobby. He was handed a box by a woman he'd never met. She smiled at him. It was full of his desk incidentals. A nice red box from a container store, he noticed, not an old cardboard box. The walk-out cliché could be stretched only so far, he supposed. At this point, leaving the building with his box, David was beginning again to take in the sights and sounds around him. Self-awareness returned. He was on the street, feeling as though he'd just walked out of the weirdest dream of his life, but his red box was there to remind him that it was quite true. He stood there on Market for a minute, with his red box in his hands and his career in ruins, and for utterly mysterious reasons. Perhaps his boss had given a reason, but it hadn't registered in those first minutes of shock. David stopped on the street corner below the far end of offices occupied by his company, several floors above. He had a vague idea of going back to ask the "why" that he'd missed but realized that would be foolish. He'd have to admit to Joy that he didn't really know why, that somehow the explanation had flowed over him without penetrating. But in all likelihood, there was no explanation, or not one that would come through the meaningless corporate gibberish. There was no point going back, and his work friends, including his immediate team of developers, would have no more idea than he did. They might be getting their own boxes. He imagined a stream of bewildered developers stumbling out onto the sidewalk, blinking in the sudden sunlight, released into the San Francisco streets with incongruously colorful cubes, carefully handling personal items of the kind developers typically care not a whit about.

David crossed the street and began the climb up Mason, holding his box in front of him as if it were an ark containing treasure of great value. A few pictures. A plant he never watered. Some coffee cups. He imagined that it also contained an unanswered question. These things, out here where they didn't belong, and his office a smooth, gleaming, empty place, giving no evidence of his successes, including most especially, the government process project. At this thought, David tucked the box under one arm and slowed his pace. He'd been reading the articles. He'd gotten some attention for this, not all of it good, but mostly he felt he'd started a civic-minded project of shining a light into dark places. A good thing, it would seem, but what if it had touched a nerve more violently than he supposed? David had guessed at soft corruption of the crony, special-interest variety. Surely the corruption could not be so deep and so virulent that it could reach out into a progressive company like his and tap him on the shoulder to be removed. Could it?

Joy was home, getting ready for an afternoon and evening shift. She'd heard him come up and unlock the door. "You're home," she said brightly, but the light in her face faded as soon as she saw David's. David set the box on the counter. Joy looked at it, puzzled. David let its contents speak for him.

"I know you didn't just quit," Joy said softly.
"No."
"What happened?"

"I don't really know." David laughed, the absurdity of it all now registering. "I just don't know."

"But they let you go?"

"Yes."

"And they didn't say why?"

"No. Well, my boss said some things, but I think it was just corporate blah-blah-blah."

"But you're brilliant! You were doing great things! How could they ever let you get away, much less fire you?" Joy had gone from encouraging to indignant. Now she went back to encouraging. "This can't be a reflection of anything you did."

"Unless I stepped on some toes."

"I thought everyone got along so well over there. I'm sure of it. It seemed like a big family."

"There was a lot of hemming and hawing. I think it goes beyond the company."

"Political?" Joy asked in a hushed voice.

"No, forget it, I'm being stupid. I'm not that important. I'm being arrogant."

"There has to be more to it. They always tell you how great you are. They like you. I can tell when we go to their functions."

"But here I am with my box."

"We'll be all right. We can make it on my salary for a while."

"We were trying to save."

"You'll be back at it in no time. This might be the best thing that could happen to you, career-wise. You've said it's the Wild West, in software."

"It is, but that doesn't mean it's okay to just get dumped like this."

"It's going to be all right."

"You keep saying that."

"It's true. You just need to absorb this for a day or two, and then we can make plans. I wish I didn't have to work tonight." She suddenly brightened. "You can meet me for my dinner break!"

"You say it like this is a good development."

"It is. I should be free around five o'clock."

"Okay."

"Okay."

"Let me borrow your computer."

"Don't look for jobs today, David."

"This isn't good for our adoption plans."

"It won't affect them at all."

"It will because it's becoming a money issue. It's just not happening the old-school way. We're going to have to adopt from Russia or China or Central America. It's going to cost a fortune. Which we don't have. I'm sorry."

"David, David, don't be sorry. It's not your fault. Anyway, God still has His eye on you."

"I hear you."

"I have to go," Joy said softly.

"I'll see you at five."

David walked over to the couch under the front bay window and looked down the street. A hand went up—Joy smiling and waving. David waved back and watched her until she was out of sight. He slumped down on the couch then pulled out his phone. It occurred to him he might be getting messages soon if others on his team were let go, but there were no messages yet. He silenced the phone and sat back in the little square of diffuse light, plopping his feet on the worn coffee table. He just wanted to sit there and be.

At five o'clock, David was at the emergency room entrance to the hospital. Joy had texted him that she was running a few minutes late. It was just as well. He had nowhere else to go anyway.

"Did you behave?" Joy said when she marched out to greet him.

"What do you mean?"

"Did you stay off the computer? The phone?"

"Mostly. I don't know any more than I did at noon."

"Good. What have you been doing?"

"Walked. Covered a lot of miles."

"I got through to Elise this afternoon."

"How's it going in the heartland?"

"She couldn't talk long. She was pretty upset. She said Tino's mother is the sweetest person."

"Well, that's not a thing to be upset about."

"But it doesn't make things any easier to understand."

"I suppose not."

"She also said she knew there was someone else."

David grimaced. "She suspected that."

"She said someone came to the house this morning. A young man. Elise was just leaving to go to the airport. He left a message that Tino should call Cassie."

"Do we know who Cassie is?"

"Elise tried to find out, but she said the guy clammed up when he saw there was more to the story, and anyway, she had to get going to the airport."

"Maybe it's nothing."

"Not on top of everything else. And then Elise landed in Louisville, and Mrs. Crocetti picked her up. They drove all around, and they talked."

"Where are we going?"

"Turner's? Is that okay? It's where I go with my shiftmates sometimes. Not too expensive."

"Sure. So Tino's not been at home, I take it."

"No, and her father is just barely hanging on, apparently."

"She's got a lot on her right now."

"Booth?"

"Yeah. Sure we have time for this?"

"They're fast. That's why we come here."

"Kind of an old-fashioned diner. I like it."

"It seems strange to have you here with me. Good strange."

"We should tighten up financially until we see how things are going to go."

"David, you could start your own company."

"I... First of all, there's no way. And second of all, I thought I wasn't supposed to think about this for the rest of the day."

"I don't want to bring you down with Elise's troubles."

"Actually, it was having the opposite effect. I was starting to feel like I don't have it so bad, that I was just feeling sorry for myself. Is there anything we can do for her? I could try to go see Tino. Find out what's going on."

"You could visit her dad tomorrow. Elise doesn't get back until late tomorrow. I switch back to days."

David shrugged. "I could, I guess. But I don't really know the guy."

"I'm not sure it matters much at this stage. He would probably recognize you as Elise's friend, and you can just say she's out for the day, and so you came to check on him. You wouldn't be expected to stay long."

"Sure, I'll do that."

"I'll text Elise to text the caretaker."

The next morning, just after nine, David showed up to have the short conversation Joy had coached him on. He found Brinkley awake, but not very responsive. David guessed it was because he didn't really know Brinkley, and there was no reason for Brinkley in his condition to put himself out for David. He just sat there looking out the window, over the top of the house across the street, as best David could tell, perhaps to the faded hills across the bay to the north; perhaps to eternity itself. David thought of himself as a poor and temporary stand-in for Elise. He wondered what Elise would do, and he found himself just sitting next to Brinkley, staring out over the rooftop like he did.

"I kept worrying," Brinkley said haltingly.

David leaned in.

"About my work."

"Mm."

"If it mattered."

"I'm sure it has, Dr. Brinkley. Neuroscience. Important."

The old man turned to David with a slight smile. With understanding eyes. His voice, though, was so soft as to be nearly inaudible. David thought he heard him say, "Potter," inviting David to address him familiarly.

"Potter," David repeated.

Brinkley shook his head. "Peter," he breathed.

Chapter Twenty

It was foreign to Tino's nature to live in the thick of conflict. He could live at its margins, and perhaps profit from it, but his role would always be the voice of reason and peace. He was poorly equipped to put on the armor and participate himself. And so now he floated in limbo. He checked his phone often, expecting a text from Elise that would not come, but not sending one himself. West Marin sometimes had spotty cell coverage, so this little routine caused him to stare at his phone screen all the more. He had texted Elise but received no answer, and that had been days before. With each passing day, Tino felt more tension, resulting not just from her lack of communication, but because it would make his re-entry all the more difficult. How to explain his absence? There was no good alternative. He would have to cite the increasing estrangement between them and fault on his own part in allowing this long passage of time with no communication. Admitting any fault would be more tortuous than the mounting tension, so Tino put it to the back of his mind.

Cassie was recovering, staying at first at their apartment in Point Reyes Station with daily visits from her mother. Tino visited daily, too, but wouldn't stay overnight. He let Cassie believe his business in the city kept him busy there as always. In fact, she seemed grateful he could be there as much as he was. The baby was only a few days old, however, when Cassie began staying overnight with her parents in Olema, shuttling back and forth to their shared house for a few hours during the day. Tino knew this pattern would not keep up indefinitely, and he assuredly did not want to visit Cassie at her parents'. Another point of tension, adding to Tino's conviction of the unfairness of it all.

Tino wasn't staying in the city, as he let Cassie believe. Instead, he conducted his business from another vacation rental in Inverness, just on the other side of Tomales Bay from Point Reyes Station. The house was modest but equipped with local art and books and touches that made it unique. The owner had put a lot of love into this little parcel of land, especially the garden behind it. The spot would be serenity itself, were it not for the turmoil Tino felt inwardly. Then, on his third day there, he realized someone was living in what he had taken to be an unused outbuilding on the parcel, at the end of a little path through the lush vegetation. Perhaps the owner herself. Tino relied on the cell coverage on the back porch until he realized the neighbor was so close and could see him there. He changed his pattern to alternate between his computer, inside, and walking out to a lookout fifty yards or so away. It was across the yard and down a long and worn boardwalk, ending at an open place in the high grass, and a bench for taking in the view, and a berm to hold back the tide, and beyond that, a wide expanse of Savannah-like grass, with streamlets here and there going in and out over the mile-wide concavity formed by the San Andreas fault. Here the boggy wetlands around Lagunitas Creek gave way gradually to marsh grass and then more gradually still to the open water of the bay. A picturesque spot between chaparral foothills to the east and the conifered slope above Inverness, to the west.

Tino's mood was increasingly ill-suited to the surroundings, however. His life was upended, he felt, as surely as if a slip in the fault had resulted in the feared earthquake. His serene surroundings did not compensate for the daily deluge of news reports about a conspiracy among hotels and vacation rental websites, the remaining question being whether the city was a victim, or complicit itself. Numerous press calls to the FBI were not returned, but that might be damning in itself. The federal prosecutor's office situated in San Francisco had issued press releases, however—more than one—confirming an active investigation. Tino's communications with Gerald had become increasingly cryptic, to the point of being incomprehensible, and then had ceased altogether. If the pressure of the investigation opened the mouths of some inside the city, it could get back to him. Same with the furtive representatives of the hotels. It seemed such a real possibility that Tino was careful about using his cell phone. His immediate surroundings were calming. The unknown about what might be happening among his former contacts was unnerving. He was experiencing a tension hitherto unknown.

Tino's mind was thus agitated when he set out for the house in Point Reyes Station on Saturday morning. He pulled onto Sir Francis Drake Boulevard, rounding the south end of the bay. He turned north onto Highway 1 and crossed the creek, slowing as he approached the main street of Point Reyes Station. People walked in the street there with no regard for auto traffic, it being the prevailing ethic that nonmotorized traffic had priority. Tino was in no hurry despite his frame of mind, however, and crept by the farmer's market which accounted for much of the foot traffic. He turned onto Mesa and in short order was at his and Cassie's house, turning onto the crunching pea gravel. Tino had, months before, put Cassie in a new truck, and the one she had used was relinquished back to her family. Neither truck was present now, however. Tino felt momentary irritation, as he had texted Cassie not half an hour before. She had most likely been texting from her parents' house, intending to show up at her house with Tino later in the day, not realizing he was so close. Not that it was a secret where she went and when. Tino realized that, from her perspective, going to the vacation house was an accommodation to Tino and not something he should be upset with. And there was no rush. No appointment going begging. No intolerable inefficiency in his work. It was not costing him money. All of that was suspended. There was a brooding omnipresence that weighed on Tino as he sat alone at the kitchen table, looking out over the neighbor's chicken yard.

It was too quiet. Tino decided to walk into Point Reyes Station. He would see Cassie if she came by while he was walking into town. They could come back to the house together, or, perhaps better, have coffee in town. Tino imagined himself convincing her that the infant would be fine outside in the mild weather. He crunched across the gravel of the drive, pointing and clicking his key fob at his car to confirm it was locked. He tried to reimagine his first response to the quiet of this place that had first drawn him to it. Tino made his way out onto Mesa Road, trying to recall the feeling he had walking this way before, with Cassie, after that first night here. He was passed by a pickup truck, rolling leisurely down the hill toward the bend in the road toward Point Reyes Station. Its brake lights flashed on, and it came to a stop in the middle of the quiet road, next to the horse pen. Tino smiled, despite the tension he'd been feeling. It was the same truck he'd seen with Cassie, months before, and just as on that occasion, the driver stepped out with apples in hand. He wore the same gray hat as on that previous occasion, and as Tino watched, he remembered Hanigan's painting. The same man. Tino continued to approach as the man fed the apples to the horse. The man leisurely strolled back to his vehicle as Tino walked up. Tino felt a kinship to the man, and to the proceedings—a fondness for what seemed a simpler time, only months before.

"You do this every day?" Tino asked as he approached.

"Nearly," the man responded. "We're pals," he said, gesturing with his thumb toward the animal.

Tino felt that there was a shared sense of peace on this quiet rural land where the California chaparral gave way to the little town and the marshes and then creek of the fault zone. For once, Tino desired this peace more than ambition, and more than power, and more than admiration.

"Here, let me show you something," the man said as he rounded the rear of his vehicle and leaned into the open driver's side door. They were sojourners, Tino felt, accidentally thrown together here in this little island of peace. Tino stood in the quiet street as the man reached into his truck from the driver's side. The man then looked back with a half-smile that flickered on the edge of a sneer. It was disconcerting. Out of place. The man suddenly snapped fully around, surging toward Tino. A flash of metal. The man's face next to Tino's. A fierce grimace. The taste of brine. As if from far away, Tino heard the door slam, and then he felt the motion of the truck.

Chapter Twenty-One

Elise had a burning desire to locate the young man who had visited and learn what she could about his connection to Tino. And Cassie. That would mean driving an hour each way at least, however, so she dithered, wondering whether to stay or go. Her father might well be near the end of his life. Elise was up early, knowing her father would make no distinction between Saturday and any other day, now. She sat with him in the early morning light while the caretaker got his breakfast. He had patted Elise's hand with a half-smile and picked up the newspaper. Elise knew he would read the paper for a few minutes, then take a break, and repeat until he tired. He seemed to be as well as he had been in the last week. Elise gently took her leave.

She was quickly on the road to Olema, her nerves alternating between steely stoicism and raw anxiety. Her marriage was likely in shambles. This trip would only confirm it. The young man had come looking for Tino but found Elise. Cassie, he said, was at the house in Olema, adding to his message for Tino's benefit "before you get to Vedanta." The young man said this before an onset of diffidence in the face of the odd circumstance of meeting not Tino, but a hurried Elise, who was quite curious, though distracted at that moment with getting to her flight on time. The young man, who gave only the name Billy, hurried off, and Elise had hung back, telling the driver to wait until she saw Billy get into an older blue pickup with a rusted topper.

Now Elise set out for Olema, with no better direction than what she remembered of Billy's fleeting visit two days before. Her desire to be at home with her father meant she didn't have time to kill wandering around west Marin County, looking for something but not really even knowing what it was. Still, she was reasonably confident of finding Cassie and finding out Cassie's connection to Tino. Olema was little more than a small crossroads, as Elise knew from her trip with the Axis earlier in the year, the day before Joy's wedding. Plus, she found online that "Vedanta" was some sort of mystic religious retreat right on Highway 1, before the crossroads. By that, the location was pretty well narrowed down already. "Before Vedanta" would logically mean south of the crossroads, on Highway 1.

On the other hand, Elise knew she might waste this entire morning riding around with no clue which rural cabin or farmhouse might be the right one, and at a time when she had a strong pull to get back to her father in his very weak condition. On the other, other hand, Elise sensed that a couple of inquiries in a small place like Olema would get her to this Cassie, or to the young man, Billy. So why not try? Elise was too eaten up with worrisome curiosity not to try.

Elise was over the Golden Gate Bridge and very soon up to Mill Valley, before Sausalito, even though the traffic was moderately heavy with sightseers and bikers and hikers and kayakers getting out of the city for the weekend. She exited at Highway 1 and hit the curves a little too fast, becoming momentarily seasick, until the road straightened and took her along breath-abating precipices far above the endless Pacific. Here Elise slowed, awed at the grandeur, even in her anxious condition. Eventually, she came down to the level of water, and then the road departed out of sight of the water altogether and began winding back and forth along intersecting creek beds in the bottoms of the San Andreas fault zone. She slowed as she sensed she was approaching the crossroads at the heart of Olema, and then saw a modest sign that read "Vedanta Retreat." She turned around and headed south, on this pass much more slowly. Elise was soon rewarded. There in a dusty turnaround, next to a modest house, was Billy's truck.

Elise paused in the middle of Highway 1, but she couldn't just sit there. She pulled in and parked next to the truck. She alighted from her vehicle and stood next to her rear bumper as if she had nowhere to go and all the time in the world to go there. From where she stood, Elise looked out around the grounds. At the rear of the little house, visible now from where Elise parked, was another, newer truck. Beyond that was a large, well-maintained, and inviting garden. To the back of that was another outbuilding, which appeared to be not a leftover appendage from antique farm life, but a well-used building with a concrete apron at the front and a large chimney at the back. While she studied this, Elise heard scuffling at the front door and saw Billy emerge. He just stood there a moment, and then said, "Hi."

"Hi."

Billy went inside again, and all was quiet. A trio of helmeted bicyclers swooshed by on Highway 1. Elise heard movement at the back of the house and saw a young woman approach the newer truck parked there. She was about Elise's age. Attractive, with dark hair. She had a baby carrier—the kind that snaps into a car seat or stroller.

"Hi! Let me just get the baby," she called out.

The girl leaned into the doorway of the truck and fastened the carrier inside. Then she reached into the carrier and gently removed the infant.

Elise stepped forward.

When the girl turned again, she was holding the baby so as to show off the child to her visitor. She had a welcoming smile. "Alessandro," she said. "Tino wanted a strong name."

For Elise, the whole setting was wrong. The sky was not dark. There was no storm. She was not swooning, but standing in the soft sunshine listening to her heart thud against her ribcage. As unwelcome as the revelation of this girlfriend was, it was not a shock. Elise had been living of late with mistrust for Tino. But in a few words this girl, this stranger, this tormentor, had confirmed the worst—a lover, a continuing relationship, *a child.*

"He's beautiful," Elise heard herself say. "You're Cassie?"

Cassie smiled. "I knew Tino had secrets," she said, smiling even bigger. "But I couldn't believe it when Billy told me he met Tino's sister. I couldn't wait to meet you."

Elise looked up. There was Billy again, this time at the back door. She could see him through the screen, looking back at her. He stepped back and then softly closed the door. Elise felt a lurch in her stomach. Her hands felt like ice, and her face felt oddly numb. The child was only weeks old. This person in front of her had been pregnant on the day Elise married Tino.

"Are you okay?" the person asked. "Do you need to sit down?"

"No," Elise managed. She tried to smile. She would not be defeated by this adversary. This smiling adversary. Elise mustered calm, willing herself to project the classical serenity that others sometimes saw in her. Cassie seemed deferential. Wanting to please her as a kind of social superior, as Elise sometimes experienced? Or more likely, to ingratiate herself to Tino's family? Elise had suspected even before now that whatever she imagined she had with Tino, it had been her imagination only. Now she saw her own delusion. "I'll be fine," she said. "I can't stay, though. I have a commitment."

In response to Cassie's puzzled look, Elise said, "I'm sorry, I thought I could make a quick trip here to meet you before a very important commitment I have this morning, but I got lost coming here. I'll be late if I don't go now. I hope you understand." As Elise delivered this lie, she became more confident in it. She felt her strength returning. She said nice things about Alessandro, who was truly a beautiful little boy.

This girl, Cassie, was no less deluded than she, but was so far happy in her delusion. Cassie alternately looked adoringly at Alessandro, and at Elise, with an expression of sunny innocence. Elise decided that no benefit would come of asserting herself with Cassie, of claiming Tino's love as if Cassie had somehow stolen it from her. This was Tino's doing, not Cassie's. And certainly not little Alessandro's.

"I'm sorry I have to go back to the city," Elise said. "I just wanted to meet you." Elise now knew what she had come to learn. She could not muster the desire to care, one way or the other, that Cassie misunderstood her relationship to Tino.

"You just came," Cassie said. Elise could see she was genuinely sorry that their meeting was to be so brief. "Anyway, I'm going over to see Tino."

"Of course," Elise said, in hopes Cassie would add information.

"He's only a few minutes away."

"I'm responsible for someone, and I'm overdue. I'm sorry."

Cassie smiled back at Elise, hugging the baby to her breast, incurious, or else not knowing what to say next, or else just considerate of Elise's privacy, or else, Elise imagined, on some deep level not wanting to know more.

"I'm glad to meet you, Cassie," Elise said, practicing it in her mind as she said it, so as not to sound curt, or ironic.

"Me too. I mean, I hope to see you soon, Elise. I'll tell Tino we met."

Elise nodded, managing a smile, and then turned to her car.

Chapter Twenty-Two

Professor Potter Brinkley, emeritus, died quietly in his sleep. At the moment of his passing, Elise was walking the streets of San Francisco, wanting to breathe the fog into her lungs, wanting to snuff out the future in her wanderings, desiring the deepening darkness. She pressed on through the night, following the paths of least light, until she was thoroughly lost in the city in which she had grown up. She stopped at a little bench that would have seemed out of place, except that it was next to a gated driveway, far uphill on what had appeared to be another ill-lit street but was actually a cul-de-sac with only a few driveways that connected to it. The bench was chained to an iron loop set into the cobbled stone of the walkway.

Elise sat and wondered at her circumstance. Had she been older, she might have wondered at how quickly all the best for her had changed. She was in her youth, however, so her changes in circumstance seemed natural, if naturally horrific. She had been the golden child, and she had conducted herself beyond reproach, and she had done only what is natural for people, pairing with Tino as she had. They had been so much more together, even, than she alone. So what had gone wrong? What did she do to deserve this? She now considered her life from a different perspective altogether. There was such a thing as pride, arrogance, a self-sufficient mastery of all, of haughtiness. Was this the real Elise, after all? Perhaps it's not enough to walk about with a knowledge of one's deficiencies and consider duty to the gods completed. Could it be that the transvestites and wanderers and drug-addled hangers-on of the Tenderloin knew something that Elise didn't? They lived life on the margin, whether a margin created by themselves or not. That margin, that periphery, might only be the shrunken distance between oneself and the dangerous razor-thin blade of reality. The thin and disappearing line between authentic man and those borrowed, ennobling characteristics of man fallen. Wings of angels, and of sinister fallen ones, hurried against the fog, pushing it about, softer than soft.

"Elise?"

Elise looked up, startled. A tall young man was peering at her, worriedly, from a few yards away. She would take it as menacing, except that two young women and another young man sauntered up behind him. In a split-second, she sized up the women, concluding that, despite the hour, they were not harpies attached temporarily to the men. So she was not likely in danger.

"You're—"

"Sorry, I don't mean to startle you. It's Tom. Widener. Tino's suitemate. We met—"

"Yes, how are you, Tom? It's the light. I didn't recognize you at first."

"Hi," chirped a young woman who stepped up beside Widener. "How're'yu?"

"Tom is my husband's officemate," Elise said in an attempt to sweep aside any obligation to deal further with the slurring young woman.

"Are you—" Tom made an ambivalent gesture, giving Elise an opportunity to explain herself, here in this out-of-the-way spot in the near-darkness.

"Lost, actually."

Tom grunted a laugh. "I can get you on the right track, I expect."

Before he could make good on this, the girl he was with set up an exaggerated remonstrance, but in actions, not words. Tom stepped toward her. She nodded toward Elise in an ambiguously aggressive way, and then Tom spirited her to a metal door in the cul-de-sac and said his good-byes to her while Elise waited. The other couple wandered along behind them, a few yards from Elise's bench.

Presently, Tom emerged from the darkness next to the girl's gate, with the other young man right behind. Evidently, Tom's date and the other's were roommates.

"Could you just get me oriented? I'm so embarrassed. This is my city," Elise said.

"Happens to the best of us," Tom said generously.

"I haven't been drinking. I've just been distracted."

"Understand." At the bottom of the street that led to the cul-de-sac, Tom said good-bye to his friend, and then he and Elise were alone.

"You don't have to walk me all the way, Tom."

"I'm going in the general direction anyway."

Elise debated within herself whether to ask the question she wanted to ask. But it was late, in more ways than one, and she felt her usual reserve slipping from her. "Have you seen Tino lately?"

"No," Tom said, drawing out the syllable a little. "I was actually about to ask you the same thing. Not my business, but I haven't seen him in a couple of weeks. At least. 'Course he's in and out all the time anyway."

"He's been busy with work. Crazy busy. And we never really kept up with... I mean our pattern—"

"Doesn't matter," Tom interjected. "Everybody does things their own way. You can be married and not joined at the hip."

Elise wanted to say something to Tom by way of thanking him for his generosity of spirit, for not taking it upon himself to judge what was right or appropriate for Elise and Tino. Among the people she had associated with all her life, Elise realized, there was a strong understood injunction against judging others, in principle. But it was a principle only. There was judgment among her set just like any other. The only variation was in the set of principles one was judged against.

"That's well said, Tom. And you're right. But of course, things aren't all as they should be, with us. I'm not in the mood to pretend it's all fine."

"You're not worried about his safety."

"Oh, no."

"I see."

There was a long pause in conversation as they cruised along the wee-hours sidewalk, both eager to chew up the distance and call it a night.

"I can ask around," Tom volunteered.

"Tom, don't." She said it with an air of finality as she slowed at the door to her father's house.

"I understand. I'm sorry, Elise. But do let me know if you need anything."

"You've been a knight in shining armor tonight, Tom." Elise held out her hand, and Tom squeezed it gently.

"Good night," he said and wheeled off in the direction they'd just come.

Elise turned to open the door but couldn't quite bring herself to do it. Her father would be sleeping. There was no point going in to see him now. She knew she would not sleep now, herself. The loggia in the pre-dawn hours had a certain appeal, but it was here, atop hers and Tino's apartment. She would not go in.

Elise and her father used a modified minivan to accommodate the wheelchair. It was in the garage, and Elise had the key.

Elise felt unmoored. She wanted to drift, to go where the tide might take her. She would indulge this hour of grief for a lost love, and betrayal, and then return for her father. She drove, in the night, and found herself drawn again to west Marin. It seemed automatic. Perhaps because she'd been there just hours before, the last place she'd driven to. Or perhaps because she wanted peace and not the distractions of the city. Or perhaps because it represented to her the source of her inner turmoil, straddling the rift of the fault line. Tino was there, somewhere, as was this other life she had been excluded from. She hated Tino and loved him at the same time. She would never return to him—that living thing between them was thoroughly torn asunder. But she felt as though a living part of her, too, had been violently torn away and continued to live here. Perhaps it might in some way be wrested back.

The Pacific was at first invisible to her except as a suggestive shimmer off to her left and far, far down. As she traveled, it brightened by nearly imperceptible degrees. With each curve, Elise thought about speeding up rather than slowing down, so as to sail out over the dark living air to the darker inky blackness down below. But she kept on, still automatically, descending with the road until eventually the road straightened and came nearly even with the surface of the lagoon next to the sea. Then she left the sight of the water, and the curves resumed, only now they were at the floor of the San Andreas fault zone. Elise took it slow. It was darker here, with the high steep ridges both to the east and west of the roadway. She longed for break of day.

In the near-darkness, Elise was insensible to the place along the road where Cassie lived, where Elise had visited less than twenty-four hours before. Then she saw the sign for Vedanta and knew she was past it. She kept going, however. That was not her destination. She felt some sense of release, continuing past Vedanta, only slowing at the oversized stop sign at the Olema crossroads. She slowed, thinking for the first time since departing San Francisco in the wee hours about where she was ultimately headed. Indecisive, she continued straight on Highway 1, headed north. She came to another stop sign. She could turn left and go out toward Point Reyes, or to the northernmost tip of the peninsula, where she had hiked with Mary and Joy on a day that seemed so distant. Or she could go straight, into the little town of Point Reyes Station, and from there perhaps further north along Tomales Bay.

There was now a faint glow in the eastern sky. Elise crossed Lagunitas Creek on the little bridge. As she rolled into Point Reyes Station, there was just enough change in light to give an eerie pre-dawn glow to the outline of the buildings on the main street. It was quiet. Was this to be her destination? Elise slowed almost to a stop in the middle of the street, hesitating. She thought of her father. Even if she were to turn around now, she would still be home long before he even arose. Elise accelerated, steering further north on Highway 1.

Point Reyes Station was a very small town, so Elise was quickly through the town and following the road again north. She was looking left, toward a deeply-shadowed savannah of grasses in the fault zone, and knew this must be the southern end of the bay. Soon she was looking in the same direction at open water, Tomales Bay proper. The road she was on rose and fell on the edge of the chaparral, sometimes at an elevation fifty or sixty feet above the bay and other times almost even with it. As the grasses of the bay gave way to open water, Elise began to see little houses along the roadside to her left, right at the water's edge, some hugging the shoreline so close that they extended over the water on pylons. At first, there was one here and there, but as she went further along Highway 1, she saw more and more. Little vacation houses.

West of Elise's highway, and across the bay, was the narrow upper thrust of the Point Reyes peninsula. But from Elise's perspective, it was a high foothill ridge dropping down to the edge of the bay. A substantial land mass. Nothing to indicate that the mighty Pacific lay just beyond. Elise pulled over to the left, on a wide gravel apron to the main road. There was a little bayside house perched on the shoulder of the road, a few yards from it. The house seemed pearly luminescent against the dark water beyond. The darker Point Reyes peninsula was a backdrop to that, illuminated diffidently by the morning sun still below the eastern horizon. Elise stepped out of the van and crunched gravel underfoot until she stepped onto a narrow grass sward at the top of an embankment. She looked out over the bay.

There is a magical time of day. It is not describable in terms of light registers, nor of tone or color value or luminescence. The time-between-times of sunset, especially at the Pacific coast, can be awesome. Garish, even. But not magical. Early morning time is when all is made new. Before Elise, the water was calm but an early morning calm, rivulets scurrying, heralding the coming day. Brushes of soft pink glowed overhead, remnants of the night's clouds catching the tentative light to the east.

But this magical sense was turned upside down for Elise. It seemed to make the pain more intense, not easier. She had longed for break of day, and now that it was here, she longed for return of the night. She grieved. She was chagrined that the physical world did not cooperate with her downward emotional spiral. The sky overhead was considerably lightened from its earlier velvet blue. Shreds of cloud in the east sky were particularly defiant to her mood, reflecting light in pastel pinks and now a suggestion of orange, as if to say that Elise must suffer alone, and the sky would not cooperate. To the west, the clouds bannered the early day sky. As yet merely suggestive, they heralded a lightness of day, and lightness of heart to come. An unbearable lightness.

Elise would have none of this. She walked up to the little bayside cottage. There was a small barque tied to the corner pylon. A ramp ascended from water's edge to the pylon and then switched back to the spot from which one might step onto the back deck to the house. Elise walked up onto the ramp. She looked over her shoulder at the back of the little house. Darkness inside it. There was no one about — on the road, on the roadside pullout, on the chaparral hills behind her, or on the shingle all along the distance to the next habitation, a hundred yards or more south. She thought of that feeling, slipping out of San Francisco, wanting to float with the tide.

With no further thought, Elise strode forward and untied the little boat. There were oars inside. They had tholepins on which they could pivot, and embedded in the gunwales, rowlocks with holes to fit the pins. She positioned the oars and rowed a few strokes, feeling the little boat respond smoothly, slipping easily and quickly into the bay. A thin, fine boat, yet with relatively high freeboard. The little house receded in front of her. She rowed several brisk pulls, and then slowed, and then rowed progressively slower. She was not interested in exercise or the air of the bay or the view. She was seated on a low middle thwart with the open bay behind her. She didn't turn around to see where she was headed, but when she thought she might have achieved the middle of the bay, she turned the oars in the rowlocks until the blades were settled inside the gunwales, and then slipped backward off the thwart, lying on her back in the bottom of the boat.

Elise folded her arm across her eyes. She felt that if she could cry, she would return the boat and cry her way home. But she couldn't cry. Tears stored up inside behind an impenetrable dam. Unmoved inwardly, she declined to move outwardly and returned her arm to her side. Elise eyed the oars resting along the gunwales. With just a flex of her thigh, her left foot touched the underside of the oar on her left. She bounced it lightly. The pin slipped easily from the rowlock. She lifted it higher. Then, impulsively, she flicked the oar over the edge with her foot. The paddle hit the water. The handle clanked the gunwale above her head then bounced away. She did the same with the right oar.

Elise looked up. She had intuited that this sensation would follow, once she was lying well below the level of the gunwales. The world had disappeared. The wide sky was before her, but not the bay or even the hills forming the sides of the Rift zone. Elise floated in this way, occasionally looking languidly about, experiencing a sense of movement from the boat, but with no visual points of reference. She lay still that way for a long time, several times closing her eyes for a few moments and then opening them to experience again the disappearance of the world. The world could just stay out of her vision, in this way, and she would float, not seeing or caring, just breathing in and out, in the bottom of the boat.

Chapter Twenty-Three

"Joy? What's going on?"

"Dr. Brinkley died."

"Okay." David sat on the edge of the bed, blinking at Joy and at the morning light. "We kind of knew this was coming, right?"

"Elise isn't home."

"What do you mean?"

"Mary called me. They called her. Because they couldn't find Elise."

"Who's 'they'?"

"The caretakers Elise hired. Why are you just sitting there? Get dressed."

"To do what?"

Joy gave David a rare warning look and then remembered herself. David was not the enemy. "David," she said more softly. "I'm worried about my friend."

"Okay, I'll be ready in a minute," David said as he shuffled toward the bathroom. "I guess church is out."

Joy was waiting impatiently by the door when David emerged. He grabbed his keys. Locking the door to their little apartment, he asked, "Why would Elise disappear now?"

"Well, you know about her and Tino."

"Yeah?"

"She texted me late yesterday. There's a girlfriend, all right."

"I hate that for Elise," David said.

"And a baby."

David mulled this for a moment. A baby. What he and Joy so desperately wanted. And here was an extra. But what a dumb thought. Maybe for Tino, and certainly for Elise, but not for the child's mother. "Probably makes it all the more painful for Elise," David said. On the street, he said, "Take the car, or walk straight there?"

"Oh, I don't know," Joy said, clenching her fists in frustration that they weren't already there.

"Car. About as fast, and if we need to go somewhere from there, we'll have it."

"Okay."

Getting the car entailed a walk to the garage on the other side of the block. "This means this was going on the whole time, even before they were married."

"What I was thinking," David said.

"I keep picturing them exchanging vows, and this is going on at the same time."

"Plus his mother."

"And his supposedly dead mother, too!"

"But wait," David said. "This girlfriend could be a prior relationship, and maybe Tino is just doing the right thing by the child. It could've been over with the girlfriend before he and Elise got married. Maybe his only sin was not being up front about it with Elise."

"No. I wish that were true, but it's definitely not, according to Elise."

"Did you text her back?"

"David, of course."

"Hey, don't blame me. Just being thorough. We don't want to overlook something obvious."

"I got hers yesterday afternoon, and I've sent her a dozen back. And tried to call."

"So I guess the theory is that she's upset and didn't come home, and so she doesn't know about her dad."

"In her text, she said she was going for a walk. I'm worried that something might have happened to her."

"We could call the police."

"I did."

They were at a stoplight. David turned to her. "And?"

"Apparently, it doesn't qualify as a missing person yet."

"Mm. I guess to them it's just an adult woman who didn't come home last night."

At Dr. Brinkley's house, Joy and David found the situation no more illuminating than what Joy had learned in her first phone call with Mary. It turned out that a funeral home had already been designated. It was part of a checklist for Potter Brinkley's hospice care. The practical nurse was overly calm, by Joy's estimation, but of course, for her, it was a job.

"I guess you've seen this before," Joy said.

"A person dying?" the woman asked. She was a beautiful and gentle thirty-something Filipina. Seeing that Joy didn't answer, she just said, "Yes, of course. But I liked Mr. Peter. He was a good man."

"Yes."

"We all die," the caretaker said, but she said it in a way that was neither flippant nor mournful nor maudlin. She spoke truth.

"You've not spoken with Elise?"

"The daughter. No, she's not here. But you're her friend, yes?"

"Yes. I called her, but I get no answer. Not like her."

The petite Filipina stepped forward to take Joy's hand and looked up at her with dark almond eyes. "There's no urgency. No emergency. Just peace. You find the daughter, you bring her. And be kind, of course, when you find her. But honey, there's no emergency." The woman looked at Joy with kind, understanding eyes. Both sets of hands were clasped together. On impulse, Joy brought the clasp up and kissed the back of the woman's hand. Then she felt sheepish. The Filipino woman erased this feeling immediately by raising their clasped hands again and pressing her cheek against Joy's hand. Briefly, but exactly long enough.

Mary arrived. Joy and Mary and David quickly found there was nothing for them to do. The body was rolled out on a gurney to a hearse, and the Filipino lady said her good-byes. They were left in the very quiet house. Together, they walked up to Tino's and Elise's apartment on the next floor, and then up to the loggia, scanning the early morning city horizon, and then went down to the garage. It was just a house. Empty. Like the mortal shell Brinkley had left behind.

"We have to find Elise," Joy said.

"We have to have a drink," Mary said.

David saw that Joy was pulling up a map on her phone, so he motioned Mary to come with him to the kitchen. David didn't drink. It had always seemed contrary to his religious principles, though he couldn't really say why. He thought that for someone who did drink, however, maybe now was a good time, though it was early in the day, and a Sunday besides. Odd that he felt this way. In an earlier day, he wouldn't have. They found a half-bottle of white wine on the door shelf of the refrigerator, and he made a show of pouring Mary some in a juice glass. She was remarkably grateful.

David returned to the main room, but Joy had disappeared. He returned to the little hallway next to the kitchen and ascended again the steps to Tino's and Elise's apartment. "Okay, where next?" he asked with bravado when he saw Joy. He said it with a certain "I'm all in" timbre. He immediately regretted it when he saw her face. She was at a loss.

"Where is Elise?" she asked David pleadingly.

David knew better than to answer. He had no idea. He knew Joy knew he had no idea. "Where we are seems like the best place to be," he said softly. "You've got your phone. We're in her place."

Joy looked at him with eyes wide.

"I feel like I'm asking a volcano not to explode," David said.

Joy smiled. She laughed. Then she cried. David tried to hold her, but after a few seconds, she squirmed free. "I'm going to see what Mary knows," Joy said.

A few minutes later, David descended the stairs and found both Joy and Mary, weepy and repeatedly hugging. Both their phones were out on the counter, charging.

"Poor David," Mary said, wiping her eyes. "He has no idea what's going on."

"Well, maybe we can take stock," David said, looking at the time on his own phone. It was almost eight in the morning. "Elise isn't here. We don't know her usual movements. Or I should say 'I don't.' If you do, say so. Where might she be?"

"Out with the seals. The ocean. The rocks," Mary said.

"What?" Joy said, drawing out the word.

"I'm just blabbering," Mary said, waving her hands around.

"Does she usually text you right back?" David asked.

"No. She's not a big texter. She doesn't even carry her phone half the time."

"Try her again."

Joy tried a text. There was a very soft ping on the other side of the room. All three turned to look.

"Oh, no," Joy said, hopping down from her stool and crossing the room. She reached for the phone, which was plugged in and resting on a lamp table.

"If I were Elise..." Joy said.

Mary said, "Try 'Tino.'"

"Of course." Joy typed the password. "Right on the first try," Joy said excitedly. "There are all my texts."

"You're quite the stalker, Joy," Mary said, looking over her shoulder.

"I see..." Joy began. "My number. My number. Mine. Mine."

"Mine," Mary added. "Mine again."

"This one comes up three times," Joy said.

"Try it."

David and Mary looked on as Joy tried the number. They heard it ring, and then stop ringing, but they couldn't quite make out the voice on the other end.

Joy glanced at David and Mary with a look of alarm when she heard the greeting. "Hi, someone there called this number. This is the phone number for Elise Brinkley. I'm her friend. I have her phone."

Joy quickly changed the phone to her other ear while she waited. Then she repeated verbatim what she had just said to the first person who answered, adding her full name and address and her own phone number.

"Well, can you tell me what's going on?" she said.

A pause.

"I know, but we're worried about her. She's gotten some bad news."

Another pause.

"It was here in her house. That's where we are now. We need to get in touch with her because her father just passed away. I don't think she knows."

A pause.

"No, he was in hospice. We've been expecting it."

Another long pause. When Joy spoke again, she tried a pleading voice but then adopted one of resignation. She repeated directions to a place in Point Reyes Station for David to write down.

When she hung up, she had little to tell, except that the calls were from the Marin County Sheriff's Office.

"Why wouldn't they tell you anything?" Mary asked.

"I'm not Elise nor her family."

"Did you tell them Elise is missing?"

"Yes, you heard me. They are very interested in talking to me."

"We heard you say you'd go there, but that's an hour away. We have to find Elise."

"I know. I didn't say I'd go immediately. But how could it not be connected?"

David said, "Anything else on the phone that might help us find Elise?"

"I'm looking. There was the Marin sheriff and us. That's it."

"Browsing history. Internet."

"Good, David," Mary said.

After a minute of searching, Joy silently held up the phone. It was a map. At the bottom, the Golden Gate Bridge. At the top, Marin County.

Joy began to tremble. "What if something awful happened? What if they found Elise?"

"If that were the case, why would they be trying to call her?"

Mary added, "And they would have said something to you. They wouldn't clam up like they did. They'd be wanting to have someone come get her. Or identify her, if she were unconscious or worse."

David said, "Look, let's think through the chronology. Elise had her phone, because she texted Joy yesterday afternoon. So at that time, she knew about Tino's double life. She was upset."

"On top of her dad being near death."

"Right, she's on edge already about her dad, but he hadn't passed yesterday afternoon. They said he died in his sleep last night. We don't know where she was during that time, but she had to have been here at some point, because she left her phone."

"My first text to her was about an hour after hers to me. That was at about 5:30."

"The first call from the sheriff was about 6:00, and it was a missed call. They called back twice more, both missed calls, so the phone was probably sitting right here. Elise could have been ignoring her phone, I guess."

"Or she could have been upstairs and not heard it."

"Possible."

Mary said, "I think she plugged it in here, and then left."

"I think so, too," Joy said. "Elise would have gone out to walk. And walk and walk and walk."

"But what about the map?"

David said, "She could have looked at that map anytime yesterday."

Joy said, "But it's the only thing we have to go on. Plus, if she were in the city, she'd be here, with her dad. And the sheriff up there wants to talk to us. We'll find out something."

"Let's go," David answered.

Chapter Twenty-Four

The sheriff's deputy shook David's hand, and then when David introduced them, Mary's and Joy's. Then he looked at his watch. "You made good time," he said.

Joy smiled, but it was a quick, worried smile. "Is she okay?"

The deputy, Smithson, held her gaze a moment, trying to read her face.

"Elise? I don't know if she's okay or not. I'd like to know where she is."

"So she's not hurt, or…"

"Not that I'm aware. She was having trouble with her husband, right? Crocetti?"

"Yes. Tino Crocetti," Mary said.

The deputy's eyes swept the faces of the trio. "When was the last time you saw her?"

Mary said, "Yesterday. Well, we didn't see her. She called me around five."

"You spoke with her?"

"Yes. No. She left a message." Joy held out her phone, and the deputy deftly took it from her but then held it by his side.

"You're all good friends."

"Yes."

"When was the last time you *saw*-saw her?" the deputy asked.

Joy looked to Mary for help. "Day before yesterday? I think?"

"Longer for me," Mary said.

"No," Joy said. "Three days ago. Thursday. Actually, I didn't see her then, either. She called me from Indiana."

"From where?"

"Indiana. She went to see Tino's mother."

"Let's go inside," Smithson said. They'd been standing in the parking lot of the building that contained the sheriff's substation in Point Reyes Station.

Inside, they sat at a cheap veneer conference table, which was too big for the room that contained it. Smithson started a pot of coffee with a practiced hand, while the others sat.

David spoke up as soon as Deputy Smithson turned again to the table. "We're worried about Elise. Do you know anything about her?"

"Again, no."

"Then why did you want to see us?" Mary asked.

"Well, I wanted to see Joy, here, because she called from Elise's phone," Smithson said, "but it's better that all three of you are here."

"What's going on?" David asked.

Smithson glanced back at the coffee pot, which was obviously a long way from being ready. "David, can I speak to you out here a second?"

"Sure."

In the hallway, with the conference room door shut behind them, the deputy said, "When was the last time you saw Tino?"

"A couple of weeks, at least. No, more. He's been separated from Elise at least that long. It's been longer since I saw him. Why?"

"How about Joy?"

"Well, she can tell you, but probably at least two weeks. Because it's been a good two weeks since even Elise knew where Tino was. And Joy wouldn't have seen him unless he was with Elise."

"Joy and Elise are buddies."

"Yes. The two of them and Mary are longtime friends. Mary lives further away, though, so it may have been more than two weeks for her."

"Could you wait out here a minute?"

"Okay," David said. Smithson had pointed to a chair, and now just stood there, plainly waiting for David to actually sit in the chair.

"I'll get you some coffee," Smithson said. He ducked into the conference room and returned with black coffee, and then bounced back into the conference room. The coffee was too bitter for David to drink. He got up, walked down the little hallway, and poured the coffee into a water fountain drain.

A little while later, Smithson stuck his head out of the conference room. "Come on back in, David." This time he sounded almost hospitable.

David sat at the table next to Joy, and Smithson took his seat at the head of the table again, squeezing into his chair in front of the coffeemaker. "Thanks for your help. You really have been very helpful. I gather the connection you all have with Tino is through Elise." By way of explanation, Smithson said, "I mean, Joy, you and Mary, you're longtime pals with Elise, right?"

Head nods.

"And Tino's relatively new on the scene."

"Right."

"But we like Tino because he's Elise's new husband."

"Well," Mary began.

"I know, I get it," Smithson said, even chuckling a little bit. "We liked him until the last few weeks. How he appears to have treated Elise."

"To say the least," Mary said.

"Got it. But none of you have seen Tino in at least a couple of weeks. And it sounds like Elise didn't even know where he was. But we don't know all of Elise's whereabouts in the last couple of days."

"Well, Indiana," Mary said.

"Except Indiana. Tino's mother. Thursday and Friday."

There was a little pause. David looked at Joy and at Mary. Turning to Smithson, he said, "So why are we here?"

"Some bad news, I'm afraid," Smithson said. "Tino's body was found last night in Lagunitas Creek."

Chapter Twenty-Five

Elise lay staring up at the sky, once in a while feeling a slight sway from side to side as she lay. Her nervous energy had been building for days and still seemed hardly to have dissipated. Then she was conscious of having had the thought, and that seemed to break the spell. She had lain rigid in the boat until now, but a lethargy overtook her, along with a desire to remain just as she was until the boat floated over the edge of the earth. The sun had risen high enough to be visible over the gunwale, and as she slowly rotated so that it was in front of her, it began to hurt her eyes. She resented the fact that the sun caused her to know her orientation, marring the sensation of floating free of the earth altogether.

She turned her head so that the sun was not directly before her, but otherwise did not move. There is such a thing as emotional exhaustion, wherein one becomes sick and tired of being sick and tired, and if the body is not also exhausted, a sort of numb normality can and must resume despite the shock that induced the emotional trauma in the first place. At the same time, the circumstantial depression can warp the senses, the judgment, the perception, so that time seems compressed or stretched. For Elise, the future beyond lying in the boat had been completely irrelevant. Now, with the sun's brightness, it intruded. She felt she had lain in the boat for days, and might lie there forever. But now reason began to emerge through the fog, and Elise considered that there had not been a nightfall since she shoved off from the shore into Tomales Bay. And she realized that she would not fetch up among the clouds, separated from the earth, nor fall off the edge and arrive at a netherworld. And after some minutes of that thinking, she realized the boat stayed attached to the surface of the water and would eventually just scrape against a sandy bottom at one side of the bay or the other, or else lodge into the marsh grass further south. And then, swimming up through her consciousness, came an image, indistinct at first, and with that image, a distant urging, barely perceptible at first. The image was that of an old man, sleeping. It came into focus, in her mind, as her father's dear face, and the urging surfaced, too, to return to him in his need. She blinked her eyes open again and now could see, as the sun was off to her left. The world remained far-off, out of view. She remained still, not yet ready to surface to reality, but resigned that she must do so.

There is such a thing as physical exhaustion, too, and the body will take over and find the repose it needs, as if to carry on with life even if the mind wills it not. Elise slept. Whether she slept a day or an hour or a minute, she had no idea, but she awakened to a more vigorous rocking of her little boat. This went beyond the now familiar sensation of movement. A shadow crossed her face. She looked up, in the direction of the prow of the little boat, and her face was shadowed again. This time she followed the shadow, and it remained a shadow, as though she had actually entered into a surreal half-life after all. But then she realized she was looking at a dark gray-black and ungainly bird, a black-footed albatross, a seeming shadow against the bright sky, flying away to her right. At that moment, she felt a push, like an airline seat on take-off. The stern of the boat dipped sharply, and she was tilted up. Suddenly, the world visually intruded in the form of the mouth to Tomales Bay, and the bay itself beyond, extending lengthwise before her as she looked south. Then the prow of the boat plunged down again. Elise's head pressed painfully against the bottom of the boat. Immediately a rush of cold seawater slapped her in the face, as though someone had thrown a bucket of it at her. The cold water served to snap her thinking into a proper timeline. She realized she had been thrown up the front of a wave, and then dropped precipitously behind it. But this was no wavelet like what she would expect in the bay. This wave told her she had drifted outside the bay altogether.

Elise put her elbows down in the water now rushing about in the bottom of the boat, and with some stiffness and much reluctance, she pushed herself back up into the world she had left. It reappeared over the stern of the boat, past her feet, which she realized, in the process, were asleep from having been elevated on the thwart. The world took the form of a long stretch of sandy beach, with breakers rolling onto it, in front of Elise and in a direction away from her. She was looking at the long beach angling from the little town of Dillon Beach into the mouth of Tomales Bay. That meant, she realized, that directly behind her would be Tomales Point, and beyond that the wide Pacific. It also meant that she was broadside to the massive waves approaching the Tomales Point rocks.

Tomales Bay is perhaps a mile wide, at its widest. From its narrow mouth opposite Tomales Point, to where it is mostly overtaken by marsh grass, the distance is perhaps ten to twelve miles. It is a long, thin, well-protected body of water. In consequence, the water of the bay is usually calm. It was this that Elise had set out into. Outside the choke point to the bay at Sandy Point, it is possible to drift beyond the breakers landing at Dillon Beach. But directly opposite that beach are the rocks at Tomales Point. Churning waves twenty or more feet high routinely charge in on the point. Massive rock formations withstand the waves. These are forty and sixty and even a hundred yards across, and the giant waves pound against them, exhilarating to watch from the point. They roll in day after day, after night after night. In among the boulder formations, waves flow in massive waterfalls and backdrafts and pools and vicious undertow. The black-footed albatross thrives there, with other seabirds, and sometimes harbor seals and elephant seals, along with great white sharks.

But never boats. Especially not small boats. Nor human swimmers. As majestic as the entire area is, it is a charnel house for a person in a small boat to wander into. The predators are not especially serious, but only because the violent crashing of many tons of deep cold water against immovable rock would decisively kill first.

Elise felt the sudden rise, again, from the left, but in her moment of hesitation, the little boat had naturally headed into the wave. The craft shot down the other side of the wave, however, and this pushed Elise further along toward the rocks. Now Tomales Point was visible to her, in all its grand beauty, but also as a spectacle of horror. Even in the moment of terror, Elise thought of how different the same scene was, for someone here, as opposed to someone up on the point looking down, as she had once done.

It also occurred to Elise that she had only minutes before been utterly indifferent to her fate. Now her every sense was taut with the will to survive. The boat now sat heavy in the water, with several inches of water inside, and no practical way to bail with the violent surging of water all around. Elise was up on her knees, gripping the gunwales, shifting from side to side to make small, pathetic attempts to head the boat into waves rather than taking them broadside. The waves here were flatter than they were a little further out, and she found herself sliding down the back of them, inexorably closer to the rocks. Ahead of her was a vast table of rock, at one moment exposed, and at another inundated by several yards of water, with geyser jets of spray sent up at the Pacific side, any one sufficient to send her little boat skyward. If she were to land on that rock by a withdrawing current, the next wave would sweep her away in a torrent from which she could never hope to reach the surface. A little to the left the water looked calmer, but there were sudden mighty gushes of it through multiple rock formations, the water rising and falling between them in constantly changing eddies and chutes and whirls and unexpected surges. Had she time to study the patterns, there would still be surprises. There was nowhere to go.

Her little barque toddled inexorably forward into this maelstrom. Elise was nearly overcome with the sheer noise of the place. It no longer registered with her as the scene she'd previously experienced from safely above, on the pointed spit of land. Down here, it was chaos. Constant churn. Death on all sides. Elise's boat was drawn away from the vast table of rock that alternately surfaced and became inundated. Instead, she was drawn into an area partially enclosed, with the tallest rock to Elise's left. The cliffs of Tomales Point's north end were straight ahead, and to her right, the uneven teeth of boulders around which froth boiled incessantly. In the middle, the water was deceptively calm-appearing. The birds would occasionally even land in this area of about twenty-five yards square. But clearly, Elise would be dashed against the taller rock by an incoming wave or sucked into the uneven teeth by a withdrawing current. And if death came by neither of these avenues, then it would come from a swirl of water cascading between the rocks and the cliffs of the headland, dashing her silly boat and her silly head against them, silencing, finally, the terrifying din.

In a long withdrawing roar, she found herself sucked seaward, but between her and the open Pacific were the grand malevolent teeth. She was pulled toward them, as by a strong magnet, and she saw a downdraft just before them, where the surface dropped and exposed the uneven base of the teeth before the next surge would come in and blast water between them. Just before dropping down into this temporary basin, however, Elise found her boat so swamped with water that it moved sluggishly, just as with those birds that dared to splash down, briefly, in the relatively benign center of the cauldron. As a result, the basin filled before she reached it, but then the opposite hazard—water suddenly elevated up the side of the teeth. Elise braced for the blast. It came, in majestic torrents of horizontally moving water, but it blasted just ahead of her and just behind, and she remained in the middle of the zone of violence, so far not smashed on any of the unforgiving surfaces that surrounded her. But then the blast of water ahead of her swirled the front of the boat to the left, and the withdrawal of the rear blast pulled her stern to the right, and she spiraled. In the midst of that twisting motion, she felt herself suddenly rising. She felt her heart sink within her as she rose so quickly that the looming tall rock to her left suddenly seemed to fall, and she was looking down on the albatrosses from above. She was, at this point, only tentatively attached to the boat. Elise attempted to jump to her right, away from the tallest rocks, but there was no jumping—only the soft push from a curved bit of the boat that was already being pulled away by the current. It was enough, though, because Elise escaped that wave, and she watched in horror as the little boat rocketed toward the black rock as though pulled from below. It splintered into several pieces, and then the pieces slid off in the direction of the headland cliff. It would have made an exploding sound if it could have been heard above the din of the surf.

She would be next. She was able to tread water for the moment, and the next pull toward the teeth was nothing like the one before. But then Elise felt a gathering undertow that would heave her back onto the rock just like the boat. Again, there was nowhere to go. She tried to push herself underwater. Perhaps the blast from seaward would miss her, and the gathering wave pass over. But she was no sooner under the water than she realized she was a rag doll in the mouth of a vicious killer, and there was not one movement she could make that would have any effect on the outcome at all. Before she could be thrown into the rock that killed her boat, however, she could feel that she would first be pulled by the backdraft into the teeth. She was looking up through three feet of translucent olive seafoam. She was being pulled toward the dark base of the teeth faster than she could climb upward. She expected never to breathe air again.

In her helplessness, Elise had a moment of lucid calm. She knew she was being carried along with the current to her death, but within a wall of water, it seemed as if she were suspended motionless. The darkness of the teeth to her right seemed to recede a bit as she was pulled from them to the opposite danger. Then she saw another dark shape, a smaller, moving shape. She wondered at the superabundance of death agents available to her. This was surely a great white shark, perhaps one small enough to navigate even these roiling waters, but plenty large enough to end Elise's life a second before the house-sized rock would.

The shark streaked toward her. The dark wall opposite seemed in the process of collapsing upon her. The shark then was not a shark, but a mash-up beast, an unnatural thing, an agent of something beyond animal or man. But no, it was a seal. An oversized male elephant seal. They were ferocious, Joy had said. This one swept under Elise's arm, and in corkscrew fashion delivered her to the surface, and then she found herself riding above the current, in defiance of it, the sleek, muscular body of the seal pressing her up from below. Elise felt the upward rise break the bond of the now-withdrawing wave, and instead of slamming against the rock like her boat had, Elise found herself still pressed to the body of the seal, but now deposited among the scattering albatrosses, atop the column of rock that stayed generally above the waves.

Elise puzzled over the strange sensation of resting on a still surface, suddenly unaffected by the movement and noise all around her. The huge seal bent toward her—surely now to devour her. She closed her eyes, helpless, exhausted, and numb and cold in her inmost being. She felt the beast's breath against her face. Through half-lidded eyes, she watched it shuffle off, look back, and then disappear suddenly over the edge of the rock.

Chapter Twenty-Six

David, Mary, and Joy emerged from the little church into the milky sunshine.

"What did you think?" David asked.

"Well," Joy began. She caught David's eye and then had to chuckle. "I feel like I still haven't been to church."

"It's not like yours?" Mary asked.

Joy shook her head and made a gesture as if to emphasize how very different.

David said, "I don't know that the gospel is at the heart of what's going on here."

"It was hard to concentrate anyway," Joy said. "Poor Tino. And what has become of Elise?"

Mary said, "I keep feeling like there's something more we have to do."

"Yeah, I don't like being in limbo like this," David said.

"It's the right thing, though," Joy said, reiterating what she'd said before church in Point Reyes Station. "Who would we call anyway? Elise is missing. We don't know anything about Tino's work, except it was connected to Elise's Dad."

"Who's also missing, in a manner of speaking."

"Right, and that leaves Tino's mother."

Mary said, "I don't think I could bring myself to make that call, even if the sheriff hadn't asked us not to."

"Better us than the sheriff, when it's time, but better than us would be Elise."

"Who doesn't even know about Tino," Mary said. "And doesn't know about her father, even."

"She had partially lost both of them, I guess you could say," David interjected. "But I'm sure the finality of it is still difficult."

"Well, David—" Mary began.

"David, that's not how it is at all," Joy said. "It's hard even when you see it coming."

"And with Tino," Mary added, "with Tino, it's worse, in a way. They're on the outs, and then there's no way to even process it—and then suddenly he's dead. No closure. Ever."

"I know, I know," David said, gesturing capitulation to the girls' point of view. "I oversimplified." He looked at his watch.

Joy reached to her pocket. "That sheriff's deputy still has my phone. What time is it?"

"One o'clock."

"This is a lovely little town, but I don't like just hanging around, under the circumstances."

"Where is Elise?" Joy asked this last plaintively, not expecting a response. "Let's go by the sheriff's office again."

"I don't think there's any point," David said. "Besides, it's just a little substation. There's probably no one there. Smithson said he'd call. He will. He knows he's got us on hold. Plus, I think we were his only link to Tino this morning. Let's just wait until three o'clock like he asked. He said he might call sooner. I bet he will."

"Nothing's changed since we talked about this before church," Mary said. "And there's really nothing to rush back to the city for."

"Oh, you're both right. I just can't stand it," Joy said, surrendering.

They were walking along the street in Point Reyes Station and had hesitated at a corner of an intersection. The sheriff's substation was ahead. The main street of the town was to the left. They turned down the main street, strolling slowly.

"Let's go for a ride," David suggested.

"We're supposed to stay close," Mary said.

Joy said, "And we don't want to get out of cell range."

"How about lunch then?"

"I don't know if I can eat," Joy said.

"Mary?"

"I don't know if I can eat, either, but it's something to do instead of just hanging around waiting."

They slowly made their way back along the main street, ending up at one of the handful of restaurants there.

They were still seated there an hour and a half later. Conversation lagged. The death of Tino weighed heavily on them. It also heightened their apprehension concerning Elise.

David said, "Elise would never—"

"What, David?"

"Well, I was thinking about the sheriff's questions, before he told us about Tino. And now he has Joy's phone."

"He suspects Elise," Mary said.

Joy said flatly, "That's ridiculous."

"Not from the sheriff's perspective," David said. "He told us Tino was stabbed. That makes him a homicide victim. So the deputy is trying to solve a crime."

"Anyone who knows Elise would know it's ridiculous to suspect her," Joy insisted.

"He doesn't know Elise," Mary pointed out, "but anyway, if you imagine it's not Elise, that it's just someone you read about in a book, what would you think? He denies his own mother. He runs out on Elise right when her father is dying. He cheats on her. He has a child with another woman."

Joy had a pained expression on her face.

David added, "And then she goes missing when they find Tino's body."

Joy began to shed quiet tears, and David scooted over next to her. Mary patted her hand and then stood up and walked the few steps to the front door of the restaurant and stepped outside. David could see her through the front window, loitering discontentedly on the sidewalk. While he comforted Joy and watched Mary out the window, he saw Smithson walk up to Mary. They talked briefly and then entered the restaurant. Smithson looked around. He was evidently satisfied that their table was sufficiently private, because he asked, "Mind if I join you?"

"Please," David said. "Were you looking for us?"

"I saw you come in here earlier. I just thought I'd walk over instead of calling. It's a small town."

Joy said, "Deputy, there's no way Elise did anything wrong, and especially not something violent."

He smiled. An understanding, disarming smile. "Don't worry. Police work isn't like on TV. We don't shoot first and aim later. We follow the evidence where it leads."

"We think," Mary began, "that Elise was upset about some things she learned about Tino."

Mary was interrupted by a loud siren, and seconds later, a fire truck went by, lights flashing. Then another.

Smithson had one hand on the radio receiver attached to his epaulet, and his head was cocked to listen to the transmission coming over it.

"What's going on? Do you have to go?" David asked.

"No," Smithson said and then listened at his receiver again, one finger held up to pause the conversation. "No," he reiterated, "but I need to stay with this. A rescue at Tomales Point."

"That's quite a ways from here, isn't it?" David asked.

"It is. But the sheriff and fire departments and Coast Guard coordinate on these things. Those guys that just passed are backing up the Tomales Fire Department, and there's a sheriff's helicopter in the air. The Coast Guard is coming over from Bodega Bay or Two Rock. Someone stuck out on a rock on Tomales Point."

"That's a rough place. I hiked there," Joy said.

"Yeah, it's like finding a turtle on top of a fence post. You have to ask, 'How did it get there?'" The deputy turned to Mary. "I think you were talking about Elise being upset at Tino."

"No, I said she was upset about some things she learned about Tino. We're her best friends. We know what she would do. She went to be by herself. But we're afraid something happened to her."

"She wouldn't just stay away," Joy added. "Her father was in bad health. Dying, actually. He passed away last night."

"Mm." Smithson cocked his head at his receiver again for a moment. "Well, I haven't called sooner because the FBI seems to be real interested in Tino. I've been tied up with them. Any of you know anything about that?"

"Well, if it's a murder, that makes it a big case, right?" Mary asked.

"Sure, but that by itself wouldn't be of interest to the feds."

"I feel like you must have some idea already," David said.

"Oh," Smithson said, sitting back and gesturing his protest, "I'm not trying to trick you, I promise. Yes, I know something about it. At least what the FBI is telling me. They have a public corruption case going. They think Tino was involved."

David sat back and looked Smithson in the eye with a steady gaze, knowing the look would communicate that he did know something. "It's in the San Francisco online papers," David said. "I've been following it. Not that they say much, just that there's an investigation. Bribery. Graft. Started with lobbying over restrictions on short-term rentals."

"Well, then you know as much as I do," Smithson said. "And I didn't know that much until the feds showed up today. How about Tino? How would he figure into this?"

"I don't know. I want to be real clear that I don't *know*-know. But he did do some kind of work for the city, as a 'consultant,' whatever that means, and I think Elise's father who just died got him connected."

"Surely Tino wasn't involved in all that," Joy said. "He was a nice guy, and very smart. And very well-liked."

"And a cheat and a deceiver," Mary said.

"Sometimes people start out meaning well and slip into wrongdoing by degrees," Smithson said. "Visit our jail sometime. You'll meet the nicest guys you'd ever want to meet. But what you're telling me, David, is essentially what the feds have told me. Do you have any other connection to it?"

Joy looked at David. "Tell him why you got fired."

David hesitated. "I think I helped set things in motion with some work I did for my employer. My employer until a few days ago, anyway. And then I was just unceremoniously let go."

"What kind of work did you do?"

"Software developer."

"Sought-after field."

"And he's no dummy," Joy added. "He was a star one day, and tossed out the door the next."

"You don't mind repeating this for the FBI boys?"

"Sure, I..." David stopped talking. Smithson was leaning into his radio receiver again, and again with one finger up to pause the conversation.

He sat up. Holding the transmit button down, Smithson spoke into the receiver himself. "Sue, 351. Could you contact our fed visitors and get them to hit me on my cell? ASAP?" Turning to the others at the table, he said, "Good news. Your Elise is alive."

The air around the table was electric. Joy and Mary started talking at once.

Smithson held up his hand as he rose from the table. "She's our turtle."

"Our what?"

David said, "The turtle on the post."

"Well, they got her off the post, and she's safe," Smithson said, beginning to make his way to the door.

"Where?" Joy asked excitedly.

Smithson stopped at the door. He looked out at his patrol car and then back to the little group assembled at the table. He had assumed an air of urgency when the transmission about Elise came over the radio. Now he adopted his more relaxed mode, for a moment, and sidled back to the table. "You've all been very helpful, and I really appreciate it. Can I please ask you to stay close, just for a little while longer? Elise is being debriefed."

"Can I have my phone?" Joy asked, as if negotiating the point.

Smithson smiled. "Sure. Here. I'll get back to you soon. We'll need to talk some more. So could you stay in the area, and be sure to stay inside cell coverage? The terrain here is tricky." Smithson then hurried to his vehicle without waiting for an answer.

"He knows we're not going anywhere without Elise," Joy said.

Chapter Twenty-Seven

Elise was huddled under a blanket. The room was adequately heated, but she still felt a deep sensation of cold. She had seen a doctor and been released. Only minor cuts and abrasions. But she couldn't get over the cold. She was still being attended by one of the Coast Guard crewmen who had been there for the rescue, the same one lowered from the helicopter onto the massive dark rock to enfold Elise with himself into a rescue basket. She was given coffee, but it was too strong. Now she stared into a Styrofoam cup of weak tea.

"Best we can do, right now, aside from the coffee," the rescuer said.

"Thank you." She took a drink of the tea, finding it weak and thinking about her own weakness, her fecklessness, and how she had let her father down. It wasn't like her to dissolve into a puddle of tears over it, however, nor could she lapse into the self-indulgence that would require. "How did you get the job of telling me about my father? Wasn't rescuing me enough?"

He chuckled. He was a young man. Brisk and businesslike as the job required, but he also had a tenderness to him. Even a becoming resilience to the protocols of military structure, despite his relative youth. He ministered to Elise. "You still haven't told me the rest of the story about the seal," he said, with a kind smile.

"Oh, yes, the seal." She said this softly, as if remembering something from long ago. "I told you about the seal."

"You kept pointing to where he was. You said he saved you. 'He brought me up from the depths,' you said. Quite poetic, given the circumstances. 'He was strong...he could have killed me.' Ring a bell?"

"I should have died," Elise said.

"Well, I'm glad we could—"

"No, I mean you guys were great. You're heroes. But I should have been gone long before you got there. I was supposed to die in the water."

"Supposed to, Elise?"

"Well, no," she looked momentarily confused. "Not supposed to, I guess. Everything happens…" She paused, shook her head. "I don't know why anything happens."

"Are you a praying woman?"

Elise had been huddled up, pondering, speaking almost as if only to herself, but at this, she looked up at the young man's earnest eyes. "I was praying in the water."

"I'm sure your father was a great guy."

"He was. I should have been a good daughter."

"I'm sure you were," he said. The young man took to a knee on the tile floor, as he had done while attending to her medical needs. He put one hand on her shoulder. "Weren't you?" He said it as if insisting she agree.

"Until he needed…" Elise broke into tears. She made an effort to restrain them. "Me," she finished, amid sobs.

"Elise, he died only last night. In his sleep. You said you set out last night." He said no more, not having the whole story already.

"I should have been there at the end. At the end is when it mattered."

"Don't be hard on yourself, Elise. It's not what we do in a moment that matters. It's what we do over the course of a lifetime."

Elise sat quietly, drinking in these words. The young man was taking his time, still next to her. It occurred to her that he was ready to go but was lingering, from kindness, to see that she was emotionally all right. "It's okay about my father. I'm okay."

The young man gave her a smile and then collected his bag and walked to the door of the conference room. He looked back, smiled again, then stepped through the doorway. Elise watched after him for what seemed a long time after the door closed.

Then she turned back to the conference room table. There had been a bustle into and out of the room during Elise's exchange with the Coastie. Now there were three men sitting at the table. One more or less opposite, two at the other end. One of the men at the end of the table was in a uniform. Khaki shirt, olive pants. A patch on his left shoulder connected him to the Marin County Sheriff's Office. He and the man opposite her had blank legal pads in front of them.

"I forgot your names already, I'm sorry," Elise said.

"Winters, Bob Winters," the man opposite said. He made a little gesture toward the others. "Rick. Kamil." Rick and Kamil both did a bobbing nod. Elise inferred from their reaction that she'd perhaps already asked them to repeat their names.

"And you're a…" she said, to Winters.

"Special Agent. FBI."

"Special. Not a regular agent?" she asked laconically. "Why 'Special?'"

Winters responded with a standard-issue smile. "That's just what it's called. Can we talk now?"

"Sure."

"We just need to understand about Tino."

"Me, too," Elise said dreamily.

"Well, can you tell us what you know?" he said.

Elise looked up at Winters and then over at the two others. "About what?" she asked.

"Can you excuse us?" Winters said.

"Sure." Elise was beginning to thaw, but her feet were cold. She didn't want the tepid tea. Maybe if it were in a real cup, she thought. The men were exiting the room. She lowered her forehead to the table.

A few minutes later, they returned. "Sorry," Winters said.

Elise looked up. Then she wrapped herself in the blanket, pulling her knees up and pulling the blanket down over her feet so that she was just a bundle under the blanket on the chair.

"You're not in custody," Winters began.

Elise looked at him blankly, then said softly, "Why would I be in custody?" She looked down. Maybe she should be in custody. Maybe she should be arrested for leaving her father at the moment he most needed to know she was there. Maybe she should be arrested for self-indulgence. Was that a crime? It should be. She shouldn't have gone walking all over San Francisco just because she was upset over Tino's mother. Everyone has problems. And Tino had a girlfriend. So what. She wasn't the first married person to be left like this. She had to grow up. It's criminal to remain a child. To act like she's the first person ever to be betrayed in this way. To have her heart ripped out of her. But he had a child. Yes, he had a child, but was that really worse? A beautiful child. She laughed, through tears, at the remembrance of the child's smile. The men at the table were looking at each other. Everyone has problems. Her father's particular problem was that he was dying. Had been. Dying. That was an actual, real problem. But what was she doing, while he was dying? She was obsessing over Tino. Or the empty place where Tino should have been, next to her. Next to her father. Next to his own mother. Elise felt hot tears rise again.

Elise's eyes were behind her hands. She remained curled up on the chair, facing one side. But she was aware that the trio had left the room again.

When they returned, there was a female officer. She was dressed like the other Marin County sheriff's officer. She had the face and figure of perhaps a former model, now in another phase of life. Still a spark of womanly kindness, Elise detected. She came over to Elise's side of the table and sat next to her.

After the men had returned to their seats, Winters clasped his hands together in front of him and began to speak to Elise in earnest. "You have the right to remain silent. You don't have to talk to us at all if you don't want to."

"Okay."

"You have the right to an attorney. If you can't afford one, an attorney will be appointed to represent you."

"Okay."

"Anything you say—"

"Am I a suspect?"

"I'm just taking precautions. And you're not even in custody, as I said."

"But what would I be a suspect for? What's the crime?"

Winters just looked at her a moment, and then over to the other men at the end of the table, and said, "Let me get through this thing. Anything you say can and will be used against you in court."

"Court for what?"

"If you wish to talk with us now, without an attorney, you may still invoke your right to counsel at any time."

"Oh," Elise said, the light dawning, "it's okay. I'm guilty. I did it."

She noted the stirring in the room.

"I'll pay for it," she said. "It was very nice, and I'm sure it wasn't cheap. And I'm sorry. Whoever's it was didn't deserve that. I'll replace it with another boat just as good, if I can find one. I hope it didn't have sentimental value. And if I have to go to jail, so be it."

The female ex-model officer turned to Elise and displayed a smile that Elise couldn't interpret. "Honey—"

Winters said, "This isn't about the boat."

Elise settled back into her blanket.

"Did you keep the checkbook for yourself and Tino?"

"No." What an odd question. Why would he care about that? "I just use the account I had when I was single. Tino gives me a set amount each month. I pay the bills for us." Then she added, more quietly still, "Same as I do for my father."

"And Tino's business?"

"He does all that. I don't know anything about it."

"You didn't handle any books in his business?"

"No."

"No work in his business at all?"

"No."

"Do you know what he did?"

"You keep saying 'did' and 'didn't.' I'm not aware that anything about his business has changed. But I don't have a clear understanding of what he does, to tell you the truth. I guess I should, but I don't."

"And what do you do?"

Elise shook her head. "Mostly Latin and Greek, at the moment."

Winters tilted his head, interrogatively.

"MA in classics. Studying for."

"Ah. Smart stuff."

Elise made what was intended as a flippant gesture with her hand, but it only made the blanket puff out a bit. She noted a lot of meaningful eye contact among the others in the room. Then the men filed out.

The female officer next to Elise turned her seat so that she was facing Elise fully. "They've left, but you should know the room is wired."

Elise nodded her understanding. She dabbed at her eyes with a shredded bit of tissue paper.

"When was the last time you saw Tino?"

"Two weeks ago. A little more."

"Do you know where he is?"

"I think he's around here somewhere."

The female officer cocked her head to one side. "Why do you think that?"

"I met his girlfriend. In Olema. She said she was going to meet him, and she said it was just down the road."

"When was that?"

Elise took a long time to answer. Could it have really been just yesterday? "Saturday," she said.

"Yesterday?"

"I guess that's right."

"And why would she tell you that?"

"I don't think she understood who I am to Tino."

The officer took a moment to process this. "So did you go with her to see Tino?"

Elise looked at the officer and made no effort to hold back the pain and despair from her face. "I went home. The city." After some mournful reflection, Elise looked the officer in the eye. Despite her efforts, her lower lip trembled. "Why do you ask?"

"Honey," the officer began.

Elise steeled herself for the next blow.

Chapter Twenty-Eight

David heard Joy greet Hanigan at the door. He was right behind her. "That was quick," David said. "Were you already in the neighborhood?"

"No, no, I just wanted to get over to see you as soon as I could. This whole thing shakes me up a little, I don't mind telling you." Hanigan looked back to Joy. "How's Elise?"

"Not great at the moment," Joy said, "but I think she'll be all right in the long run. You know her father's memorial is tonight?"

"Yes, I'll be there."

"I think it would mean a lot to Elise."

Hanigan nodded. "And what about Tino? Some sort of memorial for him, too? What do you think?"

David said, "That's a little weird in all the circumstances. But I think it's going to work out. The FBI needs some time with the body. A thorough autopsy, at least. But Dr. Brinkley's thing was half-planned already. So we suggested we go ahead with Dr. Brinkley's right away, without much mentioning of Tino until next week. Elise seems on board with that, as much as she seems on board about anything."

"Relying on you a lot, Joy?"

"Yes," David answered for her. Turning to Joy, he said, "I'm proud of how you're handling it."

"Elise is alone at home?" Hanigan asked.

Joy said, "Mary is over there right now, I believe, but Elise is going to be okay. We don't try to stay with her every minute, like at first."

"And the FBI?" Hanigan asked.

David looked at Joy and back to Hanigan. "We're sort of guessing," he said, "but we think they don't really suspect Elise of anything to do with, well, with what happened to Tino. The stuff Tino was involved with, before he died, that might be another story."

"Do they know anything more about how Tino died?"

"No, just that they believe he was dead before he was put in the water. There were signs that whoever it was tried to dispose of the body but—"

"Stop!" Joy said. She had her hand to her stomach and hurried out of the room.

"I'm sorry, Joy," David said after her. To Hanigan, he said, "She's usually more resilient than I am. She's a nurse."

"This is personal."

"Right." David resumed in a quieter voice, with Joy out of the room, "Whoever did it bungled the job of disposing of the body, apparently. Unless they find something unusual in the autopsy, it looks like blunt force to the head, but there were stab wounds, too."

"How do you know all this?"

"The sheriff's deputy told us a lot as they were finding it out. The FBI is hush-hush, but the sheriff's deputy is more on our side, it seems like. That's why I think there's no serious suspicion of Elise about the homicide."

"The FBI would be all over a local public corruption case, I gather."

"And they are. They executed a search warrant on Tino's office."

"Really?"

"Delivered a copy to Elise, believe it or not. They got everything off his computer."

"Does Elise have any reason to be worried?"

"No, she didn't have anything to do with Tino's business. But I think she's going to have this hanging over her head awhile."

"And they don't have any clues about Tino's disappearance?"

"I'm not supposed to talk about this. But heck, you'll read about it in the paper soon enough. There was apparently one witness. Not of the whole thing, but someone who saw Tino right around the time it must have happened."

"Really. Who?"

"Well, to understand this, you know Tino had a girlfriend, right?"

"So I heard."

"Well, apparently they kept a little place a mile or so outside of Point Reyes Station, which is this little tiny town—"

"Yeah, I'm familiar."

"And they would walk back and forth into town. This lady lived on the little road they would take. They would stop to pet her horse. She saw them together from time to time, but she saw Tino alone, without the girlfriend, just one time, and it was the day he disappeared. In fact, around the time they think he might have been abducted."

"Horse?"

Joy reappeared, with the color returned to her face. "Pardon me, gentlemen," she said.

Hanigan said, "No, sorry for being crass. These are your friends, not abstractions."

"Not your fault."

To David, Hanigan repeated, "She had a horse?"

"Yeah. A horse in a pen by the road. Why?"

"Just a thought. Can I have the deputy's number?"

"Sure."

"How about if I pick you both up for the service?"

"What do you think, Joy?" David asked. "Can we all go together?"

"We're taking Elise."

"If it's just Elise and the three of us, that's easy," Hanigan said.

"Thanks, Hanny."

"Happy to."

"But I'm not sure they call it a 'service.'"

"'Memorial,' then. See you around six?"

When Hanigan was gone, David asked Joy, "Are you okay?"

Joy smiled. The sparkle was back in her eye. "I'll be fine," she said.

That afternoon at about 5:30, there was a buzz from the alley gate. David hit the button to release it without looking outside, thinking it would be Hanigan. When he opened the door to the apartment a moment later, he said, "Oh. Surprise. Deputy Smithson."

"Hello, David. I'm supposed to meet Mark Hanigan here? Is that all right?"

"Sure. Come in. I'm surprised because I associate you with Marin County."

"I'm technically out of my jurisdiction, but it's okay for something like this."

"Like what?"

Smithson eyeballed David a moment then turned to greet Joy. As he did, there was a buzz again from the alley gate. David reached for the button to release it, again without looking. A moment later, Hanigan stood at the door.

"Hanny," David said. "This is Deputy Smithson."

"Good to meet you in person," Hanigan said. "Like I said on the phone, I have no idea if this means anything. I hope I haven't led you on a wild goose chase." Under his arm, Hanigan carried a flat, rectangular package, wrapped in kraft paper and twine.

"If it's nothing, it's nothing. Not for you to be concerned with."

"Well, okay," Hanigan said. "Here you go." He stepped over to the countertop extension to David's and Joy's kitchen and placed the rectangular package on it. He began to unwrap it.

Smithson looked at David and Joy. "Confidential for now? Please?"

"Sure," David said.

"How did your friend Mr. Hanigan know about the horse lady, by the way?" Smithson asked of David.

"A gift of clairvoyance," Hanigan interjected.

"Okay, right," Smithson answered. "Now what do we have here?"

"Man with a gray felt hat."

"Wow, you're a real artist. And this is a good likeness?"

"Pretty much right on, if I do say so myself. I was trying to get that certain look around the eyes."

Smithson grinned at Hanigan. "I'm a cop, not an artist. This looks highly realistic, though. Tino told you this is the guy who fed the horse?"

"That's him."

"There's only one horse pen next to that little stretch of road. I feel sure I'm looking at our suspect. I was afraid I'd get a stick figure with eyeballs going off in all directions."

Hanigan laughed and said, "I hope it helps."

"I'll take good care of it," Smithson said. "I'm glad you called me first. I've got a murder to solve. But the FBI will be extremely interested, too. They still have a few politicos and conspirators to take down. I expect this guy will end up pointing 'em out."

Chapter Twenty-Nine

Elise sometimes felt the cold, again, of that day at Tomales Point. It came to her when she actively recalled the event. The fierce cold, but also the sense of liberation. The sense that there was a force far greater than herself. A personal, caring strength. It would all be all right. Even in that turbulent and frigid motion, noise, and uncertainty, the outcome was not her responsibility. Her job was to open her eyes and accept the strength far beyond her own, the caring far beyond her own capacity to care. Elise felt the cold, but she felt the awakening that went with it. She had been asleep, these years. When she relived that sensation of cold, she also relived the sensation of profound gratitude. She had lived with dissociation, disconnection, disquiet, for so long, that when the veil was ripped from her, the reality before her seemed too real. Blinding and hard. The water too cold. The beast she encountered too powerful and too incomprehensible. The sheer raw power and energy of the waves had been beyond her imagination, but that was before her imagination was enhanced, upgraded, invigorated, empowered. What presented as an image in her mind was a view beyond the here and now—even the awesome here and now of Tomales Point. The unseen image now was of something even more vast and powerful than the violent surgings of the sea she had experienced.

She would never be the same. She was somehow more real, more valued, more *there*. And yet, she felt her place was on her knees before a loving king for Whom all this was as nothing. Life now mattered more, not less. Even in this pall cast by her shame at having abandoned her father, of having misapprehended Tino so thoroughly, of having abandoned herself to what she thought of as merely fate. Despite this, she mattered more, not less. Her eyes were opened. She received a numinous light that could only come from the presence of another and grander world behind this one. The surf and the stones and the animals in the water are not all there is. There is light—or something like light, but stronger, and more real than light—that overarches and undergirds and pervades the being-ness of things.

Chapter Thirty

David wandered over from the bay window, back to the little kitchen counter. Joy was washing dishes in the sink. "I told you I'd get that," he said. "I'm still unemployed."

"It's just a couple of things. Besides, all that changes tomorrow."

"Yeah, I was unemployed a grand total of four weeks. I'm embarrassed for thinking it was the end of the world."

"I told you you'd be a hot commodity in no time."

"Oh, so you knew this big federal investigation was about to break. That it would tie right back to my software. That there would be a perp-walk a mile long…" David was ticking the items off on his fingers.

"And that you'd be a rock star."

"You did not literally know any of that," David said.

"Are you still going out?" Joy asked.

"Well, I was going to see Hanny. We've been saying we'd get together again since Tino's funeral. Anyway, aren't you going over to Elise's?"

"Well, Mary is. And I've been over there a lot since the big swim. But I thought I might stay here with you and celebrate."

"I guess I could cancel with Hanny again. But we can celebrate the new job anytime, right?"

"Not the job," Joy said. She had a mischievous twinkle in her eye. She dried her hands and walked around the kitchen counter. She pulled David close.

"I'm pregnant," she whispered.

Chapter Thirty-One

Elise returned from her first day back in classes. She had taken a leave of absence after the loss of her father and Tino, but had then wondered whether that was the best thing to do. She hadn't really needed the extra time, and her classwork would have provided a distraction. On the other hand, what would make distraction from reality a good thing? The leave of absence had given her time to absorb this—what? Idea? Concept? Abstraction? It felt like a vision of God, but real, not some sort of dream-state apparition.

In any event, she'd taken the weeks off, and now it was time to return to life. Time to try to get the investigation behind her, if she could. Elise was beyond exasperation at the session after session about Tino's activities, during which she had learned quite a bit, but it was all new to her. She was chagrined at how little she knew of Tino's day-to-day working life. But the facts were the facts. Tino had built and maintained, in an impressively short amount of time, a whole network of corrupt liaisons. More than a bag man or co-conspirator. He had apparently constructed an entire illegal marketplace. It was understandable that there would be some skepticism of her innocence, at first, but ultimately, it had been the very speed and audacity of the enterprise that convinced the authorities she could not have had anything to do with it. That combined with the diligence Tino had applied to keeping her in the dark.

She was home from class only moments before she was on the phone with Theresa. And then, the harder call, to Cassie.

Later that week, Elise drove the van to the San Francisco airport. She worried that there were too many ways for her to miss Theresa, because Theresa didn't carry a cell phone. Elise camped out where arriving passengers would leave the secured area. Theresa walked out, looking a little bewildered before spotting Elise. They hugged tight.

"I'm so glad to see you," Elise said. "I've thought about you a lot since the funeral."

"I'm glad you invited me back, darling. It feels different this time."

"Well, let's get you home. The carousels are down that big stairway over there."

When Theresa's things were settled into the third-floor apartment, Elise suggested, "Let's go up to the loggia."

Theresa smiled her agreement. "If I lived here, I'd go up there all the time."

"Basically what I do."

In the loggia, looking out toward the bay, Theresa took Elise's hand. "Is it best for you to stay here, sweetheart?"

"You're so kind to be concerned. It's the same thing Mary and Joy keep asking. I think it's best. It's not painful to be here, and it might be if I left. I lived here for a long time before Tino. Ever since my father started having trouble walking. Ten years, at least. But what about you?"

"Nothing's different for me," Theresa said. "I've been in the same place since before Tino was born. Tino grew up there. Tino's father passed on. And then Tino left." She paused. Elise could see she was determined not to be emotional but was struggling with it.

"Maybe you would move?" Elise asked gently. "You could stay here with me."

"Elise, darling, you're very, very kind. But you're young. You have your whole life ahead of you. I don't think that's best. But you're wonderful." Theresa embraced Elise as they looked out over the city and the bay. She rested her head against Elise's shoulder.

"It's still early in the day," Elise said. "Would you want to take a ride with me? Are you up for that?"

"So mysterious," Theresa said, separating from Elise. "Of course."

"I'll be down in the kitchen when you're ready."

They crossed the Golden Gate Bridge not long after. A few minutes later, they were off the highway and headed west.

"Curvy," Theresa said.

"Are you okay?" Elise asked. "Do you want me to slow down some more?"

"No, I'm fine," Theresa said. "It's an interesting ride. The trees and grass and bushes all look so different from back home."

"Fair warning. We're about to come out to the Pacific Ocean. Are you afraid of heights?"

"Just normal afraid, I guess," Theresa answered.

"Well, the road goes right along the ocean, but high up, and it's a great view. But don't worry, I'll take it slow."

"Take it just how you want," Theresa said. "I'm fine. Oh, look over there!"

"Yeah, that's just a peek. In a minute, you'll have the whole ocean spread out in front of you."

They drove on in silence, up to the peak of the road near Muir Beach.

"Oh, my," Theresa said when they were at the top and beginning the gradual descent. "We're on top of the world." They were silent most of the way down on the road to Stinson Beach, but about midway, Theresa said, "It looks like eternity."

They were both silent again. Theresa because she must have wondered about the object of this drive. Elise because she had been preparing emotionally for this encounter for many weeks and was still not sure she could go through with it. Elise was struggling with the most difficult task she had yet undertaken, even including burying her husband in those awful circumstances.

They hit a flat stretch, next to a body of water that was obviously not the ocean itself. "Bolinas Lagoon," Elise said, without having been asked. "Now we're about to go along the San Andreas fault. We're right on top of it."

"Well, that's not very comforting," Theresa said. Then she chuckled, and Elise imagined Theresa's perspective—the oddity of desiring the comfort that the earth won't shake beneath you, or even destroy everything around you. There are no guarantees, except death, and there may not even be advance warning of that seismic event. Theresa had been battered about, emotionally. At one time, Elise would have thought of that as the product of age and experience, perhaps producing wisdom. But she knew from her own experiences that it's not necessarily just a function of age. There is no period of deluded halcyon youth to which we are all entitled. And wisdom? What wisdom had she, Elise, acquired, being on multiple counts a victim first of Tino, and then of Tino's murderer, and of hooded death so long stalking her father? Wisdom is supposed to be the consolation prize. Elise felt little consoled. None of this recent experience had seemed fair. But it had been her measuring staff for fairness that was crooked, not the events themselves. She felt numb to the pain, still, wondering if this emotional numbness was like the shock that follows physical trauma. Elise had tried, in all the hours since lifting off the rock at Tomales Point, and in the face of the aftershocks that followed, to dig into the pain, to grasp it and struggle with it and bring it to heel. There was nothing left now but to live, and to live without fear, straddling the fault line unafraid. There is more than this life. More than the ocean and the bay and the hills and the great wide earth beyond. There is more to existence. The ocean does look like eternity when one is disposed to see it that way. When one is looking for eternity already. Elise was never more so disposed than when she saw it through the jagged teeth at Tomales Point, atop her tower of isolation, with the albatrosses for friends. And that greatest of friends, there in the form of one humble instance of creation. That great huffing tusked beast who'd breathed warm into Elise's face, looming over her, and then left her, alive, itself returning to the eternity from whence it came. Elise thought of the fireworks over the bay long ago, their order and light. Unnecessary. Of no use. Except beauty. To delight. Like the best of Hanigan's art. Calling to us from that Beyond, as deep calls unto deep.

Next to her, Theresa was looking first right, to the oaks and grasses of the chaparral, and then left, to the peaked conifers that clothed the slope up to the ridgetop. Elise slowed the car and turned into a driveway, parking next to a blue pickup truck in the yard of a modest house. Theresa looked at her quizzically. Elise smiled and squeezed Theresa's hand briefly. Then she nodded toward the house and alighted from the vehicle. They spoke no more as they approached. Their footfalls clumped on the wooden steps. The screen door opened. Cassie, holding the baby. She smiled quickly at Theresa. Her gaze then on Elise. Cassie wore a look of wonder.

"Elise called me," Cassie said to Theresa.

Theresa looked at Elise. "You have a grandson," Elise said. "Alessandro."

Theresa's eyes were big. Glistening.

Cassie turned the sleeping child toward Theresa. His plump fist vibrated in reaction, but his eyes remained closed.

Theresa glanced again at Elise, then into Cassie's eyes, and then gently reached for the baby.

The End

About the Author

ALBERT NORTON, JR. is an essayist and novelist living in Atlanta, Georgia. His first novel was *Another Like Me* (eLectio Publishing 2015). He blogs at www.albertnorton.com.

Made in the USA
Charleston, SC
07 March 2017